# Bad Rabbi

A Novel

Inspired by actual events

By

Steve Levine

Published by Unsolicited Press

www.unsolicitedpress.com



For information, contact publisher at

info@unsolicitedpress.com

Unsolicited Press Books are distributed to the trade by Ingram.

Printed in the United States of America.

ISBN: 978-1-947021-16-7

Library of Congress Control Number:  2018940282

For Yvonne

# Contents

"I came from a real tough neighborhood. Once a guy pulled a knife on me. I knew he wasn't a professional, the knife had butter on it."

— Rodney Dangerfield

"All men make mistakes, but a good man yields when he knows his course is wrong,  and repairs the evil."

— Sophocles, Antigone

*He didn't see much at first. He couldn't hear, couldn't feel, but he could smell. And the smell was so strong he could taste it. In the few long, heart-thumping moments while his hand scrambled for the switch, a metallic scent caught in his throat and he gagged. His stomach clenched and bile oozed in his gut. Pulling a tissue from the wad in his suit jacket, he put it to his nose, found the switch, and wished he hadn't.*

# PART I

# Chapter 1

R abbi Louis Abrams did not get stoned today.

Often after morning prayers he retired to the cool of his mahogany-paneled office, closed the door and did a bong-hit.

Today, the morning service over, he returned to his office and just read a bit – The *New York Times* and *Haaretz*, the liberal Israeli daily he got on the Web. He went home for lunch and a nap and returned for an afternoon bar mitzvah lesson before hopping the Hi - Speedline to Philadelphia.

Louis looked forward to the exhibit opening at the Gershman YMHA, the Jewish Y some called it, where he had been a member since boyhood, lifting weights and pounding up and down its well-worn basketball court. He perused a *Philadelphia Inquirer* article about the rebirth of Broad Street on the ride over and entered the lobby just before seven.

The mid-September sun sprayed copper penny across the city as the afternoon faded and clouds rushed in. The first fat drops fell as Louis reached the building.

"Good of you to come, Rabbi," Herman Wolfe called, his right hand shooting out to greet his old friend.

Herman, a retired math teacher in the Apple Hill School District, had been a member of B'nai Tikvah for more than thirty years, longer than Louis had been affiliated with it and much longer than he'd been chief rabbi.

Tall and angular, with a jutting fuzz ball of an Adam's apple, Herman reminded Louis of a chicken. He'd also been coming to the Y for more than forty years where, in their youth, he and Louis banged elbows and shins beneath the hoops.

Considering how long they'd known each other, Louis found the formal greeting a little odd, but Herman thought it proper.

"Where's Rebecca?" Herman asked. "She's the art lover. You're just a critic."

Louis grinned at the slight.

"Old habits die hard," he said, releasing the older man's hand. "She's closing the Apple Hill store tonight. Lots to do before the holidays."

Approaching seventy, Herman was enjoying late success as an artist. The retired mathematician overlaid geometric shapes in oils creating landscapes that physically rose off the canvas.

His work had been on display at Apple Hill High School East where he'd sold a few pieces, mostly to former colleagues, but the Y opening was his first real exhibit.

"Bec will be in tomorrow," Louis assured him.

Rebecca Abrams, proprietor of Mom's Bake Shop, ran outlets in Apple Hill, neighboring Voorhees, and a new shop in the historic Reading Terminal Market, a nineteenth century train depot in Philadelphia. Where once Union armies passed through the depot by the carload, hauling prisoners and weapons of war, merchants now hawked everything from sushi to greeting cards to good French brie.

Rebecca opened her first shop after bake sale customers demanded she do more with her talent than raise funds for her sons' Boy Scout troop. The problem was, she no longer simply baked, her true passion, but was bedeviled by the fine points of running a multimillion-dollar business. With the High Holidays approaching, orders for challah, honey cake, rugelach and other sweets put a demand on her staff and her kitchens that she had to prepare for.

Herman led Louis around the gallery, stopping now and again to describe what he tried to do with various colors, shapes, and patterns. The painter was inspired by Picasso but believed his work stood on its own.

Distracted by the eight-foot vertical windows facing Broad Street, Louis caught the gaze of a homeless man whose bedraggled olive trench coat and ill-fitting pants hung from his loose bones. Why, Louis wondered, in this day and age, do we even have homelessness? Certainly, there were none around his leafy, suburban synagogue. He saw none, for that matter, lounging about the Apple Hill Mall, the onetime jewel of South Jersey for which his town was named (and not, as many believed, the other way around). He went outside, gave the man a few bucks and made a mental note for a holiday sermon.

Louis's passion from the bimah was legendary at B'nai Tikvah and played a key role in his steady ascent to the position of chief rabbi. His heartfelt sermons brought in many new members and writing and delivering them remained the most joyous part of his job, an opportunity to spread God's will through his own words.

Returning inside, Louis pushed through the lobby back to the gallery where Herman now held court.

Several students from the University of the Arts across the street pressed him on the inspiration that led to his work.

One young man openly challenged Herman on techniques he borrowed from Picasso and other cubists, but Herman, ever the teacher, quietly explained that that is what good art does. He might have rolled out a well-worn aphorism to justify his "borrowing" of techniques, but Herman just let it go. The way he saw it, if the kid didn't like his work, fuck the little pisher, and he turned to others who did.

Louis wanted none of Herman's lesson. He brushed past the group and turned his eyes toward some art of the God-given variety.

"Talk about texture," he mumbled to himself, admiring the snug corduroy pants of a young woman he hadn't noticed before.

The woman, casually making her way around the gallery, must have come in when Louis stepped outside. She was alone, but Louis couldn't tell from where he stood if she was lonely.

"Whaddaya think?" he said, sidling up to her. "Would you believe this guy taught math?"

"Looks like he still does," she said.

"Well, he taught for over thirty years, whaddaya gonna do? Old habits die hard I guess. Of course, I taught him a thing or two back in the day on the court."

"Is that right?" she said, sizing up Louis and birdlike Herman, viscerally distrustful of a bully.

Louis was a large man, six-foot-four and nearly two-hundred thirty pounds, but never a bully and he quickly sought to correct the misimpression.

"Nothing like that," he said. "We played a lot of ball as kids. My wife's actually friends with him now, but I like his work."

The woman smiled, softened by the mention of a wife and the possibility that this, for once, was just conversation.

The man obviously thought well of himself. His worsted wool suit had a trim, tailored fit and he sported a neat salt-and-pepper beard and a matching gray kippah. Louis had a raincoat folded over his left arm so she didn't see his ring, but he had obviously been hitting on her. Now, with the mention of a wife, she wasn't so sure.

The colorful, well-lit gallery, which was so often dark as she strolled home from the radio station, drew her in on this bleak afternoon. Philadelphia, the city of her birth, could be so colorless -- friendly, blue collar, but drab. Then, when she least expected it, she found fruit and color, sunshine and warmth, wherever she looked. She was astounded by the bright reds of tuna at the fishmongers, the yellow blaze of trash barrel fires in the Italian Market, the perfect azure blue of water ice.

It was there, the Italian Market, which she knew best. She loved South Philadelphia, where her family settled after emigrating from Italy and where her grandfather Giuseppe became a bread baron. It was where her father, Joe, followed in his floury footsteps.

Palumbo's Bakery was known throughout the city, its crusty, seeded loaves popular on restaurant and kitchen tables from Center City to West Philadelphia, from South Philly to the Great Northeast. But Janice had fame of her own, a minor celebrity in a city of minor celebrities. Her radio show, broadcast locally on the NPR affiliate but not yet picked up nationally, featured stories from all over Philadelphia. She extended a tentative hand, halfway hoping the man didn't know her already.

"Janice Palumbo," she said.

"Oh, how nice to meet you," Louis said knowingly. "You certainly don't have a face for radio."

She bristled.

"Why would you say that? Just because someone's in radio they're not attractive enough for TV?"

"Uh, not at all," he stammered. "Well, maybe. You never know. I mean, how could you know, ya know? All a listener knows is the voice, right? I like your voice. I'm a fan."

Louis hadn't meant to offend her but knew he was blathering.

"I meant nothing by it," he said.

Janice willed herself cool. She adjusted her bag and started to button her coat for the walk home.

"Whatever," she said, dismissing him, but Louis sought to salvage the conversation.

"You're very good," he said.

She hesitated, wondering what she was on the ropes for, but continued anyway.

"I wanted to tell stories that I was interested in, stories people would listen to, without them being distracted by *me*," she said.

You're not *that* hot, Louis thought, but he let it go.

"You've got a point," he said. "You're very distracting. That is, you look very nice."

He was stammering again and looked up just as Janice turned away, embarrassed for the both of them.

"But I'm a critic anyway," he continued. "Just ask my friend over there."

Track lighting beamed off the glossy wood floors and Herman's bald head. Glancing over, Louis saw that Herman was beaming, too. He must have made a sale.

"Actually, I'm a rabbi. Louis Abrams, of B'nai Tikvah in Apple Hill."

"Nice to meet you. My boyfriend, ex, actually, is Jewish. We met here."

Janice half hoped to run into him tonight but also hoped she wouldn't. Dr. Stephen Golding was a veterinarian whose job at Penn kept him late most nights, one of several strains that pulled at their relationship, and a chance meeting wasn't likely.

"I'll assume you're Catholic," Louis said. "Tough to make it work. I've counseled a good number of mixed couples and the Jewish-Catholic thing, always a little tough. If you're a quote-unquote good Catholic you go to Mass, take communion, and believe that Jesus was the Son of God. It's what sets us apart. I imagine that was a problem for your friend."

Janice was a lapsed Catholic but didn't consider herself any less good.

"Pretty good, Rabbi," she said.

"Well, I don't know how good. You're in this line of work as long as me, patterns develop. You see things. Didya date long?"

Janice squirmed a bit, uneasy suddenly with the conversation. Had he been hitting on her? She wasn't sure. The rabbi seemed nice enough, but she collected her things to go.

"Big day tomorrow," she said. "Nice meeting you."

Louis smiled and handed her a card.

"I hold a couple's workshop Tuesday nights," he said. "Singles come too. Nothing formal. A chance to talk issues, kibbitz a little over a cup of coffee, chew the fat and a piece of my wife's cake. Sometimes we actually say something. Bring your ex if you like or come by yourself."

Janice took the card and stuck it in the pocket of her good Burberry topcoat.

"Maybe I'll see you," she said.

"I hope so," Louis said, offering his hand again. "Nice meeting you too."

Outside, Broad Street was dark and blustery, but the skies hadn't yet opened. Tired and hungry, Janice pulled the coat about her and headed out into the night. She was within sight of her stoop when it got darker still, lightning flashed, and a deep, unsettling fear rippled through her. A legless woman atop a carpeted wooden dolly shook a cup at her half a block from her home, but tonight Janice didn't stop to put change in. She reached her door as a thunderclap exploded and brought the coming rains.

Janice closed the heavy outer door behind her, flung her coat on a stand in the foyer and glanced at the flashing red "1" on her machine. Maybe Stephen called.

# Chapter 2

Louis awoke the next morning covered in sweat, upset and trembling from uneven sleep, Rebecca already off to the shop. In his dream, one of two or three recurring dramas, he was back in sleep-away camp, happily plying the hilly, rock-strewn terrain.

Tufts of wild grass grew straight and long among the cabins, simple barracks of plain weathered plywood, their windows roughed out and covered with heavy steel mesh.

The weather that summer had been perfect – hot, bright, and minimally buggy during the day, cool and clear at night – the evenings filled with campfires crackling on lengths of seasoned hardwood fed with a crisp Canadian breeze.

His parents could afford to send Louis to camp just half the summer, but the month had been glorious once he got past his early homesickness. It was then that Louis met Kit, a young strawberry blonde from Connecticut with whom he became fast friends. Kit, who had been to camp the previous year, was the one who told Louis about "free sleep," the legendary anything-goes period after eleven on Friday nights when most campers actually *were* sleeping, but others climbed from their bunks and snuck out to re-stoke the fire and play truth-or-dare.

That last Friday he'd hoped to sneak off with Kit, kiss her on the wet grass behind the bleachers, maybe even slide his hand beneath her shirt. His heart fluttered wildly just thinking about that soft virgin terrain, tender developing mounds beneath a white cotton tee.

When the door to Cabin 8 creaked open and sprang shut sometime before eleven, Louis had already been thinking of Kit. His left hand, seemingly of a mind all its own, had fished down into his jammies and was busily pleasuring himself.

"Louis!" a voice called from across the darkened room, and he tensed, softened, and lay stock-still. Steps crept closer and he heard the voice again.

"Louis! Whatcha doin?"

The husky voice certainly wasn't Kit's, and it wasn't welcome. Donny DiCicco, a big, loud, red-headed boy from Cabin 10, was suddenly at his side, reeking of booze.

"What're ya doin!," he whisper-bellowed again, this time much closer. "You greasin' weazer?"

Louis cringed at the boy's vulgarity but said nothing, just played possum and hoped he'd go away.

"It's your last Friday in camp so we're havin' a party,"
he said.

"What party?" Louis mumbled, conversation
unavoidable. "I'm sleepin'."

"No you're not. You're pullin' rope, ya big homo.
Sleep when you're home. We're havin' a party."

So Louis, half asleep, gave in to the older boy's
demand and climbed down from his bunk. He slipped
into frayed leather moccasins and followed DiCicco in
silence out to the empty field on the other side of Cabin
10.

"Where's the party?" Louis queried.

"It's just us to start. Here, have a sip," DiCicco said,
proffering a bottle.

"What? No, I'm good."

"C'mon, *take* a sip!" the loud boy said.

Louis reluctantly took a pull on the pint of Southern
and coughed so hard he nearly puked. His first taste of
whiskey was thick, sweeter than expected, and burned all
the way to his gut.

"Take another one," Donny prodded. "And drink it
like you own a pair, Abramowitz!"

Louis tightened his lips around the rim, set his tongue at the edge and took a swig, almost spitting up but not quite as bad as before.

"Is that the best you got? Hit it again, ya big puss!"

After his fourth pull in five minutes Louis was woozy and had to sit.

"I thought you said there's a party," he said again, suddenly dizzy.

"There is," Donny assured him, and sat down in the grass beside him. "But like I told you, first it's just us."

Fishing into the top pocket of his old flannel shirt, Donny produced a half-smoked joint, lighted it, and handed it to Louis.

"I don't want any," Louis said, pushing the dope away.

"What're you, a candyass? It's your last Friday in camp!"

So Louis, against his better judgment, accepted the burning joint, took a small hit and coughed so bad he thought he'd lose a lung.

"Keep it down!" Donny said, patting Louis on the back and braying like a jackass. He took a long hit himself, then lay back on the grass and looked up at the stars.

Louis, just ten minutes out of bed, was drunk and stoned, in a state of mind he'd never been, and starting to feel pretty good. He lay back on the ground, too, and didn't even mind the dewy wetness seeping up through his bedclothes.

The unexpected attention from an older kid wasn't bad either and Louis suddenly thought himself kind of cool.

Then, without warning, Donny's hand clasped his. Louis snatched it away, but moments later the boy was reaching for Louis's sleepy johnson, pulling clumsily at his pajama bottoms.

He tried to push Donny away, but the other boy rolled up onto his chest and told him to calm the fuck down.

"I just want to try something," Donny growled. "Just lay still and it won't hurt. Tell me if you like it."

There was hate in the boy's eyes and it frightened Louis, but then Donny swung away and Louis, muttering "Stop, no," then nothing, fell back into the grass until Donny was done.

Afterward, the boys got up in silence, ambled back to their respective cabins, crept inside and went to bed.

* * * * *

As a young man Louis hadn't been overly religious. He changed his name from Abramowitz to Abrams just before entering seminary because Abramowitz sounded *too* Jewish, even for an aspiring rabbi. While the name change was hurtful to his parents, the fact that Louis changed his name didn't surprise his own family so much as his entering seminary in the first place.

But surprised they shouldn't have been.

For more than a decade Louis had been haunted by what happened at camp. Not only was he troubled by what transpired with that boy – deep down he'd never forget his name – but by the belief that it was somehow his fault. When it happened, he might not have stopped it even if he'd tried, but he didn't try. Surely there was a stick or a small rock, something with which to fend off his attacker, had he known he was under attack. But he didn't know, and didn't stop it, and finally, when at long last camp ended a few days later, when his parents arrived in their beat up old Ford wagon to bring him back home, when he cried and fell into his dad's arms too weak, almost, to carry himself to the car, he couldn't say why it was he cried so much, just let them believe he was homesick and that he wanted, more than anything in the world, just to go home.

School was starting in a few weeks and he tried to forget what happened. He shopped with his mother for school clothes and found comfort in the back-to-school TV ads, their promise of new stuff, a new year, a new start.

Louis, despite good scores on aptitude tests, wasn't much of a student during the day, but at Hebrew school that fall he began to excel. At Hebrew school there was no crazy math to solve, no Spanish to memorize, no smelly science lab and no sweaty gym class. Hebrew school, two hours a day, Monday through Friday, became a haven, and about the only thing required was a willingness to pray.

But it wasn't the prayers so much that drew him in that fall but the stories, the five- thousand-year history of which he was a part. Like him, his people had suffered, but they bounced back and prospered. And so, Louis was sure, would he.

Louis's family was secular, but they kept the holidays and every Friday evening without fail his mother carefully lit the Sabbath candles. Burning down to nubs in antique brass candleholders, the soft light emanating from the kitchen warmed the room and, no matter what the chaos of the day, calmed the household. For an hour or two after dinner the flickering light cast benevolent ghostly shadows that, Louis was sure, were the spirits of lost family members come for a Shabbos visit.

His family had deep roots in and around Apple Hill and ties to the community going back generations. His grandfather Hershel, whom most people simply called Harry, delivered ice in nearby Camden where the family settled after emigrating from Poland. They moved to Apple Hill when it was still Jefferson Township, long before the council changed the municipality's name to one they thought more marketable.

In high school, Louis was the kind of student teachers pulled aside to lecture about "potential" and urged to do more with it. At heart, he was a hedonist (though he didn't know the term then), and believed a good time always took a front seat to schoolwork.

In fact, the front seat was where Louis did some of his best work, at least until he got a car with a bed in the back. He was a lustful boy and a natural tinkerer, the kind who loved cars more than sports and who spent hours taking things apart and putting them back together.

At eighteen, Louis spent most of the bar mitzvah money he'd been saving on a 1953 Sedan Delivery. Part car and part truck, the Chevy had a long, flat, windowless cargo space that he and Rebecca put to good use two years later when they started dating.

She wasn't much interested in sex at first, but she *was* interested in Louis, a popular charmer whom all the girls thought cute. Louis was tall and gangly, embarrassed of a long, thin frame he'd have to grow into, but he had great eyes – big, wet orbs neither green nor blue with ladylike lashes. Plus, even as a teen he was roguish, standoffish, and the girls ate it up.

Parties with friends invariably ended with Louis and Rebecca in one of the many fruit orchards around South Jersey or up on Apple Hill, the one for which the mall and, soon after, the town would be named. The hill itself was now hidden under a Lowes Multiplex, the fields of apple trees long cut down and plowed under, forgotten save for a small bronze marker near the theater noting they were once there.

The Sedan Delivery had been Louis and Rebecca's private cove, and Louis made it comfortable with carpeted walls and a nice, soft bed. Now, so many years later, Louis still had the old Sedan Delivery and he still had Rebecca. The car was garage-kept, fully restored, and cherry red with chrome wheels and exhaust tips.

Over time Rebecca came to like the car, too, but she had long since stopped laying with Louis in it. She'd convinced him to stencil Mom's Bake Shop on the sides and somehow that worked for the ride.

He'd didn't drive it to shul on the holidays or Shabbos but parked the custom rod in his spot outside B'nai Tikvah every Tuesday night where it greeted regulars and newcomers alike, bright and lively as neon.

* * * * *

Arriving this Tuesday about six thirty, he set the fresh Danish, cakes, and fruit tarts in trays near the coffee urn, poured himself a cup and took his place at the head of a folding table. As always, his secretary Anita set up the pot just before leaving for the day.

Louis spread a few sections of Sunday's *Times* out in front of him but didn't have long to read when one of his regulars showed up early.

"Rabbi," Terrence Jacov called, poking his head in the open door before coming fully into view. "Got a few?"

Standing in the doorway Terrence nearly filled the frame and Louis eyed him quizzically, never quite sure what to make of the man.

"Of course, Terrence," he said. "Come on in. Grab yourself some coffee and a Danish."

Jacov filled one of the small Styrofoam cups, stirred in some sugar and Coffeemate, scooped up a big hunk of cake and took a seat near the rabbi. Squeezing himself into a child's desk, his Army surplus jacket spread tight across his back and shoulders making him look even bigger than he was, a sedentary giant.

Once, long ago, he'd sat in such a classroom for Hebrew school himself, but now, surrounded by drawings of menorahs and dreidels, he couldn't seem more out of place.

"I'm not gonna see you for a coupla weeks," Jacov started.

"Why's at?" the rabbi asked.

"Job in Cali," Jacov said.

Jacov was stateside during the Vietnam War but carried himself like a scarred combat vet. He peppered his speech with quasi military terms like "Cali," "in-country" and "mission" that at times made him sound as odd as he looked.

"Just a coupla weeks," he repeated. "I'm setting up my own thing here when I get back, which is what I wanted to ask you about."

"Oh yeah?" the rabbi queried. "What kind of thing is that?"

"Security. Who does yours?"

"My security? Who am I, the President?"

"C'mon," Jacov said. "I'm serious. The synagogue - motion detectors, surveillance cams, alarms. You're wired, aren't you?"

"Sure we are. National. We've had 'em for years."

Jacov, he knew, knew this too. There were enough window stickers and lawn signs poking up from the trim wet grass for three temples.

"Can I write you a quote?" Jacov asked. "No obligation. But I'm sure I can beat 'em."

Louis looked at him oddly, a little annoyed by the ambush pitch.

"Uh, sure, you can give us a quote. But they do it all. Of course, we've never really needed them."

"Then you can't really know, can you?" Jacov said.

There was subtle menace in the way he said this. It was a mild suggestion that he, Jacov, could protect the rabbi and his congregation from the unknown.

"You know," Jacov continued, "there was a guy, Jewish guy, believe it or not, stole Torahs from a coupla temples in Philly ten, fifteen years ago. Dude's probably out now, but he did like eight to ten at Graterford."

Louis suddenly hoped he wouldn't start finding windows broken and locks jimmied, dead cats and rabbits, and Jacov's hand out for protection money.

They met two years before when Jacov's father, a Jersey Shore businessman, died suddenly from a massive coronary. A few months shy of eighty, Irving Jacov was almost exactly the same age at which Louis's own father had died, and Jacov and Louis bonded some in the months that followed.

Jacov said the mourner's kaddish twice a day in the period just after his father's death and came to morning services for at least a year afterward, the traditional grieving period for a family member.

He had never felt especially close with his father but found solace in the daily prayers and his time spent with the grizzled old men at shul. Afterward, he'd share in their Kiddush, a small plastic shot of whiskey or wine, and a piece of marble cake left over from Sabbath services. Sometimes they even ate a little herring.

Jacov still attended morning prayers, often helping to make a minyan, the quorum of ten necessary for a service. The men could count on Terrence to come if they called him, one man short, and that made him valuable to them.

It pleased Louis that he could count on Jacov and pleasing the rabbi pleased Jacov. In Louis, an ordained rabbi and leader of B'Nai Tikvah, he saw the goodness that somehow evaded his own small life.

And so it was that Jacov became a regular on Tuesday nights, too.

"You're in security, huh Terry?" Louis remarked, aware suddenly that he really didn't know the man at all.

"Terrence," Jacov corrected. "Well, mostly security but this and that. Whatever it takes."

In fact, Jacov had done a lot of this and that since his discharge from the Army. He'd done some sales – used cars, mortgages, even mattresses – but in recent years got by on small-job handyman work and the occasional month-long gig. Security, he was sure, was his future.

Jacov was happily divorced, somewhat of a loner, and a Soldier-of-Fortune type who made Louis a little nervous. Still, he struck Louis as honest in an "I've got your back, you've got mine" kind of way and that, the rabbi knew, could always be helpful.

Though Louis would never use the expression publicly, he considered Jacov a born-again Jew, one of many he knew who'd come to prayer after losing a loved one, often a parent. Like others, Jacov rekindled a curiosity in his faith that he'd never fully warmed to as a boy, peppering the rabbi with questions about Judaism, why he should keep kosher (he didn't) and the Jewish notions of heaven and hell (it wasn't that cut and dried).

He inherited a tidy sum when his father passed, but it wouldn't last forever and that was why, after working for others for so long, he decided the time had come to strike out on his own.

Terrence still didn't know for sure if security was his calling (he wasn't really sure he had one), but it was a potentially lucrative business that he felt he had the chops for. After all, when most of his classmates ran off to college to smoke dope, bang chicks and avoid the military, he signed right up. He was relieved when the Army kept him stateside during the war and even more thrilled that he learned the art of "wet work" without having to get his hands dirty. The Army taught him how to build and diffuse bombs, how to handle weapons and any number of ways to take a man down. It just never put him to the test, and that was OK, too.

These days he literally wore his service on his sleeve, embellishing it with a Delta Force patch he bought at an Army-Navy store. He never did contact the old service buds he once thought he would, but the Special Forces patch and Army surplus jacket was his way of staying in touch.

As Louis had thought moments before, it dawned on Jacov now that he and the rabbi had known each other for years but didn't really know one another at all. In fact, the rabbi knew him no better and no worse than most people did and so Jacov, on a whim, decided to let him in.

"I never liked 'Terry,'" he said in response to the rabbi's minor gaffe and his terse correction. "The kids in the neighborhood called me Terry and it burned my ass raw. The more I said 'Terrence' the more they said 'Terry.' 'Terry Jack-Off'. I could have killed them."

Jack-off, Louis thought. Jacov, Jack-off. Yeah, he could see it.

"No need to explain," he said. "Terrence it is."

Louis glanced at his watch. The others would be along shortly.

"Kids can be cruel," he offered. "But you're above all that now."

“I am at that,” Jacov said, glancing up as a few others walked in.

“Well, good luck out in Cali,” Louis said. “And give me a call when you get back.”

# Chapter 3

Part bible study, part group counseling session, Louis's Tuesday night coffee klatch had been more popular at first but still drew up to a dozen or more attendees most weeks, mostly couples but also singles, many on the rebound or prowling for new action.

Alex and Naomi Kahan were among the regulars but she, an Abrams' devotee, dragged her husband along. Alex was a schoolteacher, his wife a nurse for the Apple Hill School District, and the couple came to reacquaint themselves with their faith and meet others looking to do the same.

Alex prided himself on his ability to read people, but there was something about Abrams that just didn't read right. His smoothness stuck in Alex's craw, and for all his big-guy bear-hugginess and "howyadoins," he wasn't very warm. Alex didn't sense anything diabolical in Abrams per se, just a vague something that felt less than rabbinical, or at least how Alex expected a rabbi to be.

Naomi's family helped establish B'nai Tikvah nearly forty years before but, like many of her generation, faith became less important as she grew into her own. She and Alex were spiritual but non-pious Jews and she'd only resumed attendance at services after her mother passed following a stroke the year before.

A renewed interest in Judaism was fine with Alex but why this, he wondered. And why did Abrams go out of his way to agree with him so much, to seek out his opinion, when he sensed the rabbi didn't really like him? Abrams barely glanced at Naomi as the couple entered the room now and, as usual, directed his attention immediately toward Alex.

"Welcome," Abrams called, his right hand reaching out. "And how are the children?"

Abrams referred, of course, to Alex's school children, as the couple had none of their own. On its face the query seemed harmless enough, but it could be read as a veiled dig at their lack of children and that was how Alex took it. Six years into their marriage the union had borne no fruit and it was for that, also, that Naomi sought the rabbi's guidance after her mother's death.

But she got more than guidance. He'd schtupped her for months and was worried, at one point, that she was pregnant with *his* child.

"They keep me out of trouble," Alex said shortly. "What's on the agenda?"

Louis liked to have a theme each week, a conversation starter. Faith, politics, the war in Iraq or the struggling U.S. economy, it didn't really matter as long as it got people talking.

"Fidelity," Louis said directly, not a touch of irony in his voice. Still shaking Alex's hand, he nodded a hello to Naomi, towering over the couple and radiating warmth upon them.

"Interesting," Naomi said to her husband. "Considering all the newly-divorced and almost divorced couples who come, it should be some topic."

"Who knows where it will go," Abrams said, pushing his shoulder blades back and standing tall and straight. "For all I know we'll talk baseball again. Maybe this is the year for Boston or, God help them, Chicago. Bats-balls, life-death, sex-marriage. It is the *human* dynamic we are interested in, how we interact and relate with one another that matters. So, we start with fidelity and end up talking home runs. Wouldn't be a first for *that* analogy, would it?"

"Not for *this* group," Jacov chimed in.

Louis gave him a look. He had a decent sense of humor but not when it was directed at him.

Which isn't to say he didn't like to have fun.

When he wasn't driving the Sedan Delivery he prowled about town in a beefed up Crown Victoria, the kind of car all the cops drove. Sometimes, as he rocketed up the New Jersey Turnpike or Route 295, other motorists even pulled aside, mistaking his for an unmarked State Trooper car, and it always made him smile.

He still loved basketball and played when he could, out at the Gershman Y or in a local men's league. Louis, a young fifty-seven, was not above throwing an elbow with boys still in high school or men half his size. In fact, he was known for it.

Louis intimated men on and off the court, but women were still drawn to him. He discovered at an early age that, despite what many said, lots of girls didn't want a nice guy. They craved rough guys, men who could protect and support them, and Louis sensed that was a desire lodged deeper in the gene pool than any Women's Issues class or *Feminine Mystique* reading. As a rule, the women and girls he'd known liked that he was somewhat aloof, that he paid compliments sparingly and stayed just far enough to keep their interest.

The exception, of course, had been Rebecca. Though a string of affairs littered the course of their relationship (all of them his) she was the one constant in his life since puberty. She didn't need his protection and could provide for herself, thank you very much. Wed now for twenty-seven years, they had two grown sons and had proven to themselves and the community that theirs was a lasting relationship.

One reason for their own union's strength was the blind eye she turned to his philandering. After so long together they'd grown co-dependent – there was no bigger booster of her bakery business than him and his rise in the Jewish community would have been impossible without her. But her lifetime with Louis came with a cost, and it cut deep.

So, while he knew a thing or two about sustaining a marriage, Rabbi Louis Abrams really knew little about fidelity and it was his decision to talk about it that made Naomi Kahan smirk. That and the fact that she knew as well as anyone just how much of an infidel he was.

As Alex glanced about the room, Louis's eyes passed quickly over his wife's body and his right eye seemed to twitch. She wondered if he actually had the balls to wink at her in front of her husband (he did), and suspected the bastard was thinking that very moment about what they used to do (he was).

"So how's the district?" he said all of a sudden. "I see the budget went down again. Carrier's been hard on you guys."

His reference to the local newspaper was not a welcome one for Naomi, whose passion for the district ran as deep as it once did for the rabbi himself. Voters almost always defeated the local school budget, the one governmental spending plan they had a direct say in. And, when they did, Township Committee made token cuts in deference to the taxpayers and overrode the vote.

But what really irked school officials – Naomi's boss, Eli Goldman, especially -- was the coverage they got in the local rag and how they came off in print.

The paper's Apple Hill reporter, Bob Jackson, had been relentless in covering the district the past several months, reporting unfavorably on how it went way over budget renovating the high school's auditorium.

Patiently, pleadingly, *imploringly*, school officials tried explaining how the district actually *saved* money with a general contractor who did the job on the cheap. They insisted that, despite the cooling economy, construction costs were high because builders remained busy and that accounted for the overrun.

The job came in well over the $18.5 million that was budgeted, yet officials maintained that was lower than what it *could* have been. The fact that it was lower than it *might* have been, to their way of thinking, made it a bargain.

Jackson didn't buy that argument and neither did the editorial board, which crucified the district and superintendent Goldman. The editors urged taxpayers to defeat the school budget and that is just what they did.

"Don't get me started," Naomi said. "They just don't get it."

"And how's Eli, my brother from another mother?" Louis said.

"He's OK. Another one not too thrilled with Bob Jackson right now, but we'll get over it."

She looked about dumbly.

"You know what I mean. He'll get over it."

Louis suspected Naomi of bedding Goldman too – a suspicion shared by Jackson, half the school board and not a few members of the public – but he knew better than to bridge the subject with her.

Like a big retriever with a bone, Naomi was relentless if not terribly bright. Louis imagined her the kind of girl whose parents urged she be bumped up to advanced placement classes over the recommendation of her counselor and, in fact, that is just what they did. And Naomi, ever resourceful, sweated it out and muddled through.

"Hi Terry!" she called now to Jacov, who still sat stuffed in the child's desk scratching its top with a long dirty fingernail.

He flinched, expecting neither the sudden hello nor Naomi's casualness. They'd spoken, sort of, across the circle in discussions, but never one-on-one, and he almost failed to respond.

"What do you say," Jacov replied.

"Not a lot, Terry. You're divorced, aren't you?"

"Uh… yeah," he said, wondering why they were even talking. "And it's Terrence."

"What's that?"

"Terrence. You called me Terry? My name's Terrence."

"All-righty, then," Naomi said, smarting dumbly. "You're divorced, TERRENCE, aren't you?"

"Does it show?"

He smiled a little, pleased with his wit, and Naomi smiled back. She was a little scared of him and paused before answering.

"Four years and counting," he continued. "Best move I ever made. Why d'ya ask?"

"My girlfriend. She went through a nasty divorce herself last year and she's trying to get back into the swing."

"Uh, let me guess. You want me to help her with that swing thing."

"May-be," Naomi said flirtatiously. "I think you'd like her."

Jacov sized Naomi up. He'd like *her*, Naomi, but that wasn't the offer. He noticed over the past few months that the rabbi liked her too and he could see why – spunky, hot little bod, a likely firecracker between the sheets.

"She's not Jewish, if that's OK, but I think you'd like her," Naomi said again.

"Oh yeah? Why's at?"

"I think she's your type. She's cute - a real looker in her day. She could lose a few, but who can't? Anyhow, I'm working on that."

"For you or for her?"

"Watch it, buster."

"Just kidding. So... *a looker in her day* and she *needs to lose a few*," Jacov parroted, flirting with Naomi even as she pitched her girlfriend. "An old fatty. Hmmm. Just my type. Gee, thanks."

"Noooo. C'mon. She's about your age. You're what – fifty-six, fifty-seven?"

"Fifty-two."

"Same difference. She's nice. She's got big boobs and a nice face. She used to be a real wild one."

Big boobs *and* a wild side? Maybe he *would* like her.

"Tell you what," Jacov said. "Bring her here. If we hit it off maybe we'll go out sometime, but I'll be in Cali till mid-October."

"Cali?"

Jacov smirked. Shook his head. Civilians.

"I've got a job in L.A. the next coupla weeks, but I should be back around the sixteenth. What's her name?"

"Rini. Well, her name is Renee but everyone calls her Rini."

"Dig it. But introduce me as Terrence, not Terry."

"Yeah, I got that," Naomi said.

There was something mysterious about Jacov that kind of intrigued her too. He wasn't her type – too redneck and surly - but rugged, kind of handsome, big. She actually thought Rini might like him.

"I'll tell her," she said.

Other couples filtered in now, helping themselves to coffee and cake and taking their places in the semi-circle around the rabbi's desk. A perfect little orbit about the proverbial sun. The time had come to start.

"Fidelity," Louis began. "Webster's says it's the state of being faithful. They also say it's about quality audio, but that's another topic."

Abrams looked around, made like he was playing a drum, the lounge lizard with a one-liner.

"Ba-dum-bum. Anyway… I say it's about being true. True to your spouse, to be sure, but perhaps, more so, true to yourself."

"You have got to be kidding me," Alex murmured, just loud enough so everyone could hear.

He had no proof his wife had cheated on him with the rabbi, this babbling tower of babble, but he had his suspicions.

"Fidelity is about faithfulness to your spouse. Period. I don't know what you're selling, Rabbi, but it ain't fidelity."

Naomi was mortified.

"Truth can be found in many places, Alex, and defined many ways. If we are not true to ourselves, our passions, our own needs and desires, how can we be true to another? Some look beyond their spouses to find completeness that they don't find in their lives and I don't just mean sex. There are other infidelities and passions that can be equally destructive and obsessive."

He paused, allowing his wisdom to wash over, to warm and educate, before moving on.

"Like work, gambling, sports. How many of us know weekend widows? Wives married to couch potatoes who waste every Saturday and Sunday parked in the living room, a bag of Doritos on one knee and a can of Bud on the other, watching *the game*?"

Here Abrams hit home.

"And that's unfaithful how?" Alex challenged, the topic suddenly personal and turned subtly on him. Of course, Abrams knew Naomi was just such a "weekend widow," that's what drove her to him in the first place.

"It may not be unfaithful in the carnal sense, Alex, but it is unfaithful just the same."

He spoke down to Alex from on high now, Samurai to serf, Jedi to Jabba, master to grasshoppa. Alex felt the urge to punch the fucker.

"When the few good hours we have to share with one another each week are spent instead watching other men battle over a football, that is, in a sense, a form of cheating," Louis continued. "It is cheating one's spouse of one's company, one's companionship."

He avoided the whole homoerotic nature of sport, the men in tights thing, patting one another on the butt, bonding over sweat and broken teeth and bones.

"It's not the same," Alex said.

"Not the same, no, but it's close."

"Not even close!" Alex nearly shouted.

"It's closer than you think, Alex. There is physical disconnect and there is emotional. Granted, extramarital affairs cause both, but there is more than one type of infidelity. That is my point."

A light rap on the classroom door interrupted the discussion just as it was getting good. Janice Palumbo stood on the other side of the safety glass and peered in. The jamb squeaked as she pushed the door open and stepped inside.

"Hi, Rabbi," she said meekly. "'member me?"

"Of course, Janice," he said, somewhat surprised to see her. "Welcome. We're just getting started."

Janice introduced herself to the group: Daniel and Ida Cooperman, Terrence Jacov, Helen Hecht, Sol and Toby Kimmelman, Alex and Naomi Kahan, Steve and Ester Frank.

"I was hoping you'd come," Louis continued. "I thought maybe you'd bring your friend."

"Stephen? No, he's working late. I told him I was coming, though."

"Maybe next time," Louis said, turning back to the group. "Many of you already know Janice, I believe. This is *the* Janice Palumbo of National Public Radio."

In fact, most did, and they also knew about Stephen, her on-again-off

-again beau, from Janice's radio program, *Driveways*. The final segment of her daily, hour-long show often explored themes and issues in her own life, personal territory rarely explored by journalists that she found game.

Unlike most other reporters, Janice thought it her duty to bring listeners into her life, a payback of sorts to both callers and subjects who laid bare their own stories week after week for her.

"Sorry I'm late," she said, finding a seat and tossing her jacket on an empty desk.

Like Jacov's experience in Hebrew school, the chairs were the type Janice sat in as a young girl in Catechism class. She remembered hating the wooden one-piece desk-chairs, shifting her body in them and, almost daily, rapping her elbow on an edge so a jolt of pain danced in her funny bone.

Janice settled into the chair and crossed her legs beneath it. Her tan khaki skirt tightened against her shapely thighs. And Louis, true to himself, couldn't help but look.

<u>Chapter 4</u>

The weeks before the High Holy Days take on a somber note for most Jews as they contemplate the New Year, the past year, and their own mortality.

Though he had his faults, a lack of faith was not among them and Louis also became introspective as the calendar wound down. These were the Days of Awe, the period between Rosh Hashonah – the Jewish New Year – and Yom Kippur – the Day of Atonement – the holiest day of the year.

For a rabbi, the High Holy Days are not just the most meaningful and important of the Jewish calendar, but a time when he or she must really be in tune with the congregation, really on his or her game. It is a time when services are most full, often attended by Jews who don't come the rest of the year – Jews who might become regular members if they are moved enough by the services over the holidays to join.

That in mind, Louis sought to deliver the most heartfelt, meaningful sermons of the year during the High Holy Days and hunted for news events with just the right connection to Judaism or the State of Israel. A certified news junkie, he found himself scouring newspapers, TV, and online media, immersing himself in current events to prepare for his sermons.

While he considered himself a true believer, Louis did not delude himself into thinking most congregants were too. Less inclined to be, of course, were those who attended services once or twice a year during the High Holy Days but did not commit to the synagogue financially or personally by joining.

It was these wanderers, these non-committed, whom Louis sought to reach with poignant, topical sermons over Rosh Hashanah and Yom Kippur. And he knew if he could strike the right balance between timeliness and holiness, he just might close the deal.

But topics were more limited than one might imagine. Sermons must be punchy but not overly political. They must entertain but return to the meat of the matter, always the meat of the matter, and what mattered most never varied much – one's faith in God and one's place in the Jewish community.

And how does one find their place in the community? For starters, they join a synagogue. *His* synagogue. B'nai Tikvah.

Perennial topics included unrest in Israel and a need for more God. Social unrest at home and a need for more

God. War (this year it's Iraq, next year who knows), poverty, starvation, homelessness, and a need for more God. Louis knew the recipe and served it up hot and tasty for the masses.

Though he wouldn't admit it, there were times in his own life when he, Louis Abrams, senior rabbi for B'nai Tikvah, community leader and upstanding citizen, harbored doubts. Not over his faith, mind you, but about his message. At such times, his sermons came off wooden and canned, as if the hand of God didn't touch him at all. Other times his certainty was Windex-clear, the spirit practically bursting from his pores. It was that energy which he sought to capture and unleash for the holidays. His goal: to let loose a contagious verve that swept up the congregation in head bobbing and belief. He'd deliver the kind of sermon that stayed with worshippers long after the benediction and led them, ultimately, to return as members or sign on anew.

The trick of it all came down to inspiration and delivery. Louis, a strong speaker if not a fiery orator, never sought the "hallelujahs" or "amens" so popular with the Baptists and evangelicals. His was a subtler, lower key approach in which he let his message flow down upon the congregation, not sweep it away. But the message had to be right, and today he was grappling with it. He was floating, adrift, and more than anything sought fresh ground on which to plant his flag.

So, Louis reached into his desk, pulled out an old Te Amo cigar box, and unfurled a small pouch of inspiration – a tight, pungent bag of weed.

The high-grade marijuana had a skunky smell that seeped through the plastic baggy and up from the box as he lifted the lid. The smell, so rich and earthy, was intoxicating even before he smoked it. He pulled the Ziploc open and breathed in the tropical musk.

"Mmmm," he snorted. "Tasty."

A buddy in Delaware scored it for him at regular intervals, usually about once every three months, and the trip down was always an experience. Not only would he cop good weed but he'd spend time in the bohemian haunts of Newark, near the University of Delaware.

Delaware babes had a style all their own, a blonde, Waspy, shiksa kinda thing that Louis really dug. His favorites were unfailingly thin with small high breasts. They were slightly snobbish, preppy and smart. Louis, had he not had to get back most days, might easily while away the afternoons among them, a hit or two of good weed coursing through his system, sipping a Starbucks latte.

When Louis smoked at home or in the office he often used a short glass bong that he bought in Newark. But his pot pipe of choice today was a "dugout," a light teak box drilled to hold a small amount of finely ground weed and a thin metal pipe fashioned to look like a cigarette. Packed with dope the one-hitter was economical and could be smoked in public, walking down the street, looking perfectly legitimate.

Louis poured some pot into the dugout, closed the bag, and packed a hit. The five-dollar lighter he also bought on Main Street threw a hot blue torch that he touched now to the end of the pipe. He closed his eyes and breathed in as the smoke expanded sweetly in his lungs and filled him, instantly, with elation. He held the thick gray cloud as long as he could and breathed out slowly, savoring the buzz.

Louis sat quietly a few minutes, then opened his desk, removed a fresh white legal pad and scrawled a few thoughts about current events. Any idea might morph into sermon material for the holidays so he'd just let it flow, stream of consciousness, when the phone disrupted him.

"Hi, Louie," Rebecca said. "How's your day, bay-
bee?"

Calling from her office, his wife's forearms were
lightly coated with flour and confectioner's sugar. Her
brow fairly glistened and she felt satisfied and content
with the morning's work. It had been years since she had
to do the baking herself, but in preparation for the
holidays she always pitched in and loved every minute of
it.

"Good, Bec," Louis answered, coughing the last
wisp of smoke discreetly into his fist. "What's up?"

"I need a favor. Could you go by the house and get
my planner? I've got my delivery guy running two hours
behind - some schmuck on the Schuylkill rammed a
school bus -- so he's stuck in Philly. And I've got three
appointments this afternoon."

"If you know about your three appointments why do
you need the planner?"

"I need it. My phone numbers, my notes,
everything's in there," she said.

"You're in Apple Hill today?"

"I'm in Apple Hill. Of course Apple Hill. Where
else?"

"Alright. Give me a half hour, forty minutes. I just want to finish up here and I'll drive home and get it."

"Thank you honey," she sang. "I love you honey."

"Yeah, yeah. Love you too. See ya in a bit."

Louis hung up the phone, scratched his beard and returned to the legal pad. War in Iraq. Bombings in Israel. Bush in office and the economy in the shitter. Good pickins. He'd settle on one, flesh it out and start writing up notes in the morning when his head was clear.

When the phone rang again. Louis let it ring a few times and hoped Anita would pick it up. He was, after all, actually *paying* her to pick it up. On the fifth ring, Louis reached for the phone, agitated.

"YES, Rebecca," he said.

"Uhh... Rabbi? It's Janice. Janice Palumbo."

"Oh, hello, Janice," Louis said, regretting all of a sudden that he'd gotten stoned at all. "I thought it was my wife. I just hung up with her."

"Oh, I'm sorry," she said. "Should I let you go?"

"No, no, it's okay. How are you? I thought maybe we scared you off the other night."

"No, nothing like that. I liked it. But Tuesdays are tough. In fact, every night is tough lately. I told Stephen I went though."

"Good, maybe he'll join us next time," Louis said.

"Yeah, maybe, but I doubt it. He's not really the club type."

"Well, I wouldn't call it a club exactly. It's more of a gang."

Janice giggled.

"I wanted to ask you something," she said. "You do conversion classes, don't you?"

"Sure I do. Considering conversion?"

"Considering it. Considering a lot of things lately, if you want to know the truth."

"Nothing wrong with that."

"It's something I've been toying with for a while. At first I thought I was doing it for Stephen, but now that's, well, anyhow I'm still thinking about it."

Louis was high. Really fucking high. And he wished he wasn't. He could function well enough after smoking, but it wasn't where he wanted, or needed, to be right now.

"Janice," he said, "we can't make anyone else happy if we don't make ourselves happy first. That's my rule of thumb."

"Good rule," she said. "Anyhow, it's not something I'm sure of. I thought maybe you could help me talk it out."

"Absolutely," he said. "My door's always open."

"OK, then," she chirped. "I'll give you a call next week."

* * * * *

By the time Louis got to the bakery, Rebecca was antsy. Her one-thirty appointment was less than half an hour away and she wanted to review her notes from a conversation with the customer from the week before.

Louis was still buzzing along, but now the munchies had set in and, entering the storefront, everything looked good, especially the little strawberry blonde behind the counter.

"New girl?" he asked Rebecca with a backward glance toward the counter.

"You behave yourself, mister," she said.

"I'm just asking."

"I know all about your asking."

He helped himself to a sticky bun and a cup of black coffee and followed his wife to her office.

"That your lunch?" she asked.

53

"Just a nosh. My delivery charge. So what was the emergency?"

"I just needed my book," she said, taking it from him. "Thank you, honey."

Louis munched the sticky bun and picked through some junk mail on his wife's desk. He thought all of a sudden of Janice.

"Got a call before from Janice Palumbo," he said.

"Who?"

"Janice Palumbo? NPR?"

"Izzat right? And why would she call you?"

The question was not why Janice would call but why he would mention it to his wife. Louis cursed himself and, for the second time in an hour, his decision to get high.

"I met her at Herman Wolfe's opening in Philly last month and she stopped by my session Tuesday night," he said. "Her boyfriend's Jewish and she's considering conversion."

"What, they got no good rabbis in Philadelphia?"

"What can I say? She likes me."

"That's what worries me," Rebecca said.

She turned from Louis, reached up and opened the hopper style window in her office. She had to step on a small, polished wood stool, a woodshop project their youngest boy made in high school, just to reach the handle.

Rebecca could be mistaken for nothing but a middle-aged Yiddishe mama but Louis still liked to watch her move. Even after all these years, he thought proudly, still a tight little package.

Louis, who didn't offer to open the window for her, stood up now and went to his wife. He rubbed a palm over her butt – firm and shapely from spin classes – and nuzzled his scratchy chin into her neck. He reached in front and cupped her breasts, but Rebecca wriggled free.

"Louis Abrams, you are a *very* bad man," she said, a wicked little grin creasing her face. She cast a quick glance at the open door to see that no one saw Louis grope her but considered closing it and letting him finish.

"You wouldn't have it any other way," he said.

"So says you, hot shot."

Rebecca thought of a new lacy black teddy from Frederick's and how maybe she'd try it out tonight. With Louis, lingerie never lasted long anyway.

"Maybe tonight I'll *let* you be bad," she said.

"Why Mrs. Abrams. A rabbi's wife, no less. But it's less fun if you let me."

He thought of their four-post bed and binding his wife to it, spread eagle, with expensive silk ties. It made him horny thinking about it.

"It's a date," he said.

Louis settled back down into a soft chair opposite her desk, took a gulp of coffee and the last bite of sticky bun.

"Just the thing for your cholesterol," Rebecca said.

"Maybe it will motivate me to go to the gym later."

He still favored the old Jewish Y in Philly, but he and Rebecca now worked out at the local Jewish Community Center. A garish, blocky building near his synagogue, the JCC was a fine athletic facility, but it made him cringe every time he saw the place. Drab gray walls topped with wrought iron fencing, the building reminded him of a prison. Or a ghetto. It put him in mind of a bleak, rainy day even in broad sunshine.

"You do that," Rebecca said.

"Is it just me or do you talk to all your customers that way?"

"Just you baby. And you ain't my customer."

Louis stood to go and Rebecca gave her husband a soft kiss on the mouth. She smacked his butt as she headed out the door into the bake shop.

"See you around seven," she said. "Maybe we'll do Chinese."

Rebecca was happy, possibly even in love. With both boys out of the house, she felt more committed to her husband than ever and believed maybe, finally, his extramarital past was indeed a thing of the past.

But Louis would always be Louis.

He gave the little blonde behind the register a quick smile as he headed out the door and she smiled back so he smiled a little more. He climbed down into the Crown Vic and gunned the engine as he left the lot, kicking up rooster tails of sand and pebbly stone.

# Chapter 5

Now that Terrence was finally committing himself to the security business it felt more right than any of the half-baked reincarnations of himself he'd ever attempted. And now that it was finally paying dividends, he wondered why he didn't get into this security stuff years ago.

Ironically, his first brush with security had been from the other side – as a twelve-year-old shoplifter scoring a bag of pencils.

The attempted heist wasn't his first, but it would have been his greatest. Previously, young Terrence took handfuls of golf pencils from Lakeview Country Club across the street from his house. He tried marketing them to the other sixth graders on the playground but, aside from the novelty – short green pencils stenciled with Lakeview Country Club - there wasn't much interest.

For one thing, the pencils didn't have erasers and without an eraser a pencil isn't much use to a kid. For another, the teachers gave out pencils *with* erasers for free.

Then Terrence had seen the oversized pencils – the type that might be appealing to a sixth grader – and tried getting his mother to buy a bag, but she wouldn't budge. They were fat, almost half an inch thick, and covered in glossy, metallic paint. And they were topped with a big, double-headed eraser so that they resembled a shiny, kid-sized gavel.

He resolved to get those pencils, even if his mother wouldn't buy them for him, and returned to the Jamesway one afternoon alone. It was winter so Terrence would have no problem concealing his haul in his bulky green and orange parka.

Terrence loved the coat – the latest trend in the mid-seventies – with faux fur hood, ample pockets and silky nylon lining. There was even a zippered pocket on the left upper sleeve that no one ever seemed to use with three additional outside pockets for pencils and pens.

The parka had a drawstring that formed a large area between his body and the coat when pulled tight and it was here, he figured, that he would stash his haul.

And it seemed so easy. He simply picked up the bags as if he were shopping, walked to the rear of the store and stuffed them inside the parka. Emboldened, he also nabbed a push button Paper Mate pen, a pair of mirrored sunglasses and a Snickers bar to eat on the way home. Then he headed to the front of the store to make his escape.

Gliding in between cashiers (he had nothing to buy, after all, just looking) Terrence stepped on the black corrugated rubber mat at the exit and the door swung open with a whir. He. Was. *Gone.*

"Hold it right there!" a smarmy little plainclothes security man roared all of a sudden. The young man grabbed Terrence above the right elbow just as he left the store, squeezing to the bone.

"Whatcha got there?"

"Nothin'," Terrence said, growing smaller inside his coat as if to absorb his stash.

The guard was thin but strong, no more than nineteen, but a full-grown man to Terrence. He couldn't tell, but beneath the white turtleneck and blue windbreaker the man was taut and wiry. He sported a wispy blonde mustache over full, red lips, and wore aviator shades like the cops on TV.

The security man touched the bulge in Terrence's coat and told him – practically dragged him – to come with him.

It wasn't until Terrence was in the security office, looking out a line of one-way mirrors opposite a bank of cash registers, that he began to cry. He didn't cry out of sorrow, out of regret for what he had done, even for the punishment that surely was to come. He cried for the sheer futility of his mission. For, from behind those mirrors, security personnel could see *everything*.

Closed-circuit cameras peered from smoky glass globes that hung from the ceiling and projected images from around the store to four large screens. Terrence had seen the large dark orbs lots of times but never realized – never thought about it, really – what the hell they were. They certainly didn't figure into his plans for a score.

Least of all did he count on there being roving security people dressed like ordinary shoppers who were watching you even though you weren't watching them. It was now horribly clear that this wiry little man/boy was one of them and had been watching him all along.

Terrence sat in the security office humiliated, waiting in silence for his mother to pick him up. The store wouldn't call the police, not this time, but don't let it happen again.

He remembered how they were nice enough and even gave him a cold can of Coke. He drank the Coke, sniffed a runny green snot that slid down his upper lip and wiped teary flakes from his cheek.

And, soon enough, his mother came to get him.

In the Jacov home, his mom was the one to fear, a tough French-Canadian who was handier than most men around the house. She didn't hesitate to reach for the belt but had been known to grab anything at hand – a wooden spoon, a shoe, even a hardcover book – to mete out punishment.

He'd heard of the legendary whuppings she'd suffered as a girl in Montreal, but it wasn't just the beatings that were family lore. She once had to squat for hours with a two-by-four wedged between the soft backs of her knees, just for skipping a day of school, and Terrence heard all about the painful blood blisters that formed there.

But his mother was not the sadist her own father had been. She punished out of passion. Now, her anger diffused by the ride over and the presence of others in the store, she hardly punished her boy at all. She stood Terrence up, took his hand in hers and walked from the store, head held high. The afternoon ordeal had been tough enough, she figured, so she took her boy home, fed him macaroni and cheese, and sent him to bed.

Years later, working his first security job at Sears, Terrence thought about his "arrest" and what he might have done to avoid it. More than that, he thought about how the kid who caught him followed him, watched him conceal his goods and never revealed himself until Terrence left the store and couldn't claim to be still shopping.

Terrence became that guy. He developed a keen eye but a soft look so shoplifters wouldn't spot him. And he lifted weights. Terrence sought steely muscles like the man-boy security guard because he never wanted to be in a position where a suspect was bigger or stronger than he.

Looking in the mirror now he wondered where that boy had gone. He vaguely recognized himself in the thickset middle-aged man staring back but still claimed to feel like a kid.

"Everyone does," the rabbi once told him. "At least that's what they say. Hold on to your youth if you can, Terrence. Treasure it. But savor your seniority."

"What the fuck is that supposed to mean?" Terrence later wondered.

He respected Abrams, sought his approval, but thought he sometimes sounded like a gusty old windbag acting out a part in a play.

Terrence, fresh now from his California trip, was high on a business buzz. He couldn't wait for the Tuesday night session with Abrams in the hope of showing off his success and drumming up more work.

The three-week trip had gone better than expected. A distributor gave him leads on several projects and he'd turned them around into jobs -- four houses and a small car dealership.

There were lots of considerations for a dealership: motion sensors, lighting, direct wiring for police and fire. He also considered gates that closed and locked at night and perimeter fencing that provided security but did not detract from the visibility of the lot. While the owner of the lot didn't go for all of it, he liked that Terrence was thinking about it so he didn't have to.

"It's value-added service," Jacov said to the man, regurgitating something he'd heard along the way. "It's what I do."

Terrence felt himself evolving from a simple technician to a consultant and liked the way it felt. Wiring a dealership, even a small one, couldn't be much different from wiring a synagogue, a library, even a hospital, and he determined to get the B'nai Tikvah business and build from there.

So, on this Tuesday, Jacov got there a little early to grab the rabbi's full attention before the others arrived.

"Good yontif," Jacov called, entering the room and putting out his hand.

Louis, seated as usual at one of the folding tables, reading a newspaper and sipping a cup of coffee, returned Jacov's wishes for a happy New Year and asked about his trip.

"It went well, better than expected," he said. "Thought I'd be back sooner but I picked up a little extra business."

"Glad to hear it," Louis said, and he was.

Jacov pressed a white linen business card with raised red lettering onto the table before the rabbi.

"Very nice," Louis said, examining the card and turning it over in his hand.

"I was hoping to resume our previous conversation," Jacov started awkwardly. He was an experienced salesman but not a very smooth one.

Abrams looked up blankly.

"The security system?" Jacov prodded.

"Ah, right," Abrams said, motioning for Jacov to sit. "We have a system. I thought I told you that."

"You did. You also said I could write you a quote for a new one, no obligation."

"Right. Well, sure you can. Of course, the Board of Directors makes those decisions, not me, but write it up. I'd say our system's fine, though. Had it ten, fifteen years."

"That's the problem," Jacov said. "Security systems don't get any smarter, but criminals do. You remember the Torah thief a few years back. We talked about him last time. A Jew, no less, breaking in, stealing Torahs and selling them on the black market."

The holy scrolls, handwritten on parchment and read bit by bit throughout the year, fetched forty-thousand or more new. But because they are singular works of art they are not so easy to fence, especially for a crack-addled amateur. Without having sold a single Torah, the man was caught, tried, convicted, and sentenced, by a devout Jewish judge, no less, who gave him the ax.

"He never actually sold any," the rabbi recalled.

"Yes, but he tried. And if you'll forgive my French, Rabbi, he came damn close."

"Well, I don't know about that. A Torah is not such an easy thing to sell. It's not a car stereo. But he did steal them."

"Exactly," Jacov said. "And it could happen again. Even here. Believe me. The thing to keep in mind is the systems of today, like everything else, are much different from those of ten, fifteen years ago. They're all digital. Laser motion detectors, silent alarms, hard wiring to police and fire. Tell you what – I'll come by Thursday morning, check out what you have and give you a quote. You can read it over the weekend and we can talk about it next Tuesday."

Louis wondered if Terrence even heard him. Didn't he just say he didn't make such decisions?

"Okay," he said. "I don't know that we need one, but you come by Thursday and write up a quote."

* * * * *

Like last time, the regulars started to arrive just as Jacov wrapped things up with the rabbi.

Alex and Naomi Kahan arrived early, she fitter than ever, and Louis couldn't help but notice. He also couldn't help but think about their times together, now several months in the past. Naomi was attractive but not what one would call pretty, exactly. She spoke with a soft lisp that made her cute, however, and she knew how to carry herself. She wore her shiny blonde hair shoulder length with short bangs and had a strong, sexy, muscular neck beneath a well-defined jaw. Her arms and torso were tight from lifting weights and her legs and butt firm from step class.

Naomi's workout attire usually consisted of a one-piece leotard, the type that was popular in the eighties and early nineties but was now dated and tired. She had complained to Louis following one of her workouts - after they'd made love several times - that her one complaint about exercise was it made her crotch sweat, but that turned him on even more. After that he had her come directly to "counseling" from the gym and they did it with the leotard half on, half off, the material rubbing when he entered.

Alex still had no proof his wife had been screwing the rabbi and she ended the affair when he began to suspect. Still, his contempt for Abrams was palpable. Now that she was no longer sleeping with the rabbi their own sex life had resumed, but she insisted on coming to Abrams' Tuesday night sessions as well as to Shabbat services to make a good show. She contended it was good for them, but figured privately if they'd stopped coming it might be interpreted as conceding the affair.

"Welcome," the rabbi called as the couple entered the room.

"Good yontif," Naomi replied.

Alex didn't so much as acknowledge the rabbi, helping himself instead to a strong cup of decaf and two lemon squares. He had nothing against *Mrs.* Abrams, and certainly nothing against her cakes.

Abrams dismissed the slight. After all, he *had* been banging the man's wife, and looked up as Janice Palumbo and Dr. Stephen Golding entered the room. Golding appeared older than Louis expected – he hadn't *expected* to see him at all – but was gladdened by the man's age.

Louis appraised Stephen stealthily from his seat behind the table, misjudging him to be in his late forties; he was forty-three. Golding was five-foot-eight, trim, and wore preppy, round tortoise shell glasses. His thinning hair did not detract from his lean good looks and he entered the room like he owned it.

Stephen had been a pretty good musician in his youth and thought he might pursue a career as a jazz guitarist but realized early on that he simply couldn't afford the lifestyle, broke and gig-to-gig.

Besides, medicine, in one form or another, had been his goal since childhood and he couldn't see trading that dream for a long shot at stardom or even a half decent living. So he jammed when he could at clubs around Philly and the few bucks he picked up for gigs covered his bar tab and after-hours sushi.

Playing guitar kept him dexterous and sharp, invaluable qualities for a surgeon, and the complex, extemporaneous jazz fed his mind and his soul. But between his veterinary practice and the jazz gigs he had little spare time for anything else, and that included Janice.

All of this made his appearance tonight all the more surprising. Louis didn't know Janice well, had met her only twice, but believed her relationship with the vet kaput. She practically said so when they first met.

"Hello, Janice," he said, rising from behind the table, the folding chair kicking back from behind his long legs. The chair's metal feet grated across the hard, commercial floor like fingernails on a blackboard.

"Louis Abrams," he said, proffering his hand to Stephen.

"Hello, Rabbi. I've heard good things about you," Golding replied.

"Don't believe everything you hear," Abrams said with a wink. "Glad you could join us."

Louis had not mapped out the starter conversation but made notes of a few newsworthy topics to get the discussion rolling.

Not unlike his flexible moral makeup, Louis's politics were a bit strange. He was a lifelong Democrat but leaned far right on some issues. For example, he believed in the presidency of George W. Bush and his legitimacy to hold office. He believed in the Bush mission, the so-called "Bush doctrine," even the name Bush. But most of all Louis believed that Bush and the other so-called neo-cons he surrounded himself with were good for the State of Israel.

Though there was ample evidence to the contrary, Louis bought the president's efforts to link Iraqi dictator Saddam Hussein to the September 11, 2001 terror attacks on America. And, though none had yet been found by U.N. investigators, he believed Saddam possessed weapons of mass destruction and that his first target, should he not be stopped, would be Israel. Saddam dropped chemical weapons on his own people and he had the capacity and the will to strike Tel Aviv, that Louis was sure of. About the only thing he wasn't sure of was why, if Saddam still had such weapons, had he not used them when he lobbed scud missiles on Israel during the first Gulf War.

Still, Louis knew in his heart that Saddam was the enemy and he believed W. would succeed where his old man had failed. Louis saw the president as honest, patriotic and a great change from Bill Clinton. That he, Louis, was a philanderer like Clinton was not lost on him, but he despised the former president all the same.

Now, as the U.S. steamed toward war with Iraq, Louis knew that mention of the impending conflict would cause opinions and blood to boil. He would be sure to strike a nerve with the handful of liberals attending.

Louis thought of Todd Beamer, the 9/11 passenger who rallied others to battle terrorists aboard a hi-jacked jetliner in the skies over Pennsylvania. "Let's roll," Beamer had said, his words carried to loved ones in his final cell phone call.

A year later, with more than a hundred-thousand U.S. troops parked in the Persian Gulf and the country on high alert, Abrams couldn't resist those words to rally his own and get the meeting started.

"Let's roll," he aped.

Naomi and Janice, having met at the previous meeting, were chatting by the coffee table and rolled their eyes when they heard it. It didn't take a tarot card reader to know what was coming next.

"My wife always says, don't talk politics or religion," Louis started, collecting the group around him. "But hey, I'm a *rabbi* for crying out loud. I am *gonna* talk religion."

A cold November wind rattled the windows and Louis walked over, turned up the thermostat, and returned to his place before the group.

"As for politics, I'm a political animal. I eat the stuff up, which I know you know. So what's it going to be, politics or religion?"

"It's your party," Alex Kahan mocked. "You tell us."

Louis ignored him. He didn't want a repeat of the run-in they had at the last meeting. He sought a rise out of people, healthy debate, not a fight.

"Anyone?" he said, scanning the half-dozen faces before him. It didn't really matter which they picked, politics or religion, because the topic he wished to explore he could reach from either direction.

"Religion," Jacov said.

"Okay, religion," Louis repeated. "Now, some people say the president is going off on a holy war. This is a Judeo-Christian crusade against the Arabs. I wouldn't say it but some would."

Golding did not want to be there, smelled a phony the moment he met Abrams, and was itching for a fight.

"If the coming war is what you want to talk about, just talk about it," Golding said. "But it ain't about religion and it ain't about politics either."

"Dr. Golding," Louis said, pivoting toward him like an afternoon talk show host. "Everyone, this is Stephen Golding, Janice Palumbo's friend. So what's it about?"

"I know I don't have to spell it out but I'll play along. It's blood for oil, plain and simple. It's about Halliburton and Dick Cheney and George Dubya and all their buddies making billions. It's about an illegitimate COWBOY of a president shoving his agenda down our throats. And it's about unfinished business from twelve years ago when Bush senior had the world behind him, but he didn't have the stones to get things done. It's about Boy George wanting to get Saddam Hussein because 'he tried to kill mah daddee.' If you want to know my opinion, I think he's a crybaby and he's going to get us in a war we can't get out of."

"Yeah, well maybe it's about terrorists, like the President said," Jacov interjected.

Golding leered at Jacov as if at a foolish child. He regarded him as simple but responded anyway.

"If this war – and make no doubt about it, we're going to war – is about getting terrorists, why aren't we going after Saudi Arabia? They're the ones who attacked us," Golding said.

"Saudi Arabia didn't attack us, a handful of Saudis did," Louis corrected him.

"OK. So a handful of Saudis did. A handful of Iraqis didn't. There wasn't one Iraqi in the planes that hit us."

"You don't get it," Jacov continued. "The I-rack-ees are training the terrorists. They're a buncha sand niggers and we shoulda nuked 'em ten years ago."

"It wasn't ten years ago, it was twelve," Golding corrected. "And I don't like that word."

"Nuke? Excuse me. We should have bahmmmmed them. We should have dropped the friggin' A-bomb on them and turned that desert into a parking lot."

"You called them sand niggers. Do not use that word in front of me."

"What, are we defending the Iraqis now? You're probably one a those guys thinks terrorists got rights, too. Well let me tell you something, fella -- we ought to burn 'em all. Catch 'em, bring 'em here, line 'em up in

Times Square and blow torch 'em. And I'd be the first to pull the trigger on every one a you liberals, too."

Golding looked at Jacov, grinned at him, practically laughed in his face.

"I'm outta here," he said to Janice, reaching behind for his leather jacket.

"Hold on, Stephen," she said. "We just got here."

"I didn't come all the way out here to listen to this redneck or his redneck bullshit. And if this is the kind of crap you pass off for an intelligent discussion, *Rabbi*," he said, "you can do it without me."

"Don't take it out on him," Jacov said, his voice rising. "You gotta problem, it's with me."

"You're the one with the problem, oaf," Golding said, locking eyes with the big man.

"If you *want* a problem, we can have one outside," Jacov said.

"Bring it, jack-off."

Stephen was up now, jacket in hand, and Jacov was fuming.

Guy called him "Jack-off". Needle-dick, bed-wetting, dog fucker would have been nicer.

Beet-red, he struggled to extricate himself from the chair and confront Golding, but he had again squeezed himself in too tight. Sucking in his gut, he lumbered to his feet, but now the small, child-sized desk was stuck, hanging from his waist like a skirt, and he sensed the laughter coming.

"Take it easy," Louis said, standing between the men before they had a chance to square off. Raising his right hand, he motioned for Terrence to sit. "You're not going anywhere. None of us are. We're all friends here."

Terrence sat, reluctantly, but Stephen moved toward the door.

"Speak for yourself," he said, stepping through.

"Any time, jack-off," he called back to Jacov, and disappeared into the hall.

Again, Louis motioned for Terrence to stay put. He went out to the hall to retrieve Stephen, but the vet was gone.

Outside the cold air felt good. Golding zipped his leather jacket around him and fished out a Marlboro from a semi-crushed soft pack in his pocket. Someone had a fireplace going nearby and the aroma of wood smoke filled the air, warming him.

In the parking lot his ragtop Jeep was parked alongside a cherry red '53 Sedan Delivery with "Mom's Bakeshop" stenciled on the sides.

"Fucking gaudy," he thought. "Has to be Abrams'."

Golding lit the cigarette and pulled hard, savoring the smoke as it filled his lungs. He expected Janice to be a step behind, but she wasn't, so he climbed into the Jeep and started the engine.

Back indoors the threat of bloodshed dissipated, but tension hung in the air, as fleeting but palpable as the smell of smoke outside.

"I'm sorry," Janice said to the group, not quite sure why she should be but feeling the need to say something. "He just needs a moment to calm down."

"It's not your fault, Janice," Louis said. "It didn't take long tonight, but we struck a nerve."

Terrence said nothing. He sat, oaf-like in his undersized chair (an apt description the others privately agreed with), a big ruddy kid with egg on his face. Not a punch had been thrown, but it somehow felt like Golding got the best of him.

"You guys sit while I see how our friend is doing," Louis offered.

"No, I'll go," Janice said. "He's probably just having a smoke."

Janice zipped her Patagonia fleece but left the lightweight jacket she brought on a chair. Six sets of eyes followed her and even Naomi Kahan, an avowed heterosexual, glanced up as she went toward the door.

Janice did not expect Stephen to blow up the way he did, but she couldn't really blame him. They expected coffee, pastry, some light conversation, not a partisan debate on the coming, and, to her way of thinking, illegitimate war.

On second thought, she should have expected the topic. It was what people were talking about, the biggest story of the year, maybe any year, and as a talk radio host, she, more than anyone, should have known that. No, she thought, Abrams was right in going for the topical.

"Know your audience," a Temple professor told her freshman broadcast class. Well, Abrams knew his.

The metal bar handle on the exterior door pushed forward with a clunk, but the door stuck so Janice turned sideways and put her backside into it. The door swung loose and wide, unimpeded by a broken hydraulic hinge, and Janice nearly tumbled onto the concrete walk a step below. There, she figured, Stephen was cooling off, but the walk was empty.

She strode to the side of the building where he might have gone to smoke, stretch his legs and get the blood moving, but that was empty, too. In deference to her he never smoked in the Jeep, but she checked the parking lot anyhow and in the stillness of the night it didn't register at first. It was kind of like how, when a man shaves his mustache, people don't notice what's no longer there.

The Jeep was gone.

"Mother*fucker*," she muttered.

Janice looked quickly about the lot thinking maybe they didn't park where she thought: under the light, next to the blood-red hot rod, but they had. Maybe Stephen moved the car, she thought, maybe he went for gas, maybe he just fucking left.

"Son of a bitch!" she said out loud.

Meekly, somewhat embarrassed, Janice went back inside to figure out how she'd get home. If someone gave her a lift to the Hi-Speedline she could be back in Philly within the hour.

"Where's he at?" Louis called as Janice entered the room alone.

"Gone," she said.

"Gone?"

"I think he left me."

Janice wiped a tear from the corner of her eye and gathered her stuff to go. A moment earlier she'd hoped someone would give her a ride to the train station, but now, realizing she didn't even know these people and that their meeting had really just started, she decided not to ask.

She pulled her cell phone from her purse to call a taxi.

"What are you going to do?" Naomi asked.

"I'm calling a cab."

"Give it a few," Louis said. "Maybe he just went for gas."

"Doubt it," Janice said.

Jacov, feeling a little guilty for his role in getting her stranded, offered Janice a lift.

"It's okay," she said, pushing open the door. "I'll just get a cab."

Louis followed her out to the hall.

"My meetings don't usually go this badly," he said. "Even last time. They get a little heated, but sometimes that's a good thing. Anyhow, listen, come back in. He'll be back. If it gets late and Stephen doesn't come back I'll drive you home myself. You don't have to call a cab."

"You don't need to."

"It's OK," he said. "Let's just wait and see."

* * * * *

Janice cringed when she got into the thing. It had heavy doors, a bulbous front end, and a long, shadowy bed area that had been used for God-knows-what since it rolled off the assembly line fifty odd years before.

Still, she liked the glossy, candy apple paint and appreciated the attention to detail that obviously went into the car. The cream colored, glove-leather seats were flawless and perfectly matched the carpeting on the floor and walls. The rear section was cavernous, van-like, and the interior bore a light, warm scent of baked goods.

The meeting lost its fizz when Stephen walked out and Louis ended it at eight-thirty, about an hour short. He tried reviving the conversation, but talk of a distant if impending war paled with the theater of near fisticuffs in the room.

Janice sat awkwardly through another thirty minutes or so before Louis, to her relief, wrapped it up. Naomi Kahan eyed the two suspiciously as she and Louis got into the old hot rod, a four-wheeled den of iniquity, and looked the other way when her husband saw her watching.

After the last of his group left the lot, Louis pulled out too, heading toward Route 70 and the bridge for Philadelphia.

"Still wondering about conversion classes?" he said, breaking the silence once they were on their way.

"Well, I was. I thought maybe it would help. Now I don't know."

Janice turned away, dabbing at the corner of her eye again.

"Maybe it could. But it's like we said the other day. If you do it, do it for you. The other thing to consider is, just because you take a few classes doesn't mean you have to convert. Learning about another religion can help you feel closer to God, however you pray to him. Him or her."

Louis was surprising, she had to give him that.

"Him or her, huh?"

"Why not? Maybe God's an It for all I know. We've never formally met."

Janice smiled despite herself.

"I'm sorry about tonight," she said again. "I had no idea."

"Listen, if anything it was my fault. My job is to challenge people. If I bore them they don't come, except for Mrs. Abrams' baked goods, but maybe not even then. But I don't want to be bored and neither do they. If I want to be bored I'll stay home and watch C-SPAN."

"Is that what you watch?"

"Not really, unless I want to be bored. Did you miss that part?"

Janice couldn't stifle a giggle.

"I mostly just flip around," Louis continued. "Lately I've been watching old reruns on Nick at Night."

"Is that right? I wouldn't have thought."

"Why not? I'm a rabbi. I'm not dead."

"Yeah, well, half the clowns on Nick at Night are."

"Hey, I grew up with those clowns," he said.

"Me, too."

"I think we're talking 'bout different clowns."

"I dunno. *All in the Family, Sanford and Son.* That's what *I* grew up on," Janice said.

"I'm talking *Mayberry* and *Leave it to Beaver.* I had it bad for the Beave's mom."

"You're kiddin, right?"

"Mmmm... little bit. Not really."

"At least you didn't have the hots for Aunt Bea," she said.

"I wouldn't say *hots,*" Louis said. "But she had potential."

"You're kiddin me, right?"

"Whatcha gonna do. Aunt Bea knew her way around the kitchen and she wore that apron like nobody's business."

Janice glanced over, sizing him up to see if he was joking, but Louis looked straight ahead.

A car was stalled just ahead but slightly to the right as Louis left the toll plaza before the bridge over to Philly, and he punched the gas to get around it. The muscular V8 roared beneath the hood, catapulting the vehicle around the stalled car and up onto the span.

Like the other bridges across the Delaware to Philly, the Ben Franklin seemed always under construction, a never-ending public works project that someone, somewhere, was getting rich off. That Louis was sure of.

"They're never gonna finish this bridge," he observed.

"That's the plan. They finish one project and start another. It's maintenance."

"Is that what they call it? I'd like, just once, for them not to be maintaining this bridge when I have to cross it."

"At least it's not falling down," Janice said.

"Your mouth to God's ears."

They reached her townhouse on Sansom Street around nine-thirty, the time at which the discussion group usually ended. Janice considered inviting him in for coffee but it would have seemed redundant, and ridiculous, considering they had just had coffee and cake.

Still, she wasn't sure how to exit. Somehow a handshake would seem odd. So she touched his hand, leaned over and gave him a peck on the cheek.

"Thanks, Rabbi," Janice said.

He didn't say call me Louis.

# Chapter 6

Rebecca arrived home moments before Louis, tired, sticky and hungry from a fourteen-hour day at the shop. She showered, slipped on a blue silk nightgown, and padded down to the kitchen for a bowl of cereal and tea.

"How was your meeting?" she called from the island as her husband came through the door.

Louis just grumbled.

He walked over, kissed his wife's cheek from behind and slapped her rump lightly, nearly causing her to drop the milk as she poured it over her plain bran flakes.

"Don't *they* look good," he said.

"If you had my day you'd be sugared out, too," she said.

"Yeah, but you already sweet," he said like a street corner gangsta.

"I know."

Rebecca carried her snack to the table and opened the morning paper. Too busy to read during the day, she caught up on the news at night but, even then, mostly just skimmed

the headlines and obits.

"Mr. Anderton died," she said, looking up.

Louis had both sides of the refrigerator/freezer open and was fishing around for something to eat. He unwrapped a waxed paper bundle of cold cuts, smelled it for freshness, and peeled off slices of thin salami.

"Do you *have* to use your fingers," Rebecca scolded.

"It's that or my toes," Louis said.

He rolled some salami in tubes, stuck them in his mouth and tossed the package of cold cuts onto the counter. Then he reached for a jar of pickle spears and fished one of those out, too.

"You're gonna be up all night," Rebecca observed.

"My funeral," Louis said.

"Speaking of which, too bad about Mr. Anderton."

"Who was Mr. Anderton? I don't know a Mr. Anderton."

"Jon's senior year English teacher," Rebecca said.

"Oh, *that* Mr. Anderton. The son of a bitch who failed him."

"Have a little respect for the dead," Rebecca said. "And Jon failed himself."

"Anderton failed him for missing too many classes."

"Well that's it. He missed too many classes so he deserved to fail."

Jon, a decent student whose morning breakfasts at McDonald's kept him from getting to school on time some days, was late twenty-two times his senior year in high school. With two lates equal to one absence, Jon had one too many absences to pass Anderton's 1st period class and had to repeat it in summer school.

Anderton, a tall, rigid man with a pocked face and ill-fitting glasses, failed Jon despite his B average and kept him from walking in graduation.

"Fucking Bullwinkle," Louis said.

"Don't say that."

"Why not? That's what the kids called him."

"Well it's not right. The man's dead. And besides, like I said, Jon missed too many classes so he deserved to fail."

"He deserved to fail? What are you, his mother or the district attorney? He did *not* deserve to fail. And he most definitely did not deserve to be kept from graduating with his class, especially if he got Bs."

"Well, that was the policy," Rebecca said. "It's not like it kept him back any."

"I don't know about that."

Jon was a local chiropractor who kept his own hours, drove a Jaguar, and had a house at the shore. But he'd wanted to be a surgeon.

"He wanted to be a doctor," Louis said.

"He is a doctor."

"You know what I mean."

Louis sauntered over to the table, turned a chair around and sat with the back facing him. He had a thing for theatrics and improv, a quality that served him well on the bimah but came off a little dumb in everyday life.

"He could have been a contenda," he said.

Their younger boy, Seth, a Temple University dental student, seemed more likely to grab the surgical ring than Jon ever did.

"Your other contenda will be home this weekend," Rebecca said.

"Good. He can help me with the leaves."

Rebecca finished her bran flakes and turned up the bowl to slurp the last of the milk.

"Ah," she said, savoring the full feeling in her belly. "Now tell me about your meeting."

"Not a lot to tell, really. Two guys almost beat each other's brains in."

"They had a fight?"

"No, but damn close. Terrence Jacov and some veterinarian from Philadelphia squared off over Iraq."

"He makes me nervous."

"Terrence? He's alright. A bit meshuggana but okay. He's trying to sell me an alarm system for the synagogue."

"Is that what he does?"

"It is now. Anyway, he may have a point. The system we have is old. We should've upgraded five years ago. The crooks are getting smarter, the alarms should, too."

"Sounds like you're already sold. Why don't you just call National. You're already paying them."

"Yeah, well, I know. I'll run it past the board. I'd kind of like to give it to Jacov, though. I think he can use the work."

"Whatever. You've got to convince the board they need it first."

Rebecca skimmed the rest of the obits and news but none of it interested her.

"So, Terrence and this vet almost had a fight. Why was the vet at your meeting, anyhow?"

"Janice Palumbo brought him. He's her boyfriend. Well, until tonight, anyway. He left her there."

"He left her? I bet we won't hear about *that* on NPR. How'd she get home?"

"I gave her a lift."

Rebecca set the paper down but could have thrown it at him.

"Why'd *you* have to give her a lift?"

"I didn't have to, I offered. Terrence offered first, seeing how he was partly to blame for her boyfriend stranding her, but I think he made her nervous, too. Besides, I was partly the reason she was there in the first place."

"Conversion class."

"You got it."

Rebecca was still suspicious as to why this Janice Palumbo, if she was interested in converting, couldn't speak with a rabbi in Philadelphia. Her suspicion was evident in the way she suddenly got up from the table and manifested in the cold clink-bump of the spoon and bowl landing in the enameled cast iron sink.

"Well, aren't you the good Samaritan?" she asked.

Louis felt the possibility of intimacy with his wife, the hope of which was inflamed by his drive with Janice Palumbo, draining from his loins.

"I'm not a good Samaritan. I just did what's right."

"Yeah," Rebecca said tonelessly. "You've got that market cornered."

Louis wasn't sure what he'd done wrong. He heard their bed creak upstairs as his wife settled in but wasn't about to follow just yet. Instead, he sat himself in a big easy chair in the living room, kicked his feet up on the hassock and flipped on the TV.

* * * * *

Louis woke with a start about one a.m., an infomercial for yet another Ron Popeil product playing on screen. The inventor was hawking a rotisserie oven that he promised would revolutionize your kitchen and your life "for just five easy payments" of blah, blah, blah.

This was precisely the kind of crap that made Louis hate TV. He abhorred commercials, couldn't stomach most of the programming and absolutely despised paying for it. Television, once you bought the set, used to be free. Now it was fifty, sixty, seventy bucks a month for cable and it was still crap. Plus, they had these damned infomercials running twenty-four-seven and if it wasn't this feel-good, smiley-faced Ron Popeil dickhead it was that cheesy bearded guy with the orange wristwatch hawking miracle soap. He clicked off the TV and went upstairs.

Rebecca, curled on her left side, slept almost soundlessly when he crawled into their bed beside her. With his right hand Louis traced her hip, up along her rib cage, under her arm and let it come to rest on her right breast.

Her quiet breathing seemed to pause ever so slightly as he brushed her through the silken gown – precisely the response he'd hoped for. Followed by a gasp or a low sensuous moan, she would turn to him, ready, guide his hand to her or, perhaps, roll over and straddle him from on top.

None of those things happened. Rebecca swept his hand away and curled up deeper into her fetal ball. Louis, long practiced in the manly arts, would have to take matters in hand if relief was to come at all.

Instead, he flipped through a copy of *Newsweek* and then turned to *Trinity*, the Leon Uris novel he'd begun for the fourth time two months before. He related to the story of Irish Catholic oppression under centuries of English rule. He thought of the empathy that Uris, a Jew, evidently felt for the Catholics, especially in light of historic Catholic oppression of the Jews.

Louis then thought of tonight's meeting, of the fight that almost was, and of Janice Palumbo, a Catholic who thought she might want to become a Jew. He counseled scores of converts over the years and thought he knew what she must be feeling -- conflict, confusion, doubt, loss. Laying there, his mind returned to his car, the drive across the bridge, the smells of cookies, challahs, and Janice. She touched his hand. She kissed his cheek. He slept…

Sleep came easy to Louis, as it always did, when he was in faithful mode. His breaths fell into rhythm with his wife's, rising and falling as he drifted off to dreamland.

Louis preached faith - to God, to oneself and to one's partner, believed in the words, but simply had a hard time keeping them. And when he lost faith he fell hard. A handful of indiscretions marred his union with Rebecca like traces of tar on a clean white carpet. Over the years they'd nearly destroyed his family but also nearly destroyed him.

Every encounter simply added to a web of lies that consumed him, his whereabouts and his cover-ups. The lies worked at his psyche, manifesting themselves in a sham of order as flimsy and transparent as Plexiglas.

During an affair, Louis, always a neat and well-groomed man, became fastidious, compulsive, a reflection of his attempts to keep his trysts a secret.

His cars gleamed. His work space became so clean and ordered that it took on an air of timelessness, a museum quality that made it appear as if no one actually used the space but simply came to see it.

Likewise, his yard. He had the best-groomed grass on the block and took to cleaning his driveway, every day, with a gas-powered leaf blower. Even in the rain.

Louis thought himself capable of being faithful but often lost the will to stay so. It wasn't just Janice, whom he hadn't touched, but even the girl in the bakery, Rebecca's young employee, the tasty strawberry blonde he'd ogled that very day.

But for tonight he was faithful, he was good and he could rest. He rolled on his side, placed a hand on the small of Rebecca's back and slept.

# <u>Chapter 7</u>

Janice had neither seen nor heard from Stephen since the night of the meeting. Now, three weeks later, she went out of her way to avoid him, exercising in the morning when she knew he wouldn't be at the gym and immersing herself in work. Her family noticed a change, and it wasn't for the better. She became sullen, withdrawn, depressed.

Her grandmother, Sofia, had tried to console her.

"Honey, that man, he wasn't a no good for you," she said.

Sofia had been in the country sixty years but still couldn't shake Italy from her accent. Her biggest beef with Stephen was that he wasn't Italian. But he wasn't even a Catholic, and Sofia wanted Janice to have big, Italian, *Catholic* babies.

For Janice, that wasn't even an issue. At thirty-five her biological clock was ticking right along, but her maternal drive barely had a pulse. Sure, she told herself, she'd like children, but she could be a happy aunt. She was already the cool, fun aunt and she never had to change a diaper unless she wanted to. Which was pretty much never.

As her time away from Stephen grew, Janice visited her family more, spending time in and around South 9<sup>th</sup> Street, the century-old Italian Market. While many Philadelphians found comfort foods there, she found simple comfort. The historic market spoke to her senses and she drank it in, from the earthy produce on either side of it to the deep, overpowering aromas wafting from the cheese stores.

Janice especially loved the vision of crate fires set by produce vendors in steel drums near their stands. Sitting on a stoop outside the family's bread shop, a hot cup of coffee warming her hands, she'd marvel as giant SEPTA buses navigated the blazes on their way up 9th Street. It was a sight she never bored of, a real-life vision of Dante, as the buses, too big for the street to begin with, emerged through canned fires, headlights aglow like hellish white eyes.

Janice hadn't thought much about conversion these past few weeks but wondered, suddenly, about Rabbi Abrams. He had been kind to her after Stephen drove off. He didn't have to drive her home. He...

"Janice! Give the man his change!" Rosie practically shouted.

Janice absently closed the register after taking the customer's money and was helping herself to a slice of Sicilian but forgot to finish the transaction.

"I'm so sorry," she gushed, handing the man his eighty cents.

She'd only stopped in to say hi, but Saturdays were a mad house at Palumbo's Bakery and, of course, her family put her to work. Now, two hours later, the rush had died down a bit but customers were still two deep at the counter and she was famished.

"No problem," the man said, taking the change for his $1.20 semolina loaf.

Janice loved the bakery but unlike Rosie had never planned on working there for life. Now Rosie acted like she owned the place and, in time, she probably would.

Four years younger, Rosie was pure South Philly. She dripped gold (practically sweated it, really), wore garish painted nail tips and absolutely *loved* the Eagles (pronounced in these parts "iggles.") She married, surprise, surprise, a guy named Tony from the neighborhood and they had two young children, Tony Jr. and Roman, both of whom adored their cool aunt Janice.

With the rush finally eased, Janice pulled a waxed paper square from a blue cardboard box on the counter, picked up the slice of pizza and went back to eat it. She propped her butt up against a floury countertop where she once did school work, made pizelles and daydreamed of her fairy tale wedding. It seemed more out of reach now than it ever did then.

"Whatsa matter?" Rosie said with a mock accent and a hand gesture that was her impression of non-Italians doing Italians.

She followed Janice back with a cup of black coffee and cannoli, her ear tuned to the bell should a customer come in.

"Nothing. Just out of it, I guess."

"Ya think?"

A delicate eater, Rosie took small, measured bites of the cream-filled shell and sipped the bitter coffee.

"I was like, 'Yo, Jan, give the man his change', and you're like, duh, all glassy eyed and what not."

"I'm alright," Janice said. "Just tired, I guess."

"You're tired? You work on the friggin' *radio* for Chrissakes! Try doin' *this* six days a week."

Janice fingered the cheese on her pizza, considered the fat grams and calories she was consuming.

"Yeah, Ro, you've got it real rough," she said flatly. "You don't even have to work. Tony G. would be more than happy to support you."

"Yeah right. And be his little baby make-uh. Let me tell you somethin' girlfriend, that factory is ca-losed."

"Is that what he wants?"

"Hell yeah that's what he wants. He wants more kids, but he ain't havin' em without me. So guess what - he ain't havin' em."

"Could be worse, Ro. At least you've got someone at home."

Here we go again, Rose-Ann thought; she didn't say a word, but the I've-been-dumped-again bit was getting a little old.

Janice reconsidered her slice. She tore off half the cheese and dropped it in an old five-gallon spackle bucket that served as a trash can. She really just liked the tomatoey bread.

"It's true," she said. "You bitch about Tony, but at the end of the day he's there for you. I don't see him stranding you in Jersey like Dr. Dickhead. I'm, what, 35 ..."

"Pushin' forty."

"Thanks. Pushin' forty and I've got zee-ro prospects on the horizon."

Rose-Ann neared her breaking point but held back. The girls had always had similar looks -- flawless olive skin, satiny black hair, great boobs, but the boys always liked Janice better. Rose-Ann became matronly after having children, filling out in the hips and legs as women do, and Janice still had her shape.

The conversation was nothing new, really, a retread of talks they'd had since their teens. Janice always liked playing the victim. There was a string of bad breakups in her wake going back to high school and always, it seemed, there was drama.

Still, Rose-Ann felt bad that her older sister was down and indulged Janice a bit more.

"You've got prospects," she said. "How 'bout the clown you almost just beat for eighty cents? He was starin' so hard he almost forgot his change."

"*I* almost forgot his change," Janice corrected.

"I woulda sold him another loaf."

Janice smirked because she knew her sister would.

"You wanna know the truth? I don't even want another guy," Janice said. "I'm tired of it. It's like a merry-go-round anymore."

"Yeah, but you always did like to ride," Rosie said, sucking the cream from the end of her cannoli.

"You are BAD, Rose-Ann, BAD!" Janice said.

"I know it. But I gotta get it out here. If I go home talkin' like this Tony'll think I want some."

They sat for a moment in silence, Janice polishing off her slice, Rosie crunching the last of her cannoli and washing it down with coffee.

"So it's over, you and Stephen?"

"Looks that way. Jerk off left me in friggin' New Jersey, for Chrissake!"

"Yeah I got that part," Rosie said, now definitely bored with the I-Got-Left-in-Jersey bit, too.

"Fuck him," she said.

"Yeah," Janice said. "Fuck him."

She really did hurt because this one, she thought, might have worked out. They had lots in common – political views, professional standing, great sex – but she had to let it go.

A light pitter-patter of rain bounced off trashcan lids in the alley and the sound brought Janice back to her youth. As a girl she'd lie in bed at night listening to the rain and, for the longest time, thought Mr. Ciccone next store was out banging on the lids. She couldn't remember how old she was when she finally realized it was just the rain.

The shower moved through quickly and, when it had, Janice decided she'd had enough of the bakery for one morning. She kissed her sister and stepped outside into newly washed 9th Street.

The make-up of the neighborhood changed a lot since she grew up there, especially in the last fifteen years. Italian Americans still held a slim majority, but Vietnamese, Korean, even Cambodian immigrants had taken a foothold, setting up shops and eateries in and around the market.

Vietnamese restaurants like Dong Phuong now competed with venerable Anastasi's, a family name in the market for a hundred years. There were even mom-and-pop Mexican joints serving up the real thing – arroz con pollo, tamales, carne asada, and rich, creamy refried beans.

Janice turned up 9th Street toward Center City and made a quick left on Catharine. At the next intersection, a four-way stop half a block up, a taxi got too close to a beat-up Hyundai and bumped it. The punk South Philly native at the wheel of the Hyundai jumped out, fist pumping, ready for a fight.

"I'll knock your friggin' head off, sand nigger!" he shouted.

The dark-skinned, middle-aged taxi driver, a Pakistani or Indian, cringed, gripped the wheel, but did not move. He had been listening to music from home and wasn't paying close enough attention to the car in front of him.

The Hyundai's driver inspected his bumper, saw no damage, looked the other driver square in the eye and gave him the finger. Then he got back in his car and sped off, nearly causing a second collision as he tore through the next intersection.

Sand nigger.

The phrase stung Janice like sleet. It was the same expression Jacov used, the one that nearly touched off the fight between him and Stephen, the one that got her stranded. These are angry times, she thought; angry, dangerous times.

Bush is stirring the pot, choosing up sides, like world affairs was a middle school game of dodge ball.

"Either you are with us, or you are with the terrorists," he'd declared September 20, 2001.

"Illegitimate cowboy of a president," Stephen had said.

The dickhead was right, she thought. Bush's actions are making things worse, around the world but even here at home. Like many, she believed the war he was itching for would deteriorate America's standing in the world and stir up more terrorist attacks. Like whacking a hornet's nest, someone had said. And the biggest, saddest irony was that no Iraqis were even involved in 9/11. The terrorists were almost all Saudis and the Bush family is in bed with them, has been for years.

It's all connected, she thought -- Stephen, Jacov, the punk in the Hyundai and this poor immigrant taxi driver.

The cabbie pulled past the intersection and stopped, peeled his hands from the wheel and dabbed a colorful handkerchief at his face and neck.

Janice stood there a moment looking at him. She hadn't seen a fight since she was a little girl but now, in the span of three weeks, almost witnessed two. And they both involved the phrase "sand nigger." She wasn't sure, but the taxi driver appeared to be crying. He was on a phone, probably with his wife, when she turned to walk away.

# Chapter 8

Terrence arrived at seven a.m., an hour ahead of his two-man crew, to prep for rewiring the alarm system. Upgrading had been an easier sell to the board than Abrams expected and the suggestion to hire one of their own, as opposed to giving more money to National, actually helped close the deal. (Of course, they'd still have to pay National or someone else to service the system, but the capital expense was the upgrade.)

Jacov had been a synagogue member for two years, since his father passed, and what he lacked in piety he made up for in enthusiasm and a desire to belong. He found himself embracing his once denied, long-suppressed Judaism, and it felt good.

In addition to joining the rabbi's Tuesday night coffee clutch, he became active in the synagogue's Men's Club. The group met two Sundays a month to discuss charity events, fundraisers, scholarships, and the like. Similar to the Women's Club, it presented each bar or bat mitzvah with a gift – a silver plated Kiddush cup if it was a boy or a set of candle sticks if it was a girl.

Jacov's blue-collar sensibilities were somewhat ill received among some of the more "intellectual" of the

Men's Club members. First off, he was a Republican – a clear minority. He was also burly, somewhat unkempt and, to some, an obvious gun nut. The latter they divined by means of the NRA sticker on the rear window of his work van. In fact, the combination of work van and NRA sticker, to these older Jewish men, screamed redneck *and* Republican.

Still, he was generally well-liked. While Jacov could be oafish - as Stephen Golding accurately noted - he could also be generous. He was often the first to volunteer to get the Sunday morning bagels or to help make a minion, if called.

Jacov could also be funny: his self-deprecating sense of humor was endearing, especially with the smaller men, who were otherwise intimidated by big guys like him.

Ritchie Kohn, a Voorhees retiree who played in a YMHA racquetball league, brought Terrence to the gym as his guest recently and recalled the highlight of the Philly trip before the last Men's Club meeting.

"So we're in the weight room, right, and Jacov's checking out this hot shvartze babe, right. She's hot, like Halle Berry hot. Or, who's the shvartze cokehead? Whitney Houston? Right. Whitney Houston, before all the blow. So he's on the bench and he's pushing up 225, 230, a lotta weight. And I mean he's pushing -- face red, back arched, like he's having a friggin' baby, right, when all of a sudden he lets loose this fart. I mean, he ripped one! It fucking *reverberated*! You could practically see it, it smelled so fuckin' bad."

"I think I burned the bench," Jacov deadpanned.

"You burned your chances with that little Halle Berry babe, I'll tell you that," Kohn said.

"I don't think my odds really got any worse," Jacov said.

"No, boychik, but they didn't get any better."

Kohn, a former homebuilder, liked Jacov for his honesty and his ability to take a joke. It also didn't hurt that Kohn, like Jacov, had been a blue-collar working stiff, too. He found his first construction job — as a laborer —in the nineteen-forties and by the early sixties had his own company. By the late eighties he was loaded and retired.

Though he skipped college, Kohn was extremely well read, spoke some Hebrew, and kept an apartment in Tel Aviv.

He did not look down on Jacov because he didn't have or do those things and even liked him well enough to give him a nickname.

"You're all right, Kid," he said.

Soon many of the other men, most of them veterans of World War II or Korea, called him Kid, too. He was, after all, a kid to them, thirty to forty years their junior.

"Hey, Kid – what's this I hear about you and some dog doc knocking heads?" Sammy Juacucha said.

He and all the others had heard about Jacov's run-in with Golding at the Tuesday night coffee club.

Juacucha, the Men's Club president, was born and raised in Mexico City. He married his wife Mona and converted to Judaism in the early nineteen-seventies.

"We didn't knock heads, but I was this close," Jacov said, raising two fingers to show them.

"You gotta watch it, Kid," Juacucha said, grinning. "You not a kid no more."

Working quietly by himself, Jacov smiled now, recalling the warmth of the room and the fellowship he shared with these old men. They were kind, Jewish and they liked him. Like old men everywhere, they had stories to tell from their youth, hard charging and victorious, tales belied by the spotted, saggy flesh that hung from them now.

At the end of the meeting they always had a little schnapps, cheap whiskey out of plastic shot glasses, and a few pieces of nice, fat herring. Most of them, cardiac patients to a man, knew they'd be better with the herring in wine sauce rather than the opulent sour cream, but they ate it anyway. They reminded Jacov of his father and Jacov, never close with his old man, found now that he missed him.

He carried heavy spools of wire, touch pads, black metal boxes, motion sensors and other equipment for the job from his van to the building. With most of the gear unloaded, his men could just get to work.

He sat on a concrete stoop, pulled a schematic of the old system from his jacket, and gulped a tepid cup of Wawa coffee when Abrams swung into the lot.

"You're early," the rabbi called, stepping from the Crown Vic with a wide, shallow box of baked goods.

"Early bird and all that," Jacov said.

"Good man. I knew you wouldn't let me down. Donut?"

"I shouldn't."

"You should. They're fresh."

The donuts were still warm and Jacov helped himself to a soft, round jelly with a generous dusting of powdered sugar.

Abrams pulled a big key ring from a pocket, found the right one and opened the metal door.

"Come in, sit for a few," he offered, and Jacov followed him in.

Jacov had never been in the rabbi's study before and it was just like he imagined: dark paneled walls of books, a slight musty odor from an old Persian carpet and a heavy smell of leather.

Louis loved leather furniture and his office was dominated by it. There was a big oxblood leather couch, two matching chairs and ottoman, and a good leather office chair behind a big oak desk. The desk was immaculate, bare save for a phone, a Cross pen and pencil set in a gray marble base, and a leather-framed writing pad.

A pungent trace of something else also seemed to hang in the air, but Terrence disregarded it, figured it couldn't be.

"Haven't seen you in a few weeks," Louis said.

"Been busy."

He chomped the last bit of donut and licked the sugar from his fingers.

"You or your friend either. I thought maybe you and he ran off and got married."

Jacov smirked. Of course he meant Golding.

"I should have kicked his butt."

"No, you should not have," Louis said paternally. "You did the right thing."

Louis helped himself to a donut and offered Jacov another.

"Naomi asked about you last week," he said. "Something about a date with her girlfriend."

"Mmmm. Forgot about that," Jacov said. "I'll ask her about it Tuesday night."

"Good man."

Jacov recalled the conversation, Naomi's description of her friend and his reaction: Big boobs, wild side, just your type.

"So this is what, two-day job?" Louis inquired, returning to the business at hand.

"Yeah, maybe less, depending on what we run into. Shouldn't be that tricky. You're staying with National for servicing?"

"Probably."

Louis considered the glass bong at his foot beneath the desk. He tapped it with his shoe and almost knocked it over, spilling the smelly pot water.

A second van with Jacov's workmen pulled alongside his own followed by several cars of worshippers for the morning service.

"If we can't make a minion I might pull you in," Abrams said, glancing across the lot.

"I'd offer to bring Hector and Luiz if I thought they'd count."

"You're welcome to bring them," Abrams said. "But unless they're circumcised and had their bar mitzvahs, they won't help with the minion."

* * * * *

Louis did not need to call Jacov for the service. B'nai Tikvah, like most conservative synagogues, now counted women for the minion and allowed them to come up and read from the Torah, too. It was a relatively recent trend, the past 20 years or so, but a huge leap forward for the Jewish women's movement and the community at large.

For the first time in thousands of years, women were being called to the bimah to open the ark, to hold the sacred Torah scrolls and, most significantly, to read from them.

114

The Reform movement was the first to allow women to read from the Torah and it even ordained women rabbis. The conservatives followed them, at least in respect to reading from the Torah, but the orthodox and ultra-orthodox held to tradition: no women on the bimah, none reading from the Torah and, especially, no women rabbis. During prayer they still sat separate from the men, segregated by a wall, a glass partition, even a cutrain.

Abrams, to the surprise of many traditionalists in his congregation, embraced a greater role for women early on and was instrumental, long before it was fashionable, in calling women to read from the Torah.

This morning's worshippers included not one but three women, two of whom recently lost a parent, and they were counted as equals.

Returning to his study following the service, Louis thought of this now and was glad he came down on the side of inclusion early. The synagogue had lost a few members, mostly old, traditional men, when this upstart young rabbi changed their congregation. But it picked up lots of new members, entire young families with women who had been bat mitzvahed and who had young children, boys and girls, who would attend Hebrew school and be bar and bat mitzvahed there, too.

Louis knew, instinctively, that modern women would not stand for being treated like they were half as good as men and would go where they would be treated as equals. So they came and prayed with him. They opened their hearts, their minds, their souls. They opened their checkbooks, too, for memberships, Hebrew school, tutoring and special events. And, for handsome, charming Rabbi Louis Abrams, some even opened their legs.

He clicked on the television, flipped to CNN, and took his seat behind the desk. Louis was reaching for his bong when the phone rang.

"You son of a bitch!" Rebecca screamed in his ear.

"What is it? What did I do now?" Louis said, genuinely wounded.

"Not what. Who. You're fucking Naomi Kahan, you bastard!"

"I'm doing no such thing," he said honestly. "Would you kindly give me a break and remember where I am and what I do here? Naomi Kahan is a member of the congregation, a friend, a worshipper. Nothing more."

"Right, Lou. I long suspected her of worshipping you, and you of her, but now I've got proof. She couldn't even look me in the eye."

"What are you talking about? And what kind of proof is that?"

Naomi had left the Apple Hill bake shop moments before where she'd stopped for rugelach and donuts for a parent-teacher meeting. She always avoided Rebecca but bought pastries for school functions there because Superintendent Eli Goldman told her to.

The superintendent's trysts with Naomi stopped two years before, when she became involved with Louis, but he knew more about her affair with the rabbi than he let on. He wouldn't fire Naomi – couldn't, really, without just cause – but his petty torments were merciless, one of which was to put her face-to-face with the rabbi's wife whenever he could.

"Are you or are you not sleeping with her?" Rebecca demanded.

"I am not," he answered truthfully.

Louis, always smarter than whomever he was talking to, especially his wife, could not let the conversation end on a safe note. He had to push it, give her the opportunity to challenge him, to seek out the truth even if it meant revealing it, which of course he would deny.

"I never have."

Rebecca hated him. A lifetime of devotion, of family, of joy, of sex, of illness, death and sorrow came down to this. Her marriage was a farce. A happy front. And she wished he was dead.

"You're a liar, Louis," she said calmly. "You've always been."

The door to her office was open and Ferdinand, a middle-aged Mexican whom she'd hired six years before, was standing outside of it. She paid the man twelve dollars an hour off the books, far more than he'd make in a restaurant kitchen, and he loved her dearly for it. He had not been listening but heard his boss clearly upset and poked his head in.

"Wood ju like some coffee, meesus?" he offered.

His shift started at four a.m. and now, five hours later, it was half over. A light resin of flour coated his thick hands, arms and neck and turned his gray hair grayer. Ferdinand's home in a small village outside Oaxaca was little more than a memory now, but still he supported his family, who never emigrated to the states, with wages from the bakeshop.

"No thanks, Ferdi, I'm good," she said.

Ferdinand smiled wanly and shuffled off, worried about his benefactor, boss, and friend.

Louis heard Terrence and his men checking gear and running lines in the hallway and envied the simple satisfaction of their work. He assumed their lives modest, an uncomplicated existence of a day's work for a day's pay, cigarettes, cold beer at happy hour and a good, plain woman at home in a modular or mobile home somewhere in Salem County.

His own life, of course, was anything but simple, a series of overlapping, crisscrossing events that swept him along like the Delaware. He was but a chunk of wood just above the surface with all the other bits of detritus. Seeing things this way enabled him to feel powerless and, therefore, blameless, as he washed along the river of life.

"What do you want from me?" he asked. "I'm trying my best. And I am not sleeping with Naomi Kahan."

Rebecca was beyond tears. She was beyond doing this, too, but here she was again. She fumbled with a sharp, heavy brass letter opener on her desk that she'd won for high single game in a bowling league two years before. For the briefest of moments she thought about plunging the damn thing into her own throat. Let that be the bastard's punishment. The point was sharp and she pushed on it hard till it nearly burst through the soft pink flesh of her thumb but dropped it with a clang on her desk.

"I want you out," she hissed.

<u>Chapter 9</u>

There was no reasoning with Rebecca when she was like this so Louis didn't even try. He'd seen it before and she'd always gotten over it.

Yet somehow things felt different. The last time, shortly after her surgery three years before, she slammed down the phone so hard she hurt his ear and, he presumed, broke the handset. Now her rage was gone, but the slow-boil anger that replaced it sounded a bit more menacing.

But really. Where did she expect him to go? They were married. Her house was his house and his house was hers.

He'd win her back. Flowers. A ride down the shore and a bottle of wine. Nice seafood dinner followed by gentle, meaningful sex. Maybe he'd even go down.

Louis felt triumphant in his quickly hatched plan and got a stir in his loins just thinking about it. He treated himself to a bong hit.

He'd barely expelled the smoke from his lungs, sensed the first pleasurable response as the drug coursed to his brain, when the phone rang again.

121

Anita wouldn't be in for another half hour so he'd have to get the phone himself and risk dealing with Rebecca again or just let it ring and bounce into voicemail. But he hated the cursed voicemail. You couldn't call anywhere anymore where someone simply picked up the phone.

"Yes, Rebecca," he breathed.

"Uh, Rabbi? It's Janice Palumbo."

"Hi, Janice," he said.

"Every time I call you think it's your wife."

"That's how it is with old married folk, Janice. How have you been?"

"I'm good actually. Haven't heard from Stephen, but that's okay, too."

"Maybe it will still work out."

Louis couldn't care less if things worked out between her and Dr. Fucking Stephen Golding, but he was high now and somehow that sounded okay. He felt generous, magnanimous, good about himself and his world.

"Anyway, that's not why I called. I'm still interested in conversion class if you'll still have me."

Louis nearly choked on her choice of words.

"Of course, we'll still have you," he said, "if that's what you want. How does your family feel about this?"

"It's not up to them. I mean, they'll support me. I'm the black sheep, remember? The one who left the neighborhood?"

"Leaving the neighborhood's one thing. Leaving the flock, even if you're the black sheep, is quite another. It's not like skipping communion or dating a Jewish man. You'd better be sure on this one."

"I thought you'd support this."

"Sure I support it. I just want you to be sure. It's kind of like a tattoo – or, better yet, getting married. Once you go through with this thing it's a little hard to undo. It's a bulb you don't unscrew."

"I'm not one to turn back. When I do something, I do it."

"Way to be," Louis said.

"But speaking of marriage, Stephen turned out to be a real shit, don't you think?"

"Not for me to say," Louis said. "He seemed a little high strung, but I only met him once. And Terrence can push buttons. Is that where you thought it was going?"

"Part of me did. We didn't talk about it much. I guess he wasn't interested. Anyhow, he did turn me on to a good thing."

"Yeah, what's that?" Louis said, short on words now but high, high, high!

"Judaism!" Janice continued, mildly peeved he didn't know what she meant. "When I went to synagogue with him I felt a connection. I don't know how to describe it. There was a feeling of community, inclusion, a reverence for a higher power without being beaten over the head about it."

"I think you just did."

"Did what?"

"Describe it. You pretty much summed up the essence of Judaism."

"That's how it felt. I loved the services, the wine and cake afterward – "

"— the Kiddush."

"Right, the Kiddush. In a way, it reminds me of communion."

"Well, there's wine, but the similarities pretty much end there," he said.

"I know. But it's nice. To tell you the truth, the whole body of Christ thing always freaked me out a bit, even when I was a girl."

"It's a ritual," Louis continued. "The Catholics have their sacraments and we have ours. I suppose if they didn't we'd all still be Jews."

Neither said a word for a moment.

"So, anyhow," Janice said, "I just thought I'd let you know. What's the next step?"

"That's up to you. I have regular group classes as well as private lessons. Group is nice because you're in with others going through the same thing as you. Issues come up and we tend to have nice conversations. On the other hand, it tends to be something of a couple's thing. Private is good, too, because we can get more in depth, explore issues and topics that interest you and make the experience more meaningful."

"I've always been more of a private lessons kind of girl myself," Janice said.

"Whatever works best. Why don't you call me in a few days and we'll set up a time for you to come in and talk."

"Will do."

Placing the phone back in its cradle Louis rubbed his whiskery chin in wonderment and possibility. The events of his life were once again crisscrossing and overlapping.

A powdery layer of beige-green pollen lay thickly upon his windowsill, visible evidence that late spring had come.

It was unseasonably warm and dry the past week and the yellowish gunk was everywhere, coating Louis's cars and flowing in silty pale streams down storm drains when it rained, which wasn't enough. The pollen was so thick it caught in his throat and gunked up his contacts, forcing him to wear glasses.

Louis wiped the sill with a Kleenex and thought seriously about another bonger when a scream rocked the morning peace.

Rushing to the door he found chaos in the hallway and Jacov shouting, "Aqui! Aqui!"

One of the Mexican laborers had touched a hot wire with a long screwdriver as he installed hardware for the new alarm. The jolt seemed to have run up one arm and burst out the other. His shirtsleeve caught fire and an acrid smell of burnt hair and flesh floated in the hall like a malevolent ghost. The man still gripped the screwdriver so tightly his fingertips were white, but he lay on the floor quivering, his mouth open but dumb.

Louis, cell phone in hand, dialed 911 as Jacov reached down to the man, touched his neck for a pulse and leaned close to check respiration. He pinched the man's nose, blew two successive breaths into his mouth and straddled him to start chest compressions.

"What happened!" Louis screamed, but Jacov didn't seem to hear.

"Nine, ten, eleven, twelve."

He counted fifteen, swung off the man's chest and blew two more breaths into his mouth, then returned to his chest and started compressions again.

Louis saw the man was badly hurt but wondered now about the bong. The police were on their way. Was it safe beneath his desk or should he hide it more securely? Did he dare leave the scene, he the chief rabbi, for anything in his office, or be here, official and presiding, when the cops arrived? The dope addled his thoughts and good, focused decisions did not come.

The other laborer stood over Jacov and the fallen man and Louis could see worry on his face.

Louis hadn't noticed before, but the men looked a lot alike. The standing man was ashen and peered on in silence as Jacov struggled to save his brother.

Louis stepped back into his office and fumbled under his desk for the water pipe but knocked it over, spilling foul-smelling liquid into his carpet. He stashed the bong in a closet and returned to the hall just as the police arrived.

"I couldn't find a pulse," Jacov was telling one of the cops.

The policeman knelt to feel the man's wrist and knew he had to shock him.

"Grab the AED from the trunk and check on that bus!" the officer told his partner.

Louis never cared much for cops, sensed their hostility and hair-trigger readiness to do something, anything, to feel more cop-like, to ease the boredom of sitting somewhere in a parked car waiting for shit to happen. Listening to the officer now, he thought the guy sounded as if he'd seen one too many cop shows for his own good.

After all, he thought, we aren't all part of some lame ass plot line but smack in the middle of an actual emergency. He knew "AED" stood for automatic defibrillator unit and bus, in police parlance, of course meant ambulance.

While the second officer scrambled for the defib unit the first tossed his hat to the side, pulled on latex gloves and went to work on the patient's shirt. He cut it down the middle with a small pair of good chrome scissors he pulled from a case on his belt and felt the man's neck again for a pulse.

A moment later the officers had electrodes attached to the injured man's chest and shocked him as the ambulance rolled into the lot. Voltage from the machine made the man's entire body flop and a tiny "bleep" indicated the return of a heartbeat. The EMS guys left the electrodes on as they wheeled the man away.

"You saved his life," Louis heard the first officer tell Jacov.

"Just did what I had to do," Louis heard him say.

Maybe so, Louis thought, but he was impressed. He saw the intensity with which Jacov worked to save his man, knew he had seen a side that he, Louis, and lots of others, didn't know existed. Beneath all the camouflage and Army-guy bravado was a man who knew what to do when the time came. Jacov was not the oafish buffoon people took him to be but a man of action.

"Mazel tov," Louis said, patting him on the back.

Jacov, sweaty and panting badly, did not know what to say. He wiped his glasses with a red bandanna and dabbed it across his forehead.

"What you did was a mitzvah," Louis continued. "These are the things God remembers in the Book of Life."

"I just did what I had to do," Jacov repeated humbly.

"My point exactly."

Jacov and Jorge, the uninjured worker, called it a day and went to check on Jorge's brother in the hospital. Simon Gonzalez suffered second- and third-degree burns that ran from his left hand across his chest to the other hand. His skin was inflamed, blistered, and charred in the worst places and doctors at Kennedy had him in guarded but stable condition. The most important thing, they told Jacov and Jorge, was that Jacov kept Simon's heart going until help arrived.

For Louis, the morning excitement gave way to a predictable afternoon lull. His buzz wore off around eleven and left his mind sluggish and gray as Jersey shore fog. Reading meaningfully was unthinkable and the TV news bored him so he took an early lunch, drove home and napped.

Louis woke with a start two hours later. The phone had been ringing but so deep was his sleep that he absorbed the sound in his dreams. There he heard Rebecca's last words reverberate again and again: "I want you out... I want you out... I want you..."

She hadn't caught him in the act, but in her mind she might as well have. The look she read in Naomi Kahan's face that morning was confirmation that the little strumpet was, or had been, fucking her husband.

Rebecca and many of the other PTA mothers suspected Naomi of having an affair with her boss, Superintendent Goldman, and it was something to kibbitz about after school board meetings. Though it wasn't her job to do so, the feisty little blonde defended Eli tenaciously against attacks from parents, over reports in the press, even rogue school board members who had the gall to question him, and it fueled their chatter.

These days, her boys several years out of the Apple Hill school system, Rebecca didn't deal much with Eli or the district and couldn't care less about him and Naomi, what they did or didn't do. But what she wouldn't tolerate was another broken vow in her marriage and that is what Naomi Kahan personified. Serving Naomi herself that morning, she slammed the cash drawer shut and didn't so much as thank her for the twenty-eight-dollar order.

Louis resented his wife's anger but, more than that, privately resented her growing independence. His salary was decent at \$110,000 a year plus bennies, but her income was far better, and growing. While her initial Voorhees storefront sold just a few items at first – Jewish apple cake, rugelach, and challahs for Shabbat – as her business grew so did her offerings. She also now sold good sticky buns, deep, New York-style cheesecake, a variety of fresh breads, soft, delicate snowflake rolls, pies, muffins, and cookies.

Despite his resentment, Louis appreciated his wife's business acumen, the popularity she enjoyed with her customers and the financial freedom she built on her own. Sure, she inherited a tidy sum when her parents passed, but Rebecca was self-made.

All of it, however, made her words more meaningful as he replayed them in his head, for the third time today, driving back to the office. How would it look, the chief rabbi of B'nai Tikvah, separated and facing divorce over an extramarital affair, thin though the evidence may be? Surely, they wouldn't keep him, would they? Rebecca would survive, but, how would he?

Louis's mood soured further by the time Jesse Kornhauser rapped at his door for a four p.m. bar mitzvah lesson.

Jesse wasn't a bad kid, but he needed to be kept in line. Cantor Isikoff wouldn't see him anymore, not after the condom incident, so Louis bore responsibility for getting Jesse up to speed for his bar mitzvah. And time was running out.

"No more condoms, right Jesse?" Louis said.

"No more condoms, Rabbi."

Two weeks before, Jesse pulled a prank that would land him in B'nai Tikvah Hebrew school lore. As Joshua Hecht's bar mitzvah date drew ever closer the boy still struggled with his Haftorah, a Hebrew prayer recited during Torah readings, the chanting of which essentially constitutes one's bar mitzvah service, so he spent extra time studying with the cantor.

The days were already light well past five o'clock when most Hebrew school classes ended so if anyone approached the windows outside the cantor's office they would have beenl seen.

Still, Jesse wanted to fuck with Joshua, to crack him up in the presence of the bearded, humorless old cantor. So, hugging the outside wall one afternoon, he crept up and placed a condom on the window sill.

The prohylactic was torn from its package and oozed a thick, viscous blob of Elmer's glue, an effect even Louis found amusing when he heard of it.

The cantor most assuredly did not.

All he saw was a boy's small hand reach up from underneath and deposit something on the sill. Picking it up the cantor screamed like a little girl, dropped the oozing rubber on the floor of his office and rushed to the restroom.

"You are done, done!" he screamed at Jesse moments later after Joshua, fearing the cantor's wrath, ratted him out. "Forget your bar mitzvah because you are done here!"

Of course, Jesse was not done. His father, Dr. Leonard Kornhauser, served on the synagogue's board of directors and was a generous benefactor. If anyone was done it would be the surly, overbearing cantor, but for now Louis would train Jesse for his bar mitzvah himself.

"So why'd ya do it?" Louis asked the boy now, as casually as he could.

"I dunno. I guess just to do it."

Louis liked the boy, saw in him the impish, daring qualities he enjoyed himself at thirteen, and didn't really begrudge him a bit.

Louis's problem was that despite his successful career as a rabbi he never fully outgrew the impish, thrill seeker of the boy he'd been. Thus the cars, the fast driving, the womanizing, the weed.

But Louis more than anything sought to put his womanizing ways behind him, to live the life of faith and mitzvot that he preached, and so, returning home that evening, he bought the prettiest, fullest bouquet of flowers ACME had in an effort to make things right with Rebecca.

He jettisoned earlier plans for a romantic drive down the shore because he doubted Rebecca would get in the car with him, but knew she couldn't resist a home-cooked meal after a long day in the shop. He bought pencil-thin asparagus, the kind Rebecca liked best, a packet of hollandaise sauce mix, some beautiful filets of sole, fresh cherries and vanilla ice cream. To wash it all down he stopped and bought two nice bottles of wine.

But Louis now saw that he bought too much. Waiting for him, instead of his wife, was a suitcase and a sticky note.

"You pack or I will," the note simply read.

The soft tan suitcase was part of a five-piece set they bought for their honeymoon, the only luggage they'd ever owned. Now, instead of representing the promise of a new marriage, the empty valise symbolized the crumbling of an old one.

Louis set his groceries on the oaken kitchen island and sat ponderously on a stool before it. He once believed Rebecca would never leave him, no matter what he'd done. Least not over a fleeting dalliance with Naomi Fucking Kahan. *Especially* since there was no real proof he even had one.

He slumped on the stool, pondering his situation and a martini. Several shots of gin, a hint of vermouth and three fat olives would help. The anticipation would be almost as good as the drink – chilling the glass, splashing in the booze from a shaker of cracked ice, breathing in the sweet, piney juniper before that first sip.

But the drink would have to wait.

Buster, their two-year-old pit bull, was scratching at the back door and wanted in. Louis loved the dog. His smile – pit bulls really do smile, Louis told people – cheered him no matter how low he felt.

He and Rebecca adopted Buster as a puppy, just five weeks old and so small he nestled in a fleece blanket in the top of a copy paper box. He was now a seventy-pound bruiser but gentle as a bunny. Louis despised the stereotype of the breed, the perception that they are inbred monsters born to attack other dogs as well as people, and paraded him around as much as he could, the pit bull ambassador.

Louis let the dog in, but his thoughts turned back to Rebecca. They'd weathered so much that he still didn't believe she'd leave him. After all, they'd known each other since they were kids, raised two boys, had grandchildren together. They'd loved through births, deaths and near deaths. She was his backbone when his father was felled three years before by a stroke and Louis was by her side when Dr. Ferri found the lump.

In fact, Louis believed, his brightest moment may have been when he encouraged the reconstructive surgery and told her again and again how beautiful she was.

But now he just sat there, wondering where she was.

He considered the bake shop (unlikely, since she'd already come home and set out the valise); the health club (she hadn't been there in weeks); even Jon's chiropractic office (but how much time could she really spend there? And why would she?).

Louis aborted plans for a martini and opened one of the cold, wet bottles of wine. Just for kicks, he called Jon's office and was surprised when Jon answered the phone himself.

"Slummin it tonight, son?" Louis said.

"Hey, Pop. What do you mean?"

"Answering the phone, like the old days."

"Jenny called out. Nance was here for a few hours, but she and mom went back to the house to light the grill. What're you, in the dog house again?"

"Woof."

All couples fought, some more than others, so Jonathan and his brother Seth never gave it much thought when their parents went at it, especially once the boys were out of the house. Their parents were busy, successful people, so if they brought a little stress home they were entitled.

"So, what was it this time?"

"Not a thing," Louis said. "I've been good."

"You gave mom shit about something. What'd she do, back into the mailbox, burn a roast?"

"Nothing like that. Everything's fine. But listen, when you see your mother, have her call home."

"Why don't you just call her?"

"Nah, but if you see her just have her call me."

"You got it, Pop," Jon said, but both he and Louis knew everything was pretty damn far from fine.

# Chapter 10

When Jacov returned from the hospital that afternoon it was so hot that the parking lot outside Apple Hill Towers radiated heat in waves. He saw the heat rising from the soft, warm asphalt and breathed in the deep, pungent, manly aroma lifting off the pavement.

As a rule Jacov didn't use air conditioning in the van, no matter how hot it was, and his face was red and pimpled with sweat when he parked and headed for his eighth-floor apartment.

Along the way he saw Mrs. Nettles, a loopy senior who had been trying for months to set him up with her mildly impaired daughter, Nadia. Walking a wooly brown poodle he heard her call Cocoa, or sunning herself fully clothed by the pool, the girl grinned at him whenever he saw her about the apartments.

Passing the pool now he couldn't help but notice Angela Agnew, a pretty Temple Law student who lived next door to him. He knew her name only because he'd gotten her mail once or twice, but they hadn't really spoken in the ten months since she'd moved in. She was polite enough, nodding or returning a hello if it came down to it, but quickly ducked inside her apartment if they found themselves alone in the hall, fumbling for their keys.

Jacov concluded correctly that Angela wouldn't give him the time of day. If she gave him any thought at all, it was that Terrence seemed harmless enough, a big lummox who might have been handsome eighty pounds and thirty years ago, but that was a lot of years and way too many beers.

Now, between his four-inch jelly roll and the blackheads, curly hairs and zits propagating along his neck and back, Jacov had about as much sex appeal to her as road kill.

And yet she had wondered, seeing him haul bulging white Hefty bags to the Dumpster while she sat poolside, her nose in a law book, what it would take to make this man attractive. He was kind of rugged in an overweight, over-the-hill, *boy I really must be getting sun-stroke* kind of way, and she thought under all that blubber there might just be a man.

Terrence was not unique in the mental makeover she performed on him, a habit she couldn't resist on both men and women who let themselves go.

Angela called these intellective exercises Regis treatments. They were named, of course, for the morning talk show host and his perky sidekick who couldn't resist giving an on-air makeover, typically to some stay-at-home tubby from Tulsa with four young boys and a waste can full of shitted diapers.

Regis and his co-host would drag little Miss Tulsa into the studio, let a troupe of stylists go to work on her and, by show's end, she was an honest-to-God hottie.

Angela didn't like the show, especially the cutesy poo hostess who replaced the True American Bitch, but she couldn't get away from it.

Lately, as the reality TV craze infected nearly every aspect of programming, entire shows dedicated to makeovers gained traction. There was *So You Want to be a Slim Guy*, a show that might appeal to men like Terrence if he'd only give it a chance, as well as *The New You*, in which a top-notch plastic surgeon worked wonders on truly cursed beings. This often involved teenagers with cleft palates or accident victims, poor souls who had no means to afford the treatment without the help of a benefactor. The program she most despised, however, was *Extreme Contours*, a show in which doctors (and deep pocketed producers) helped young women get the look they wanted and what they wanted never varied:

big boobs, tiny waist and a hyper-white pearlescent smile.

Angela had been blessed with a small waist herself. As for her boobs, well, lots of guys liked them small.

To her extreme displeasure, she sensed her neighbor lumbering over now so she donned as bookish and busy a face as she could, hoping the big lummox would just get the point and go. She tried willing him back to the building, back to the elevator, back up to 8B, a single unit exactly like hers but not quite far enough away. But the big beef spied her, white bikini-clad in a white plastic chaise, and couldn't resist the opportunity to amble over and offer up a goofy hello. And *gott-damn* if he wasn't fucking goofy!

"How do, neighbor," he said, more *Green Acres* than even she expected.

His eyes tried in vain to ford the big legal book that hid her bikini top but, repelled, found a sunny wisp of down just north of her bikini bottoms. But the wolfish eyes didn't stop there. Foraging back to the hollow of her navel, he scanned up past the book and settled on her pretty WASP face.

Angela squirmed, but figured she'd better say something or the oaf would just stand there, eyeballing her like food.

"Just trying to study," she said. "Finals next week."

"Law school, right?"

Angela curled an eyebrow, screwed up her lips and waved an open hand at the ten-pound ethics tome.

"Right," Jacov answered himself. "It's Angie, right?"

"Angela."

"Oh yeah, Angela. You know, Angela, I wanted to be a lawyer."

"That right?"

"That's right. I started out going for the law but went in with the Company instead."

"What company is that?"

"*The* Company. You know what I mean."

"Not if you don't tell me I don't," she said.

College kids. Jacov could see she was a little slow on the uptake so he fed her a bit more intel.

"Colonel North, Neek-ar-agua, Sand-an-eest-as, you know what I'm saying. I can't really talk about it."

She thought of the rickety white van he drove, its patches of rust eating through the sheet metal like cancer. She didn't believe someone who drove such a piece of shit could be so much as a Wal-Mart supervisor, let alone a professional spook.

"Iran-Contra," she said. "I remember reading about it. Reagan breaks the law, sells weapons to Iran, funnels money back to the Contras in direct violation of a Congressional order and forgets the whole fucking thing."

Jacov scuffed the cement with the bottom of a dusty, cracked boot and bellowed a knowing huff.

"Civilians," he smirked. "If it was only that simple."

"And *you* were there," she said.

"I was there. But I can't really talk about it."

"So you said."

Jacov sensed he should have kept walking straight to the building, straight to the elevator, straight up to 8B, but here he was, hot, sweaty, and tired in his dirty work clothes, at the end of a really stressful day, trying to make an impression but things were going less than great.

"So you're, like, a plumber?" Angela continued, eying the tool belt Jacov rolled into a bundle and carried in his meaty right fist.

'No," he said, peeved to be mistaken for a drain-clearing, shit-smelling, sludge-wearing plumber. Even if they did make bank.

"I'm a security consultant. Doing a big job for Rabbi Abrams over at B'nai Tikvah. Technically I'm still a G-man 'cause you're never really out, but I'm more of a freelancer now, if you know what I mean."

The day was coming to an end, but the sun was still hot in the western sky and new beads of sweat broke out across the dirty crust on his forehead.

"To tell you the truth, I don't," Angela said. "Listen, a..."

"Terrence," he said.

"I don't mean to be rude, Terrence, but I'm trying to study."

"No, no, I see you're studying. I'm down with that. I just wanted to say hi."

"Okay, well, hi," Angela said, returning her eyes to her book.

Little fucking snot! Snobby little cunt! And MOVE THAT FUCKING BOOK!

"OK, then," he said, holding his tongue. "I'll catch up with you later."

"OK, then."

Angela tried re-reading a dreadfully boring passage, but Jacov just stood there a moment too long and Angela felt a threat from the big man above her she hadn't felt before.

It was only a moment or two, but still he stood there, perspiring, his big face reddened by work, beer and sun, his gut enormous, his stink like a garbage truck. He reeked of hard cheese and deli meat, like a big, garlicky kosher salami.

And then it hit her. A big, wet, smelly drop of Jacov. Viscous, oily and full of his scalpy DNA, the drop merged from several on his forehead, ran together and flew from his nose like a ski jumper. It slipped under the bridge of his glasses, gathered momentum on the slope and hurtled from his nose for a perfect ten-point landing on her firm young thigh.

"Jesus CHRIST!" she screamed, dropping the book. "You're DRIPPING on me!"

A big, wounded animal, Jacov stood there immobilized a moment, then tried to help. He reached for her towel, but she snatched it back and wiped so hard that her flesh reddened.

He didn't know what to do and so he just stood some more, ham-handed and dazed, sweaty, smelly, and helpless.

"I've *got it*," she said, as if to a bad child. "Just go!"

As he turned Jacov saw a handful of other young up-and-comers around the pool peering over their Ray-Bans at him. The flat-bellied boys in bright surfer shorts and caps with rounded bills; the nubile young girls in thongs and bikini tops. In his misplaced confidence approaching Angela he hadn't even seen them, wasn't certain they'd even been there, but they were sure there now and staring at him like he was a molester, a dirty old man.

He turned and high-tailed for the door.

Angela waited until he was gone and gave him a full five minutes to ride the elevator, get to his apartment and go inside. But now she sensed him leering at her from behind the smoky dark glass and it spooked her.

So, in one smooth motion, she set down the book, gathered herself in the plush mint and white striped beach towel, stood and made for the elevator. She reached her apartment, bolted the door, and locked the bathroom for a long, hot shower.

<u>Chapter 11</u>

The first night or two were kind of like a vacation, except he couldn't go home. Louis set himself up at the Apple Hilton, plush, comfortable, and pricey, but for the few days it would take Rebecca to cool off he could afford it.

It seemed unfair, his banishment to a three-star hotel, for something he'd done so long ago. It also seemed his platonic pleadings about Naomi Kahan infuriated Bec more than if he'd come out and admitted adultery, but the A-word sounded so serious, so *biblical*, that he refused to acknowledge the crime even to himself. Banging, schtuping, screwing, fucking. Those words he could handle, but he would not concede adultery.

Though he'd tried, pre-banishment, to convince her, nothing he said would persuade Rebecca that his relationship with Naomi was nothing more than that of friend and mentor.

And so, defeated for the time being, he resigned to enjoy his stay at the Hilton where, surprisingly, he ran into few locals despite its location in central, sprawling Apple Hill Township.

His hometown was the kind of outer-ring no-man's land that felt like everywhere and nowhere at once, as tasteless and American as supermarket pie. It had its mall, several Starbucks stores, a Barnes & Noble and a Boston Market but so little flavor of its own— especially for a place with fruit in its name – that someone passing through might never know they'd been there.

Ironically, passing through was about the *only* way to know one had been there. A huge faded water tower off Route 295 proclaimed "Apple Hill" to motorists whizzing by at seventy-five mph and bore an unimaginative apple motif.

More notably, drivers heading north or south on 295 always smelled coffee and its source confounded them. The eight-lane artery dividing Apple Hill into East (the more affluent section) and West (more blue collar, still good, but with an inferiority complex to the east), concealed a massive coffee roasting plant just off the highway. There, day and night, workers roasted Columbian, Kona, Hazelnut and Chocolate Raspberry beans and the aroma floated down into the cars of passing motorists. Winter, spring, summer or fall, drive through Apple Hill and you smelled coffee.

As for Louis, ensconced now in the Apple Hilton, he smelled only soap and it sickened him. His bathroom reeked of almond and English oatmeal and the scent filled the cold dry air of his non-smoking room. Fresh cakes in crisp tan and cream boxes appeared daily atop a bundle of neatly folded washcloths and the sight of them, intended to make guests feel special and homey, actually made him homesick.

A few days were closing in on a week now and he still hadn't spoken with Rebecca. Calls went unanswered and his excuse to office staff for staying at the hotel, that he and Rebecca were having work done and were *both* holed up there, was starting to wear thin.

The weekend passed uneventfully but now, Monday morning, he became anxious about his Tuesday night rap session because free bakeshop goodies had become part of the routine (if not, he'd hate to admit, the draw itself).

Abrams was at an impasse. Admit to his wife that he had been banging Naomi Kahan and he was not just an adulterer, he was a liar. Hang onto the lie and he was, well, still an adulterous liar but homeless to boot.

It was more than evident that phone calls wouldn't work so he decided the time had come to plead his case in person. So he fired up the Crown Vic and stopped in to the Apple Hill store where Louis knew his wife would be working.

"The meesus she no want to see you," Ferdinand said the moment Louis came through the door.

Louis ignored Rebecca's trusty manservant, went to the counter and rang the small bell by the register.

Their six days apart had been the longest they hadn't seen each other in thirty years and Rebecca, answering the bell herself, looked tired and drawn.

"I tell heem you no want to see heem," Ferdinand said.

"Thank you, Ferdi," she said. "It's okay. Why don't you get some lunch."

Rebecca was compassionate despite her weariness and the sight of her personally answering the bell, rung by her louse of a husband, brought a lump to Ferdinand's throat.

But Rebecca, tired only from work and not, as Louis presumed, a lack of sleep, was fortified by a clean conscience and Louis weakened before her. He was, for the briefest of moments, genuinely sorry.

"Hi, Bec," he said.

His wife's big dark eyes were soft and wet but unyielding. She opened the register and withdrew a bundle of twenties and checks for the afternoon deposit.

"I know you didn't come by just to say hello," she said.

"No, I did not," Louis said. "I came here to say I'm sorry."

"What are you sorry for? You didn't do anything, remember?"

"I'm sorry for walking out."

"Walking out? You have *got* to be kidding me. You didn't walk out, Lou, I threw you out. Now is that it because I've got work to do."

"Can we talk?"

"We just did."

"In your office."

Rebecca wrapped the checks and cash in a red rubber band she rolled off her wrist, turned on her heels and stepped back to her office. Inside, a window air conditioner hummed quietly, efficiently, but she turned up the fan and closed the door for privacy.

"Your man doesn't seem to like me," Louis began.

Rebecca opened the fireproof safe near her desk, put the money in and slammed the heavy door shut.

"What's there to like? Besides, he's not my man, he's my employee. A good, *loyal* employee. Loyalty's hard to come by these days."

"Bec..."

"What, don't you agree?"

Louis felt as if his nuts were in a vise.

"If you say so."

"I do say so. I want *you* to say so."

"Rebecca..."

Their week apart had been hard and lonely, but it gave her time to think.

"What do you want, Louis? You want me to say it's ok, it's alright that you fuck around on me? Say the word, Louis. Loyal. I don't think you can. I don't think you know the meaning of the word."

"Rebecca..."

"That's right. Rebecca is loyal, Louis is not. The thing of it is, I'm getting to the point where I don't even care, do you understand me?"

"What do you want me to say?"

"There's not much *to* say, Lou. You were FUCKING Naomi Kahan. I know you were because I saw it in her face. You don't think that's proof, but I am a woman and I can tell you it is. You were FUCKING

Paula Stephenson - our son's GOD-DAMNED TEACHER! You were FUCKING Miriam Kornbluth! You think I don't know? I know! But the thing is, Lou, I'm about done with you and I just about don't care."

"Rebecca..."

"For God sakes, Lou, for a man who speaks for a living, you don't have a lot to say. But that's okay. I've got a call out to Jackson and you can speak to him."

Her attorney, a nebbish WASP named Jackson Pollard, did all the work for Mom's Bake Shop, but he wasn't exactly a hotshot divorce guy.

"What are you calling him for?"

"Louis, I am not going to play this charade with you anymore. I will DI-VORCE you, do you understand me? I will leave you and save myself a whole lot of grief and embarrassment."

"Rebecca, listen. I've made some mistakes. I am a man and I made some mistakes."

"Do not give me that 'I am a man' shit! You want to talk about a man? *Ferdinand* is a *man*. He works his *balls* off and sends money home to support his family. *That* is a man."

For the first time in their life together, a life that dated back to high school, romps in the fruit orchards, marriage, children, failures, successes, he felt small and pitiful before Rebecca.

"I've made some mistakes," he said again, wiping the corner of his eye. "I'm sorry."

Louis reached across the desk to the hand of his hurt but vulnerable wife. She let him hold it for a moment but snatched it back suddenly and swiveled in her chair to wipe a tear of her own she hoped he didn't see.

"I can't keep doing this, Lou," she said.

They sat there quietly, the hum of the air conditioner mimicking the breath between them. Louis blew his nose on a clean cotton hankie, dabbed his right eye again and returned it to his suit pocket.

"I want to come home," he said.

"I'm not ready for that and neither are you."

"Rebecca, it's my home, too. We haven't seen each other in a week and I want to come home. We can work on this together, in our home."

"No. Not yet."

Outside, heavy overnight rains had stopped, but it was hazy and humid when Louis and Rebecca left the bakeshop together and walked toward his car. He unlocked the door and reached again for her hand, but it was damp and limp, unresponsive to his touch. He tried kissing her on the mouth but she turned her head and allowed him to press his lips to her cheek instead.

A thaw.

He was still relegated to the hotel but sensed his banishment coming to an end.

* * * * *

On Tuesday afternoon Louis visited his wife's original shop in Voorhees, a glass-faced, low-rent storefront bookended by Butts 'N Betts and Glamour Nails. He knew Rebecca wouldn't be there and paid for that evening's sweets in cash.

He was meeting Rebecca for a bite after the night's meeting so he was determined not to nosh too much himself but maybe, if things went well, there'd be a little noshing back at casa Abrams later.

Attendance at his Tuesday night sessions had flagged the past month or two so Louis decided to freshen it up a bit with a guest speaker. But having neither time nor money to find someone really special (someone he'd have to actually pay) he asked Janice Palumbo, who hadn't been to a session since Stephen abandoned her eight weeks before. She didn't return partly out of embarrassment, partly because of her schedule and partly because she didn't know if she belonged now that she and her Jewish boyfriend were splits. Louis, calling her on short notice Monday morning, assured her that she did.

As a guest speaker, he told her, she'd be perfect. After all, she was a professional radio host, she was already known to the group and she was confused about conversion, a trip many in his group had taken.

But her doubts were not unfounded.

"What's so special about her?" Naomi Kahan hissed in her husband's ear that evening, after they'd helped themselves to coffee and cake.

Alex would rather they didn't come at all, no matter who the speaker was, just stay home with a pizza, drink beer from the can and watch the Phils.

Jacov also wondered what was so special about Janice Palumbo, but he had no one to voice his concerns to so he squeezed back into his desk chair, munched some coffee cake and fingered the swizzle sticks in his cup.

In her two earlier sessions Janice sensed that some of the members, particularly the women, resented her, and she couldn't have been more right. She was, first off, a celebrity (again, for Philadelphia). But she was also well-dressed, well-groomed, well-built, under forty, unmarried and un-Jewish. In short, thought Naomi Kahan, everything most men wanted.

"When Rabbi Abrams asked me yesterday to address the group I wasn't so sure," Janice started. "It isn't that I lack for things to say but I'm a little out of my element here. So I thought, rather than talk *to* you, maybe I'd just talk *with* you."

The conversational tack wasn't what Louis had in mind when he asked her to speak, but it was a little late to turn the boat now. After all, moderating the group was *his* schtick, but he sat back and went with it.

"As you know, I am not a Jew. but I think I might want to become one, and I thought speaking with you, without a moderator (a glance at Louis), could help me make the right decision."

Louis didn't mean by having a guest speaker he'd have no role at all. He also thought she'd actually *speak* about something – her radio show, the media, Jews for Jesus, some friggin' thing, -- but he played along.

"Who, me?" he mouthed but remained silent as an observing school principal in one of the tight children's desks toward the back of the room.

"It's been a while, but those of you who were here the last time will remember Stephen, my now ex," Janice continued.

"How could we forget?" Alex mumbled.

Janice flipped her bangs but barely glanced up.

"At any rate, Stephen and I came because we were thinking about a lot of things – marriage, conversion, maybe even getting a dog. Well, the good news is, I may still get the dog."

She grinned awkwardly and leaned back against the heavy metal teacher's desk.

"Yeah, yeah, get the dog," Jacov panted. He smiled up at her, but his eyes, as usual, worked their way south and settled on the front of her blouse.

Janice straightened her back and moved on.

"Who knows, maybe I'll make my parents happy and get married someday, but probably not to Stephen," she continued, expecting another outburst from Jacov but getting none, just crinkled foreheads, pasty faces, sips of coffee and blank stares. "What I'm less sure about now is conversion."

Naomi did not feel generous.

"So you were with a Jewish guy, it didn't work out, he moved on. Maybe you ought to do the same, honey," she said.

"Maybe you didn't hear me, so I'll go slow," Janice said. "I did move on, but that's not what I'm here to talk about. I'm still considering conversion and Rabbi Abrams thought that's a topic some of you could relate to."

Fact was, about half of the eight or nine couples who often attended his sessions included a partner who converted. Two men converted for their wives, one wife for her husband and one woman started the process but never quite finished.

"I relate," said Donatella Lapedis, an Italian immigrant who married her late husband just after World War II. "But the question is why? Like Naomi said, you not wit-a dat man no more, so why go through it?"

Janice wondered, too, not just about converting but about laying herself open to these people. She didn't know them and sensed hostility, especially from that Naomi bitch.

"Maybe I just want to do it for me."

"Do it for you? What do it for you?" Donatella said. "You family make-a the bread, right? I buy from you family forty years, every time I go to-a the Italian Market. They from old country, like me. But when I marry my Joshua I convert because that's whadda you do. For the children. But you? You convert and not marry that man then you really alone."

"Excuse me. But you don't know my family," Janice said. "And you certainly don't know me. Again, I am not here to talk about whether or not I'll marry Stephen. I mentioned it as an aside because being with him exposed me to Judaism. What's a matter, do you regret converting?"

"No, I no regret," Donatella said. "I'm Jewish, my children are Jewish. God willing, my grandchildren will be Jewish, too. But this is a decision I make fifty years ago. I was just a girl, twenty-two years old. I was in love. And in Roma, Rome, I knew Jews and I saw what happened to them. These were good people and I felt for them, especially after I meet-a my Joshua."

Olive skinned like her, Donatella reminded Janice of an aunt or distant relative she never knew. Her clothes spoke of taste and New World success – creamy, off-white leather shoes, fine linen suit, a nice watch on one wrist and a thin gold herringbone bracelet on the other.

"I'm glad it worked out for you," Janice said coldly. "But whether I get married or not, whether it's to a Jew or not, again, this is a decision I will make for me."

"So why talk-a to us?"

Janice was about to respond when Jacov distracted her, pulling, twisting and cracking his fingers until the digits popped like twigs. He thrust his big hands forward so his elbows and his wrists popped, then manipulated his big heavy head and his neck cracked, too.

"What about your family? Don't you care what they have to say?" Alex asked, participating despite himself.

"Of course I care, but it's not up to them," Janice said. "If I did what they wanted I'd be my sister."

"What's your point?" Naomi said.

Janice winced. This woman was getting on her last nerve and she, Naomi, did not want that. Janice forced a cold half smile and answered as civilly as she could.

"If I wanted to be my sister I'd have married a guy from the neighborhood, bore him a coupla kids and lived in a row home one block from the house I grew up in. That is my point."

There was silence for a moment, but it was broken by Anna Libman, a spry Holocaust survivor who met her husband after he and a division of GIs breached the German line and liberated Bergen-Belsen.

"Good for you, madel," she called from the second row.

The octogenarian spent eleven months in the "unofficial" concentration camp and it nearly killed her. Sixty years since emigrating to the U.S. she still peppered her speech with Yiddish and it pleased Janice to hear Anna use it toward her. This frail woman was a survivor, a walking miracle who tended to quote her Nazi captors because she outlived the bastards and doing so reminded others of what she'd been through.

At eighty-three she was still feisty and wore her sleeves pushed up so the prison camp serial number tattooed on her sinewy forearm showed for all to see.

Anna remembered the sooty skies above Bergen-Belsen blackened by the smoke of the crematoria, the piles of mangled human corpses – grotesque haystacks of mottled gray flesh stacked up and waiting for the oven.

And she remembered Commandant Josef Kramer, a pockmarked SS man who looked like he shaved with pruning shears. Under Kramer, Jews died by the thousands of diarrhea and dysentery. The commandant, who cared far less about dead Jews than the mess they left behind, saw a solution in starving the prisoners.

"They don't eat, they don't shit," Commandant Kramer had said, and so he refused to feed them.

Anna, courage incarnate, respected at once the young woman standing before her now, a lovely South Philly girl willing to leave everything she knew – family and friends -- for something that felt right. She would be a Jew.

"Please join us," Anna said.

"Excuse me?"

"Convert," Anna repeated. "You belong with us."

# Chapter 12

After the meeting Louis met his wife as planned at Olga's Diner, a twenty-four-hour Route 70 landmark just east of Apple Hill.

"Hi, Bec," he said, sliding into a booth opposite his wife, twenty minutes late. He leaned across and kissed Rebecca's cheek. "You look great."

Dog-tired, she didn't want to come out this late but couldn't very well blow it off so she washed her face and drove over.

"Who are you kidding, Lou?" she asked. "I look like a frump."

"Yes, but you're my frump."

Rebecca thought on this a moment, her husband's missed opportunity to say something right given the shit he was in, his cocky use of a possessive with regard to her.

"Ever the charmer," she said.

Fact was, despite the twelve hours she'd worked that day, Rebecca did look good. She didn't sleep well the first few nights they'd been apart, but the last four or five had been wonderful.

She wasn't preoccupied with planning, shopping and cooking for two so she was eating less, barely at all some days, and the eight pounds she'd lost brought out her jaw line and took in her waist.

For two hours late in the day Monday she treated herself to the spa and her cut and colored hair fairly glowed now, framing her face.

Louis might have guessed she did it all for him, but he'd have been wrong. Not unlike Janice, there were some things Rebecca did just for her.

"You do look good, Bec," he said again.

"I know."

Louis spied two couples in far corners of the restaurant whom he had married and one of the men, noticing, waved over to him.

"Eli Goldman's daughter and her husband," Louis said, waving back. "I married them two years ago."

Louis couldn't remember the other couple's names but hoped they didn't stop over. He, a good-natured tax attorney, had the paunch and pate of a man hitting middle age the hard way. She, an Irish Catholic who hadn't even considered conversion, divorced two husbands and buried a third. Seven or eight years older than her new man, she aged even worse than he: loose, reptilian skin and bad breath. The woman was a heavy chain smoker and, Louis presumed, an infrequent brusher. He pegged her for a shrew, a hanger on, the kind of woman who doesn't work and trades in the only currency she's got. Problem was, by the look of her, even that was drying up fast.

Neither Louis nor Rebecca wanted the topic of marriage to surface so quickly, but here it was, like ants at a picnic, which they could neither avoid nor ignore.

Fortunately, their waitress bought them some time.

"Youz guys ready or you still need a few?" she said.

She placed two short glasses of ice water before them and pulled a lined, pale green order book from the pocket of her apron.

Louis sipped his water, crunched a cube in his back teeth and took the lead.

"I am," he said. "Two eggs over easy. Whole wheat toast and a cup of decaf tea. No potatas."

"Decaf coffee and the fruit plate, please," Rebecca said.

"You got it, sweetie," the waitress said, scribbling in shorthand and popping her gum. The polished floor squeaked beneath the soles of her red Chuck Taylors as she stepped away.

"Fruit plate? What kind of dinner is that?" Louis said.

"No worse than eggs over easy, sleazy and greazy."

"You've got a point."

There was serious business before them, but neither wanted to jump right in so they danced a little longer.

"How's my boy?" Louis asked.

"He misses you. He just lays by the door looking out, his chin on his paws like two little hands."

"I miss him, too."

A phalanx of boys and girls from Apple Hill High School East filled a six-top in the wide marble center aisle and Louis and Rebecca glanced over, seeing themselves in other people's children. The boys, evidently upper classmen, sported varsity letter jackets, too much cologne and premature facial hair that belied pretensions of manhood. The girls swooned anyway.

Faster than expected, their waitress returned with plates of food and Louis went to work, breaking the yolks and sopping them up with torn, buttery hunks of toast. When the yolks were gone he cut the whites in squares, salted and peppered them, and slurped them up too.

It was after ten and Rebecca assumed he had dinner, plus snacks at his meeting, but here he was eating again. She shook her head and grinned into her fruit plate.

"I went to the spa yesterday," she said.

"That right? I said you look great," he said as he chomped. "And you do."

"You always say that, especially when you want something. And you always want something."

"What, can't a man tell his wife she looks good?"

Rebecca, her eyes still low, played with her food now, too, spearing a juicy yellow cube of pineapple and a grape, seeding a piece of watermelon with her butter knife.

"You hurt me, Lou," she said.

"Bec, I think we've been through this."

"I want you to know you hurt me. At this point I don't even care if you admit it, but I want you to know. I've thought about it a lot this week and I'm tired. Do you know what I mean? I'm tired and I'm tired of being played for a fool."

"You're not a fool, Rebecca."

She seethed.

"Then grow the fuck up and stop treating me like one."

The nearby clink of silverware on plates reminded them to keep their voices low. The meal was ending and Louis, his bags packed and already out in the car, did not want to return to the hotel. But if the conversation didn't take a turn for the better, and soon, that's where he was heading.

"So what do you want me to do?"

"What I want you to do is to change, Louis, but I don't think you can. I want you to honor me. Do you remember vowing to honor me?"

"I remember."

Rebecca was close to tears again, steeled less by the anger she nurtured all week than she hoped she'd be. She blew her nose into her dinner napkin and cleared her throat.

"I want you to honor the vows you once took – the same vows you recited to Eli Goldman's daughter and son-in-law over there, and every other couple you marry. I want you to take them as seriously as you make them out to be. You say that shit with a straight face, Lou, and I'd like to know if you ever hear a single word you're saying."

She paused.

"What I want is for you to not need me to explain this to you. For God sakes, Louis, you're the rabbi! What I want you to do is start acting like one."

"I can do that, Rebecca."

His wife stared out across the parking lot to the intersection of routes 70 and 73 where motorists swarmed through one of New Jersey's last remaining suicide circles. Cars entered the circle like healthy red blood cells flowing from one artery to the next, avoiding the oncoming crush of vehicles as if they were giant, dangerous leukocytes. Rebecca wondered if the drivers were happy, if they led upright, faithful lives, if they trusted their husbands and wives.

"I want to come home, Bec," Louis said.

She pushed the watery, homogenous fruit pieces around her plate and wondered how, like her dinner, life with her husband had grown so tasteless. She looked out the window and dropped her fork resignedly.

"Then come home," she said.

# PART II

<u>Chapter 13</u>

They arrived home separately, seconds apart, and Rebecca bee-lined for the bedroom, leaving Louis with Buster, their seventy-pound pit bull.

"No push-push for Lou-Lou, huh boy?" Louis said, greeting the dog as his wife shut the door behind them.

Buster sensed something wrong, felt tension in the air, but greeted Louis warmly and with a big grin, his whole body wagging with his tail. He was so excited at seeing Louis that he nearly knocked him over, bounding through the room like an incoming wave, and smiled, genuinely smiled.

The dog's unrestrained joy at seeing him was so pure and unconditional that Louis nearly wept; it was a reaction he drew from no other living thing.

"It's OK, honey," he said. "Daddy's home."

Louis rubbed the top of the dog's thick, broad head and Buster sat there grinning. Then he jumped up into Louis's lap and practically begged for more. Buster loved playing rough, wrestling and snorting and grunting, and Louis encouraged it more than he probably should have.

"Who's the big dog? Not YOU, bitch!" he'd say, pushing Buster away and letting him charge back again and again, exercising the both of them.

He'd tie Buster up in loose approximations of old wrestling moves he learned at the Y, never hurting the dog but holding him down just long enough to show that he, Louis, was in fact the big dog.

Louis tried to ignore the situation at hand – that he'd be sleeping alone tonight, the ninth night in a row, but was overjoyed at seeing his boy nonetheless. He knew the dog would slink up onto the pull-out bed after he, Louis, was close to sleep and lay there at his feet till dawn.

Louis did not understand the bedeviling these dogs got in the press but recognized from whence it came.

The media pricks who ran the stories were jackals, pure and simple. They'd eat their own if it sold a few more papers and the bigger, juicier, more startling the story, the better.

So a dog bite today, a car crash tomorrow, a corruption case the next, it didn't really matter. Today's news, tomorrow's trash liner, and around and around.

The pit bull is the demon dog du jour, he concluded; there have been others, but today it is the pit. And he had almost bought into it.

When his liberal neighbors, Alfred and Toni Sachs, adopted their first pit bull after returning from two years on a kibbutz, Louis and Rebecca were horrified. They feared a bloodletting in the neighborhood and knew it was only a matter of time before the dog mauled every pet, child and letter carrier in the area.

What they expected was a snarling, aggressive uberdog, the canine equivalent of Mike Tyson, bulked up and turned loose.

What they didn't expect was to fall in love.

Sasha, a brindled brown female, hardly barked at all and they never heard her growl. She was so gentle she didn't even use her teeth to accept treats that Louis and Rebecca began feeding through the chain link.

When the Sachs got a second pit to keep Sasha company, Louis and Rebecca were broken. The cuddly brown puppy who could be named nothing *but* Ginger so thoroughly won them over that they had to have one.

Louis researched the breed, found they'd been among the most popular dogs in the country for decades and had a long and proud history. The dogs were bred for courage, strength, tenacity and companionship, a cross between bulldog and terrier, and the more he read, the more he liked. He learned that, despite the beating they took in the press whenever some jackass abused one, pit bulls had always been bred as family dogs, that aggression toward humans was selectively bred out of them.

His online research was almost all positive: experts crowing over the gentle nature of the dogs, their intelligence and willingness to please (and how that was a trait that could also turn them into terrors). He read about their comic qualities, their tendency to grin when they are happy, their showmanship and pluck. And he read, surprisingly, that pit bulls love to cuddle.

Still, the local daily rag ran story after story, playing upon the blood lusting stereotype. It ran pieces about urban thugs in Camden raising the dogs as weapons, siccing them on other dogs and on rival thugs, posing them street side as spike-collared trophies.

The editors at the *Carrier*, a once strong daily that, like most papers, was now hemorrhaging readership, ran pit bull stories from halfway across the country that they picked off the wires, playing them big and ugly, because that's what they thought sold papers.

"Beloved Pet Mauls Elderly Mom."

"Pit Bulls Savage Pizza Boy."

"Child Loses Eye in Dog Attack."

What didn't make the papers were stories about the many more bites from so-called family dogs, Louis noted. Like the Cairn Terrier that bit Louis's own sister in the face when they were kids. Or the pet Schnauzer that mauled Jerry and Elaine Goldfarb's young daughter's hand. And there was nothing in the paper about the Saint Bernard that broke through a screen and attacked a paper boy, his enormous maw closing on either side of the poor kid's torso.

In a five-minute Google search Louis found that there had been many famous pit bulls, from Petey of *Little Rascals* fame to Sgt. Stubby, whose World War I heroics made him one of the most decorated dogs in American history.

There was Nipper, the RCA Victrola dog, who was also a pit bull, as well as Tige, the dog in the early Buster Brown shoe ads.

Perhaps the name Buster lodged in his mind from his research, but it seemed to fit the spry, tough, lovable little dog he and Rebecca adopted.

And, now that Louis was home, it occurred to him that he and Buster had more in common than he knew on the ride home. They were both in the doghouse.

Louis sat heavily on the couch in the den, a frayed relic he and Rebecca bought as newlyweds, and thought about watching TV but stood up suddenly and readied for bed. He tossed the couch cushions in a four-high pile near the TV and pulled at the old fold-a-way bed tucked inside it. The dusty blue strap, so long out of use, strained and nearly snapped as Louis tugged on it, but the bed came up with a twang. He pushed the lower third of the mattress toward the floor and extended its splayed, reluctant metal legs. Louis stared at the bed, resented it, loathing the night ahead, the metal crossbar wedged in his back, the thin, worn cushion little more than a membrane between him and it.

When he did sleep it was fitful and thin, the right house but the wrong room. Buster snored contentedly, but Louis tossed side-to-side, wresting blankets from beneath the leaden dog.

Later, during the long, gray period of night that Louis most loathed, the time when he felt most vulnerable, he dreamt he was barefoot on a beach. He was a young man. Sharp pieces of shell cut the tender skin between his toes and the sun blinded and burned him. Yet he walked along, solitary and free.

As so often happened in his dreams he soon found himself aloft. He floated over the beach, transcendent and calm. He understood life and all its complexities so clearly from up here but, like overnight haze, the wisdom always dissipated with the coming dawn.

Still, he enjoyed it while he could, un-tethered by gravity or obligation, and wished he could fly forever.

He breathed deeply and soared, but soon the thick salt air filled him up and forced him down. He crashed on the beach with a thud.

The brilliant golden hues of his dream were gone, replaced by a morning that broke dull and overcast, a gummy gray film over everything. As he assumed it would, his lower back ached from the bed's steel support bar and he cursed the thing yet again. It wasn't the hard landing after all.

Outside, the low, masculine roar of a lawn mower growled from a few yards over and the high-pitched trill of insects filled the space between his ears.

Louis rolled out of bed marveling how he could feel so bad and yet Buster, occupying the same quarters, slept so well. Louis accidentally kicked the dog as he swung his long legs free, but Buster snored on.

Louis stretched, arched his back to will some relief to it, and hobbled toward the kitchen for coffee.

Stuck to the oak island was a note, un-addressed and unsigned, but it was cordial nonetheless.

"Hope you slept well. We'll talk later."

"You bet we will," he growled, deciding there and then that he would not spend another night on the friggin' pull-out couch.

Along with the note, Rebecca had left him half a pot of coffee. He poured himself a cup, jumped in the shower and sped off to synagogue for services.

<u>Chapter 14</u>

In the weeks that followed, Louis and Rebecca shared the house but not much more.

He refused to admit a relationship of any type with Naomi Kahan despite his wife's rock solid "proof" of an affair.

Louis insisted Naomi's look in the bakeshop, her quick departure and failure to return, could have meant anything, and proved nothing.

But with another round of holidays approaching Louis and Rebecca had other concerns. For him there were sermons to write and plans to make. Jacov and his crew had finished the alarm system, but now the main air conditioning unit was on the fritz, the synagogue's handyman had quit and they needed an HVAC guy, like, yesterday. Orders poured in and Rebecca, ever busy, got busier still just struggling to keep up.

Banned from his bed, Louis took up residence in Jonathan's old room, still decorated in 1970s kitsch.

From the wall above his son's bed Farrah Fawcett smiled down in a ruby one-piece, stomach flat and firm, million-dollar grin.

There was an old florescent black light above his son's desk that still worked and a lava lamp that didn't, its waxy blob just sort of floating, motionless, suspended like an oily dump. And, along a shelf, Louis found long-drained airplane bottles of scotch and whiskey that he'd never noticed when they were full.

For the sake of appearances, he and Rebecca remained a couple, but the blood felt drained from their marriage and the strain wore upon them. Neither wanted to believe their thirty-two-year union was coming to an end, but there seemed little left to discuss.

Even at the gym, where Louis worked out and played racquetball as usual, buddies could sense something amiss.

"You look like shit, Lou," his long-time racquetball partner, Shelly Tannenbaum, greeted him courtside one morning.

"Don't sugar coat it, Shel," Louis said. "Tell me what you really think."

A scrappy Haddonfield lawyer and a big wig with the Camden County Democrats, Shelly Tannenbaum was a long way from the Bed-Stuy block he'd grown up on but loved talkin' trash like the old days. Friends called him "Brooklyn" and knew the trim ex-boxer could still mix it up.

Louis spent enough time on South Philly street corners to talk the talk, too, but he'd always be just a big Jewish kid from suburbia.

"You know I don't like to pry, Lou, but you sleepin' awright?" Shelly asked.

His Columbia education and law degree aside, he still loved the vernacular and inflection of the workingman and peppered his speech with it.

Louis sidestepped the question along with his friend and entered the polished wood court. They had only a half hour reserved so they had to get to business.

Shelly grunted as he served the small rubber ball, stepping out of the way so Louis could try to hit it. Louis returned the volley, won the serve but still didn't answer.

He served the ball powerfully, remembering to follow through, a move Shelly did automatically.

Shelly, more agile and athletic than Louis, stepped back and struck the ball like a pro. Louis returned the shot, but barely, and Shelly pounced, slamming the ball back to the front with such velocity that Louis could barely get his eyes around it, let alone the racquet.

He put both hands on his knees and leaned over for breath, severely winded.

"You don't like to pry? Who you kiddin'? You're a fucking yenta," Louis finally answered.

Shelly caught the ball on a bounce, leaned up against a wall and caught his breath, too.

"Whadda ya mean, yenta? I've known you half my life."

"Yeah, and half your life you've been a fucking yenta."

Shelly served the ball savagely now. It struck the front wall at an angle, hit the side and ricocheted off the floor before Louis even got a swing at it. He flailed wildly, missed and fell on his ass.

"Good shot, buddy," Shelly said, offering Louis a hand up.

"F.U., Brooklyn," Louis said, taking the hand. "Serve again."

"Why, Rabbi Abrams. Your language offendeth me."

"Cut the crap, Shel. Serve the ball or I'll 'offendeth' you with this fucking racquet."

Their games were generally closer, but today Shelly walloped him 15-6 and 15-7 before they called it quits.

They left the court drenched, toweled off and grabbed a small table near the track. There they would grab a cup of coffee, talk trash and watch the new moms in short shorts run themselves back into shape.

"So what's the story, you sick? You played like shit," Shelly said again.

Louis swept his wet hair back and rubbed the graying brown whiskers on his chin. His beard needed a trim.

"I'm awright," he said. "Not sleeping great lately is all. Bec and I are paddling some rough waters."

"Paddling rough waters," Shelly marvelled. "What are you, a fucking Indian?"

Louis would take such talk from few people, especially over something so personal as his foundering marriage, but Shelly Tannenbaum happened to be one of them. Louis smiled despite himself.

"Yeah, I'm an Indian," he said. "Big Chief Kick Your Ass."

Shelly went for the coffees and in his absence Louis turned his attention to a big middle-aged Russian pummeling a heavy bag near the track. He was among a wave of Russian immigrants pouring into the Philly metro area, a trend that started across the river with the fall of the Soviet Union and was making its way over to Jersey. Rumors swirled about them, that they had been black marketeers or the Russian mafia, driven out when Putin became president, but it wasn't true. For the most part.

The man hitting the bag had sparse strands of hair pasted back over his scalp and every time he laid into the canvas sweat flew from his head, neck and shoulders.

"Here you go, chief," Shelly said.

Louis looked up and took the coffee. He stirred in two sugars and two creamers.

The Russian continued pounding the bag, but he was slower now. He'd strike it low and powerfully as if throwing a body shot, turn an elbow and shoulder into the bag, then hit it again with the other padded fist.

"So what's going on?" Shelly asked again.

"You really are a fucking yenta. You know that, right?"

"Whatever."

Louis stirred his coffee some more and held back, still watching the big man strike the bag.

"Rebecca and I are separated," he said at last.

"You're separated? What are you talking about? I saw her at shul with you just last week."

"I'm talking about we're separated. It's been three weeks, give or take. I'm at home, she's at home but it's separate rooms, separate meals, separate everything. She won't even wash my clothes."

"I didn't know. But that's not exactly the legal definition of separated."

"Believe me when I tell you," Louis said. "And how could you know? You're the first one I'm telling."

Louis sipped his coffee and thought about the pickle he was in.

"She knows about Naomi Kahan."

"Naomi Kahan? You still banging her? That was like two years ago."

"No I'm not 'still banging her' you friggin' barbarian. I am being good. The idiot stopped into the shop a few weeks back, took one look at Rebecca and high-tailed it out. Rebecca took that to mean I'm still fuckin' nailing her."

"What do you mean still? She knew?"

"She knew and she didn't. I never admitted but she isn't a fool. Naomi and her putz of a husband still come to my Tuesday nights so in a way I'm still seeing her but not like I used to."

"She *is* a hot piece of ass."

"You have no idea."

Louis gulped his coffee and both looked up as a young woman less than half their age jogged by. The word "East" was stenciled in white across the back of her pale blue shorts and it jiggled with each leggy stride. She was out of high school, but not by much.

"So whatchu gonna do?" Shelly asked.

"I don't know."

"You're not talking divorce, are you?"

"No. Well, I don't know. We're not really *talking* anything."

Louis looked toward the snack bar longing for something sweet - a cruller, a brownie, even a bran muffin, anything but those nasty Power Bars they couldn't sell enough of.

"The first week I stayed over at the Apple Hilton and since then I've been home in Jonny's room," Louis said. "So I'm home, but barely. The thing of it is, she knows. She knows about Naomi Kahan and she knew about the others."

"Paula and Miriam?"

"She knows. I don't know how, but she knows. I'm about one fuck-up away from divorce court."

"Jesus Christ, Lou. If it was Kim, I'd a been out on my ass. No comin' home. No Jonny's room. No second chances."

"If it was Kim I wouldn't be looking."

"Don't you believe it, Louie. You're just like the rest of us. Every now and again you just want a little strange."

But Louis was not like the rest of them. For him it had never been every now and again, but all the time. He considered trying a twelve-step program, but they all seemed too desperate, too much of an admission, too not him.

He didn't even know if there were twelve-step sexaholic programs, but if they were anything like the narco group he tried they definitely weren't for him, that much he was sure. That scene was nothing BUT a pick-up joint.

One Saturday afternoon that summer, his head intermittently cloudy from weeks of on and off dope smoking, he snuck off to a Narcotics Anonymous meeting at a Black Horse Pike Baptist church without telling even his wife. But there he felt out of place, somehow way under-qualified, like a guy with a stuffed nose in a cancer ward. For once, his lack of mental clarity seemed trivial as one after another the druggies raised their hands and rattled off real tales of woe.

Some had been to prison or lost their homes over drugs. They lost families, jobs, futures. They were all "clean and sober"— at least for today – and for that they thanked their sponsor, their program and their Higher Power.

Which was all well and good but what really got to Louis was all the hot chicks. One of them, a mousy little thing who simply *had* to be a school teacher, stared goo-goo eyed as "Joe" told how he'd recently gotten out of Bayside State (prison, not university), come home to a crappy little Camden rent-a-box and set out to find gainful employment.

Clad all in white, the colorful ink on Joe's sinewy arms, shoulders, chest and neck stood out in relief. He wore a white "wife beater" tee, crisp white jeans, white leather Reeboks and a K-Mart courtesy counter's worth of silver chains, baubles and bracelets.

Joe carried himself as a badass white kid from the streets, but back at Bayside State, Louis was certain, he was just another bitch.

"My name is Joe and I'm an addict," Joe told the group.

"Hi, Joe," the group responded.

"Hi, bitch," Louis thought.

"I'm here 'cause I wanna be here, ah-eight?" Joe said. "But it's also a condition of my parole, I ain't gonna lie to you."

Louis thought little of the punk, but he sure seemed street. A poor man's Eminem.

"I did some bad things, things I ain't proud of, I ain't gonna lie to you, yo," Joe bragged, dying to get some cred if it killed him.

"And I paid for it, you know I'm sayin,' yo? I ain't talked to my moms in two years but I don't blame her. All the lyin', the stealin', the cheatin'. I be slingin' dope, pimpin'. I did what I had to do, but I hurt the people who loved me and now I'm about as alone as alone can be."

With this, the group (minus Louis) got behind poor Joe with all the "amens" and "tell it, bros" he could handle.

"But it's all good, you know I'm sayin', yo, 'cause I am not getting high today."

Heads bobbed in unison and more than a few ex-offenders and drug addicts smacked high-fives. One big black dude – head shaved, ears ringed – even gave Joe some body love.

"Mah nigga," the man said, bumping fists and hugging him deeply. Joe hugged him back but had to go on. There was still more to share.

"In my old life I did whatever it took to get high 'cause that's what I was about, you know I'm sayin'? It wasn't like, 'Joe, today we gonna bus' some ole lady over the head for twenty bucks so we can get high,' you know I'm sayin'? But that's what I did. And, like I said, I ain't proud."

He certainly didn't *seem* proud, Louis thought. In fact, Joe seemed about to cry and the other hoodlums and junkies just stared, rapt, a little weepy themselves.

Louis himself couldn't turn away from the drama, an episode of Maury or Springer come to life. But what really mesmerized him was what seemed to be developing between the confessed druggie-robber-thug, and the hot little teacher type – with her tight little bod, small high breasts and rimless glasses - who evidently wanted to mamma poor Joe. If he lived to a thousand he'd never get why such friggin' hotties were perpetually drawn to such utter, fucking losers.

"Anyhow," Joe said, "I'm clean now and I'm not gonna get high today. I thank my sponsor, my program and my higher power. As-Salaam-Alaikum."

Oh, for fucks sake! Louis thought. A white boy Muslim? Now I've seen it all.

"You with me, Lou?" Shelly said, drawing Louis back.

"Yeah, pal," Louis said. "I'm sorry. Just a little distracted."

"That's alright buddy. You're gonna get through this. You just gotta keep your eye on the ball, something you didn't do in that court today. But no more talk of divorce. I see enough of that crap at work. Speaking of which, I gotta fly. I got deps in an hour."

What Louis couldn't tell anyone, even Shelly, was that Janice Palumbo's conversion lessons had started. And those crazy old feelings had come again.

# Chapter 15

Like many rabbis, Louis conducted most of his conversion classes in a group, six or seven couples entering the process together, often before marriage.

He instructed the women on what it means to keep a kosher home, how to bless and light the Sabbath candles, and about the key festivals and rituals throughout the Jewish year.

Many would-be converts found the experience to be just what they had hoped, warm and welcoming, as comfortable and renewing as a hot bath.

He taught the men about reciting the Kiddush over wine before meals as well as about their traditional role leading the Passover service. While most of his male students had been circumcised, the men also learned the meaning of the brit milah, the b'ris, a ritual cutting of the foreskin performed when a boy is eight days old.

Men and women alike studied the sanctity and meaning of the bar and bat mitzvah, the portal into adulthood when, at 13, boys and girls are called to the Torah to read from the Holy Scriptures for the first time.

They studied respect and tolerance for all peoples and the long history in which those principles were denied the Jews, from the Pharaohs in Egypt up through the Spanish Inquisition, the pogroms, the Holocaust and modern-day anti-Semitism.

And they had an introduction to the prodigious liturgy that commands, to varying degrees, how every Jew leads his or her own life.

On occasion Louis also instructed singles who, for one reason or another, pursued conversion for themselves alone, without a partner. Louis preferred the group format, the interaction and fun of shared new experiences, but often found the singles to be more curious and probing in their search for God.

It was into this latter category that Janice Palumbo, recently estranged from her fiancé Stephen Golding, came into the fold.

While her separation from Stephen was recent, Janice had long before broken from Catholicism. Church icons she thought beautiful as a child disturbed Janice as she got older and struck her, from her late teens forward, as idolatrous.

She thought churches in general, and the Catholic church in particular, held far too much sway politically and were corrupted by power and money.

It was not as if she stopped believing in Jesus, in the basic kindness and goodness of the man. She just wasn't sure about the whole "SON OF GOD" thing and saw, in Judaism, a bonding of sorts with Jesus through the sharing of his faith.

She still smirked, recalling candidate George W. Bush, as he answered the question of who is his favorite political philosopher during one of the 2000 presidential debates.

"Jesus Christ, because he changed my heart," Bush said.

She thought the former governor a jackass then and a shithead now, partly because he reminded her of Stephen, a Bush disciple even before he stole the presidency.

"I can be a Jew for Jesus," she told her boyfriend at the time, happy, in love, but confused.

Now, rid of Stephen for good (she hoped) and stuck with Bush just for the time being (she prayed) she wanted to become a Jew for its own sake.

Her belief in Catholicism was shaken by any number of things, chiefly among them an intractable dogma that demanded devotion to an ancient, oppressive and hypocritical creed.

Among Catholicism's greatest hypocrisies, Janice believed, was the confessional booth. There, earnest worshippers went to admit everyday sins to priests who, more and more, seemed some of the biggest sinners of all.

In recent years the courts and newspapers became so blackened by lawsuits over sexual abuses inside the priesthood that new allegations, no matter how horrific, failed to shock. And the Pope himself seemed to look the other way!

She herself had done half-hour radio shows featuring men and women so damaged in their youth by fondling, touching, *penetrating* priests, that they were simply broken as adults, damaged beyond repair.

"You're a sap," Stephen told her following one of the shows in the twilight of their relationship.

"What, for airing their stories?"

"No, for believing them. They're out to make a buck. Can't you see that?"

But Janice didn't see that. She believed their stories, felt them viscerally, and longed for the victims to win in court as much for themselves as for her.

It wasn't as if Janice thought all Catholic priests were child molesters, but their fondling of children was so common in her South Philly neighborhood that those who did so acquired a special nickname: didlers.

Thus, Father Joseph was a didler; Father Peter was not.

Uncle Anthony, now *there* was a didler, but we never talk about that, do we Janice?

"You be a good girl." …

Everyone loved Uncle Anthony, Goombah Tony they called him on the block, Mamma's older brother from Italy.

… And how he died, such a sin.

Your Uncle Anthony loved you.

"Nice and clean, little Janna."

Just a little girl.

Sundays after church.

"We have to bathe you now, Janna."

Thick, strong butcher's fingers.

"Be a good girl, Janna" …

Janice screamed so loud and long one night that the cops came, thought she was being murdered. She hadn't used Ivory soap in forever. Momma never bought it and neither did she, but what the hell. Five for a buck at Super Fresh on South Street.

Good day. Nice meal. Hot soapy bath. And then it hit her, the thick cloying smell of virgin white Ivory filling her tub, her nose, her eyes, her …

Thrashing about. Screaming. *Wailing*!

She called Momma, wanted to scream at her for what her bastard brother did, dead now six years and never paid a fucking dime for it or a day in jail.

"Whatsa matter?" Momma wanted to know. "You fight with-a that Stephen again? Stephen no good. He make-a you cry."

"It isn't that, Mamma," she muttered. "Stephen makes me happy."

"But you no sound-a so happy. You know I love you."

"I love you, too, Momma."

In the end, of course, she couldn't burden elderly Momma with what Uncle Anthony did thirty-five years before. She probably wouldn't believe it anyway.

Poor, dead Uncle Anthony. Father, husband, brother, uncle. Felled by a stroke while eating a fucking canoli on his motherfucking bench. That God-damned bench where all the old goombahs gathered day in and day out in front of Anthony's house at 9th and Catherine.

They talked about everything, those old men, but surely not *everything*, Janice was certain, not if he knew what was good for him, not in *that* neighborhood. He looked kind of rabid when she saw him last, the crusty pastry stuck painfully in his throat, a frothy mix of sugary cheese filling and saliva foaming at his lips. Eyes bulged like a fucking dead fish – open, cloudy, gone. She couldn't help but smile.

<u>Chapter 16</u>

"Thank you for taking me, Rabbi," Janice said at their first meeting, settling into one of the lush high-backed oxblood leather chairs in his chambers.

"You're quite welcome, Janice. Like I told you before, group is nice, but individual works better for some and I think that will be the case for you."

The heavy masculine smells of leather, cigar smoke and drug store aftershave made her head swim, but she breathed deeply, crossed her legs, and settled into the chair. She absently rubbed the polished, textured brass rivets that fastened the smooth upholstery to its frame.

"We use the same texts, cover the same material, but I think one-on-one allows for greater penetration, a deeper understanding of the work," Louis continued. "And as your work progresses you can always come by the group classes to meet others going through the same thing as you."

In the months to follow they'd work through three basic texts: *What is a Jew?* by Rabbi Morris N. Kertzer; *Jewish Literacy* by Rabbi Joseph Telushkin; and *The Complete Book of Jewish Observance* by Leo Trepp. And, if Louis had his druthers, they'd also explore his true meaning of penetration.

"You know, even before I met Stephen I felt a connection with Jews, with Judaism, that I don't think I ever felt in my church," Janice confessed, unable to shake the old habit in the presence of clergymen. "Too much structure and ritual. Eat the body of Christ, drink of his blood."

She shuddered at the thought of communion, a rite her family considered sacred and beautiful, one she had taken part in hundreds of times herself.

"Taking communion is indeed among the holiest of Christian sacraments, but it is not for everyone," Louis pontificated. "As Jews we do not believe in blood rituals, in fact just the opposite. Do you know much about the Laws of Kashrut?"

"I know what it is to keep kosher, if that's what you mean."

"It is," Louis said. "Keeping kosher is an integral part of Judaism that dates back before the time of Maimonides, one of our great medieval scholars. Maimonides interpreted Biblical dietary laws as health-based, and many of them are. The meat of swine carried trichinosis, for example. Shellfish are scavengers of the sea, living off detritus as bottom dwellers. A Jew who practices kashrut does not eat pork, nor does he eat lobster or shrimp."

"What's that got to do with communion?"

"Getting to that. Jews also do not eat blood. The Torah dictates we do not consume blood because the life of the animal is contained in the blood. We do not eat it and we certainly do not simulate drinking it."

"Gotcha."

The priests she had known all her life and Rabbi Louis Abrams had something in common that neither, she presumed, ever gave much thought to. It was the power of their conviction, a certainty that whatever they say or do is better than OK. Their actions are ordained, God's will, the same fucking rationale that turned priests into pedophiles – or, at least, absolved them for it.

From the beginning, Abrams projected a sureness that startled and offended Janice yet comforted her too. It was a quality that could welcome and warm her, provide answers, keep her safe.

"And the milk and meat thing?" Janice asked.

"Again, the Torah instructs us not to mix the two and, as Jews, we obey the Torah. As it is written, you shall not boil a kid in its mother's milk. The scholars interpreted that to mean you do not eat meat and milk at the same meal.

"We'll get into all this," he said. "The thing to keep in mind, Janice, is you do not have to be a Holy Moses, you should pardon the expression, to be a good Jew. You do right. You live a good life. L'chaim! To life! That is the essence of being a Jew."

Louis practically shouted this, startling Janice with his throaty roar.

"I like it," Janice said. "But what does it mean to lead a good life?"

"Ah, that's the question, isn't it?" he said, leaning forward on the leatherette writing pad that cushioned his Spartan desktop. "Somehow I doubt we'll get to the bottom of it tonight. To hear Spike Lee tell it it's fairly simple. Do the right thing. If you ask me, he's a bit of a racist, but in that case he wasn't too far off the mark."

"I like him," Janice said meekly.

"Sometimes I do, too."

They would meet twice a week, Mondays and Thursdays, moving through the material in a steady, if cursory, fashion. After all, thousands of years of Jewish history and law could not be boiled down to a few short lessons, but Janice would become a diligent student.

Louis gave her the texts she needed, assigned the first readings and walked her to the door. Janice offered her hand and Louis took it, shaking a bit too long, she thought, before letting go.

But Louis was impressed by her. Her small, soft hand produced a grip that was surprisingly competent and strong, qualities he hadn't sensed in their first meetings. In her eyes he saw a spark he hadn't noticed when she and Stephen first joined the Tuesday night rap session. She was a grown, sensuous woman, but in her bright wet orbs Louis saw a lively girlishness that had been stifled under the husk of a bad relationship. She smelled musky, womanly, warm.

Later, in Jonathan's old bedroom, in his son's old bed, Louis couldn't help but think of her some more. He tried as best he could to quiet the creaky old springs, to somehow settle his weight between them so his wife in the next room wouldn't hear, then fell asleep to visions of Janice.

<u>Chapter 17</u>

Leaves streamed down like rain, falling from trees and blowing about in gusts that swept them up and moved them about again. Some of the more stubborn gathered in pools on the grass or clung together in pairs or desperate singles as Jacov toiled with the old bamboo rake to collect them.

Working in his mother's backyard he thought the rake fragile, like mother herself, its ancient brittle tines like lost and broken teeth.

Though he despised the work ahead – collecting and hauling the leaves out to the curb - their warm autumn colors soothed him for a while, cascading to earth in a gentle ballet of browns, golds, crimsons and yellow-greens.

The futile, perennial chore frustrated Jacov as a boy and he hated it no less now, struggling with the same leaves in the same yard, even the same damned rake.

All aspects of the job depressed him, from the inevitable blisters he'd get from not wearing gloves to the grime and sweat he'd be covered with when he was done. Even the joy of the colors faded fast for Jacov as they quickly lost their splendor in heaps upon the ground, blending with one another in a lifeless, undefined, brown-gray mass.

Of course, as in all areas of his life, Jacov had choices, and what appeared easiest wasn't always the case. He had to rake the leaves, for if he didn't it wouldn't get done, and the tools at hand were the old bamboo rake or the rusted cast iron one in the shed. He could have driven to Lakewood Hardware for a new one, or, better still, an electric leaf blower, but he would make do.

"Terrence, you wanna tuna sandwich?" mother called from the kitchen window just as he got started.

"I'm doing work here," he said.

"I know. Do you wanna tuna sandwich?"

"It's ten-thirty in the morning for Christ sakes! I just had breakfast."

"Well, I been up since five and I'm making lunch. Do you wanna tuna sandwich?"

"Don't *bug* me!"

The old woman dismissed him with a wave of her hand and forced the creaky aluminum window shut.

"Ya don't want, ya don't want," she muttered, not offended by her son's brusqueness and glad he was helping at all.

Tonight was Shabbat, the holiest day of the week, and she hoped he'd stay for dinner of roast chicken, kasha with bowties and canned peas and carrots, but knew he probably would not. Since Irving's death she'd spent more Shabbat dinners alone than she wanted to remember, but next week was yontif, the start of the high holidays, and she knew her boys would be home for that.

Jacov had always been more of a loner than his brother Rueben, six years his junior, but they remained close. Reuben, who lived ten minutes away in the thickets of Jackson, had a family of his own now as well as a house and a yard and his own damn leaves to rake. He and Jacov would sit with Mother at shul during the holidays, maybe pass a joint in the afternoon following services, but, as for the yard work, Jacov was on his own. And he wished he had a joint now.

So, on the spur of the moment, he climbed into his rusty beater van and headed down to 4th Street, the old black area where they used to cop nickel and dime bags from hoodlums on the street.

"Nickels," he mused. "Damn. I *am* dating myself."

Some of the dealers he'd gone to high school with were long dispatched to prison. Others were dead. One had found religion and done well, televangelising against "the life" on cable TV. And two, not so ironically, became cops. They always had the best shit and, Jacov presumed, still did.

Driving up Clifton Avenue he hooked onto East 4th and drew stares, just like in the old days. Back then a slow drive past Clifton and 4th and the briefest of eye contact was all it took to draw two, three, four black guys in hooded sweatshirts scrambling to the car for business. Even when it was dry – when none of his own contacts had dope – he could almost always score with the brothers on 4th Street.

To Jacov's surprise, as he drove up 4th Street, the Pookies, Tyrees and Spanky Bs of his youth were gone now, replaced by Mordechais, Davids and Chaims, none of whom were evidently pushing pot. His rickety van still drew looks, but these were from newcomers to the block, Orthodox Jews who purchased broken down shanties and vacant lots in the nineties and built massive, non-descript, three-story houses. He *had* been away awhile.

The homes, block after block of them, were utilitarian fortresses designed for the large families that fertile young Orthodox women churned out.

Jacov watched as girlish mothers pushed sturdy blue baby carriages, small contingents of older children in tow, the lot of them excited about the fast-approaching Sabbath. There would be sweet wine with dinner and golden braided challahs, roast chicken and vegetables, honey cake with hot tea and lemon for dessert.

Jacov listened as men in black coats and payis – traditional curled earlocks – met in the street after morning prayers and wished one another a "Good shabbos."

He sensed joy in the air - richer, denser and more gratifying, it seemed, even than a dime of good weed. On an impulse he parked the van and got out, not even bothering to lock his doors.

"Good shabbos," he said to a bent, bearded ancient headed his way.

The man, stooped by arthritis, looked up in surprise. His first impression was to take Jacov for a goy, a non-Jew, and he had not expected the traditional Sabbath greeting.

"Good shabbos," he returned, offering Jacov a gnarled, bony blue hand with a surprisingly strong grip. "Jeweesh?"

"Of course I'm Jewish," Jacov said with a start.

The old man looked Jacov over.

"Of course? Vy of course?" the man said.

He was so stooped he had to crane his neck to bring his buggy blue eyes up from the sidewalk, but, when he did, he seemed to be grinning. His cracked old lips revealed a set of big, crooked teeth.

"So vhat is it, boychik, you lost?"

"No, not lost," Jacov said. "I was looking for someone. I think maybe she moved."

"A yiddishe madel?"

Jacov didn't quite hear him or didn't understand what he meant.

"Come again?"

"Eh Jeweesh girl?"

Jacov thought of Leslie Bruckner who had lived nearby when they were in high school. At the time she was Jewish in name only, a cute, plump, party girl who gave it up, and fast. Leslie had a black boyfriend for a while and she had done it with Jacov's buddy Kevin, a scrappy, wiry son of alcoholics whom, to Jacov's puzzlement, a few hot chicks dug.

He, Jacov, never got into Leslie's pants, but oh how he wanted to. He was as surprised as anyone when, senior year, she dropped out of school and married a Chassid, one of the ultra-orthodox Jews who, in many locals' opinion, were now taking the town over, house by house and block by block.

"Yes," Jacov continued. "I knew a girl who lived around here once, but it's been a long time. Back in high school. Thirty years ago."

"So you think she's still here now?" the old man asked.

Now Jacov was sure. He was fucking grinning! This crooked old man was screwing with him. Jacov thought about whacking the old bastard on his head, climbing back into his van and getting the hell out of there but thought better of it.

"Probably not," he admitted. "I dunno. Maybe."

"To me you seem lost, boychik."

Jacov hadn't noticed, but they were stopped in front of the Chabad house, a movement within the orthodox community known for recruiting secular Jews like himself into a more pious life.

"Abraham Goldstein," the man said, offering Jacov his hand again, before going in.

"Terrence Jacov."

"Yacov," the man said, pronouncing the name biblically and pulling at his scraggly beard. "I am

Abraham and you are Yacov. We are both named for our patriarchs. Come in, Yacov, and sit with an old man."

Jacov knew about Chabad, had seen their houses in Philly and New York, but had never ventured in. The man's offer was friendly and warm, sincere, but Jacov's mission had been pot, not piety, and he still had the leaves to do.

"Maybe another time," he said.

"Vhat, you're here now. Come, sit."

"Nah, can't today. Maybe another time."

"Vell, maybe you come tomorrow after shul? Vee have a little schnapps and some herring. Maybe vee help you find-eh that madel."

"Maybe I will," Jacov said, turning back toward his truck.

"Okay, Yacov," the old man said. "Vee see you tomorrow."

Jacov climbed into the van and drew the belt around his gut. He started the truck and pulled a Phillies Blunt from a pack stuck in the visor, lighted it and drove back toward mother's. There, her Friday night soup was already a-bubble, filling the house with rich smells of simmering chicken, diced carrots, celery and onion.

He might have stopped at the hardware store on the way back and bought a new rake with the ten bucks he saved on dope, but he did not. He parked the van, went directly to the backyard and fished out a pair of his dad's old brown work gloves from the shed. Pulling them on he felt closer to his father, sensed him looking down, proud Jacov was helping his mother without having to be told. He picked up the rake from the grass where he'd dropped it and fell into a rhythm with the leaves.

"Terrence, you wanna stay for supper?" mother called moments later from a narrow slot of window. It was just past noon and dinner would be at five.

Thinking he hadn't heard her, mother struggled with the inner pane of the forty-year-old window frame, metal on metal, which didn't slide so much as rock side-to-side when she tried to move it further.

"Terrence! You wanna stay for supper?" she called again from a slightly wider crack.

"Jesus Ka-rist," he mumbled. "Can't you see I'm working?"

"You're working, you're working. I'm making supper. You wanna stay for supper?"

A bead of sweat trickled from his hairline and down the side of his nose and he wiped at it with dirty fingers.

His fingers left skid marks on his cheek, but Jacov let them be, not displeased with the effect, like camouflage on an infantryman. He swept a pile of leaves as if driving a ball.

"Terrence! I'm talking to you!"

Try as he would to ignore it, the voice would not let him be.

"Terrence!"

"What!"

"You wanna stay for supper?"

"Yes, mom," he said finally, peering over the tops of big round frames. "I want to stay for supper."

<u>Chapter 18</u>

The next morning Jacov stood up the crooked old man from Chabad and hoped not to run into him the following week when he returned home for Rosh Hashanah, the Jewish New Year, one of the holiest of the High Holy Days.

But another chance meeting wasn't likely. Like every year, Jacov would be late and, when he finally made it to synagogue sometime around noon – three hours after services began – Jacov would half-heartedly follow along, not really part of the service but not completely apart. He'd sit, stand, read and chant along with the other worshippers, but his involvement in the service would be mechanical, vestigial, a tenuous carry-over from his youth.

Still, Jacov couldn't help feel like he was changed somehow by meeting the old man in the street, Abraham the Elder, as he now thought of him.

While he hoped not to run into the old man, to be gently pressured into joining him at Chabad, Jacov felt good about his warm offer of fellowship, and by the knowledge that it still stood.

"We are both named for our patriarchs," Abraham had said.

"It resonated," Jacov told Louis the following Tuesday evening, arriving, as usual, a few minutes ahead of the others.

"As well it should," Louis said in his best rabbinical tone, Tevya from *Fiddler on the Roof.* "You are a young man, Terrence. It is not too late to do right by your God, by yourself, by your people."

I'm forty-eight, Jacov thought, maybe five years younger than you, so save the "wise old rabbi" routine for the Hebrew school crowd.

"Do-Right," Jacov parroted. "I hear ya. I can be Dudley Do-Right."

"Look, I'm trying to talk to you as an adult," Louis warned. "If you want to act like a child I'll treat you as I would a child."

"I'm sorry, Rabbi," Jacov said. "I'm just playing."

"I'm not."

* * * *

Returning to Lakewood the next week for Rosh Hashanah, Jacov knew his first stop should be his mother's house and the unfinished yard work but detoured instead to the rebounding downtown, just blocks from where he sought weed the week before. His destination was still not the Chabad house but a Jewish-style deli near the police station where, one day before the New Year's holiday, he figured on finding an easy table.

Driving east through Jackson, Jacov could practically taste the Center City's hot pastrami, three inches thick and mounded on thin marble rye. His mouth watered for the sour pickles and tomatoes in white plastic vats upon the table, all you can eat, just like at the great Manhattan delis on which the Center City was modeled. He'd also have to get a knish.

The deli was finished to look old and lived-in – hardwood floors sanded raw; sturdy, conventional chairs salvaged from some New York sandwich shop, chrome legs shiny but pitted, red vinyl seats; and, swaying from chains above the service counter, yard-long Hebrew Nationals six-inches thick.

Jacov entered the deli around two – after lunch but well before the early birds – and was seated right away.

"All set?" a young waitress chirped before Jacov barely had time to scan the menu.

"Not really, no," he said.

"Not a problem, hon," she said. "Coffee?"

"Yeah, Heineken."

As the waitress wheeled away for his drink she offered Jacov a quick view of her plump little rump and he actually, for the briefest of moments, thought he had a shot at it.

"Gimme an order a *that*," he mumbled as she sashayed away.

The little red head was freckled, cute, and wore a green cotton t-shirt that read: "Manischewitz Kosher for Passover" but Jacov sensed false advertising. She was evidently trying hard, but she and the two other servers seemed out of place, like mayo on a salami sandwich.

"Can I ask you a personal question?" he said on her return.

"You can ask," she responded, mildly vexed.

"I'm trying to guess what year you were born. I say nineteen-eighty-two."

"I don't *think* so," she said, rolling her eyes and flipping her hair.

"Nineteen-eighty-three?"

"No."

"Nineteen-eighty-four?"

But now he was just boring her with empty, safe flirtations both knew were going nowhere.

"You ready to order?"

Jacov puffed up his chest.

"Born ready. Hot pastrami, extra fat, extra bread. A potato knish. And another Heiny."

"You got it."

Turning from him the waitress glanced at her girlfriend across the room. The girl stood with her butt against a stainless steel countertop, eyeballing perfectly airbrushed nails. From the other girl's expression Jacov was sure his waitress mouthed "eeeewwww" over his order, his flirtations or both.

She returned moments later with his food.

"Here ya go," she said.

"I was just trying to be nice," Jacov told her. "I'm not a dirty old man or anything."

"Whatever," she said.

Cognizant of the young girls eyeing him like a letch, Jacov wolfed down his meal almost joylessly, paid the bill, and pretty much fled the scene.

# Chapter 19

Mother was out of the house by nine the next morning and settled into her seat fifteen minutes later with most of the other observant and semi-observant Jews. For many, one of the biggest thrills of Rosh Hashanah was the sounding of the shofar, the ram's horn, a tradition that preceded the destruction of the Temple in Jerusalem. In ancient times, Jewish warriors rallied their troops by blowing the ram's horn and the distinctive sound – harmonious when blown right, hair-raising when blown wrong – today rallied the faithful, as well as those who were faithful three days a year.

Jacov looked forward to hearing the shofar blast, echoing as it did around the temple of his youth, but for him it was more nostalgic than religious, an auditory transport back to Hebrew school and his crush on Amy Goldfinch.

Amy was the daughter of a local urologist who met her mother in the waning days of World War II. Both Jacov and his buddy Larry asked her out on a bright spring afternoon their final year in Hebrew school and she considerately mulled both offers, ultimately accepting Larry's.

Of course, it didn't mean much, hand holding at best, but Jacov was crushed, certain no woman would ever be as hot as Amy at thirteen.

They didn't speak much in the decades to follow, but Amy never lost her heat: glossy chestnut hair falling about her shoulders, flawless skin speckled with dark beauty marks, great rack and a slim hourglass shape. A light mustache barely fuzzed her upper lip and matched a feathery down that played upon her cheeks and arms but, to Jacov's eyes, these imperfections made her all the more beautiful. Even as a child Amy didn't speak so much as breathe her words and her tone made one lean forward to listen, forcing intimacy in the most routine of conversations.

Through his divorce and hers, Jacov never stopped thinking about Amy, but seeing her two, three times a year across the sanctuary he froze, never once working up the nerve to go over and talk. And so, as the years wore on, polite hellos fell away to distant smiles, smiles became nods, and nods, ultimately, looks the other way. The High Holidays would forever be a class reunion of sorts as grown men and women who knew each other as children caught up a few times a year, but Jacov's hopes for rekindling a crush flared out long ago.

Now he just served his time – one or two hours, two or three days a year – and shot the shit outside with guys he'd known since boyhood. Larry Bowman, his onetime competitor, didn't attend services anymore, but his brother Harry, a Delaware chiropractor, still drove up to worship with their parents. Most years, Jacov, Harry and Jacov's brother Rueben still slipped away after services and burned a bone in the parking lot, just like they did in Hebrew school.

What Jacov hadn't planned on this year was Lori Steinmetz remembering him - or he her. Three years his junior, Lori started a Jewish dating club when she was single that developed into an online matchmaking service. JungleDotCom reportedly bought the thing for like three million dollars, but the same success that gave her financial freedom helped destroy her marriage. Her schlump of a husband, a failed musician who taught piano for a living, ran off with their Mexican pool cleaner and half the couple's cash.

Fred Steinmetz was always one foot out of the closet, but Lori never thought he'd come all the way out, especially after they'd had children. And she definitely didn't think Juan, who was even more fem than Fred, would be her husband's type. Last she heard, Juan was a pre-op cross dresser and the two found moderate success with a gay porn web site.

After the split Lori collected her dignity and turned her attention to her boys and her faith. She became active in the sisterhood, attended services and was always the first to volunteer for Chinese Auctions and other fundraisers. She visited Israel, considered making aliyah – relocation to the Holy Land – but decided to wait for her sons to finish school and to do what she could, meanwhile, for the synagogue.

And her efforts did not go unnoticed. Within three years she was appointed to the synagogue's board of directors and, one year later, to be its president. That exalted position, which she now held, enabled her to sit on the bimah near the rabbi during services.

Taking a break from her seat at the front of the congregation, she stood outside the hall's huge wooden doors handing out leaflets for Yizkor, the memorial service, as Jacov walked up.

"Good yontif," Lori said, handing him a leaflet.

The white four-page printout contained the names of the congregation's departed, Jacov's father among them, and prayers for the short service of remembrance to follow.

Jacov didn't recognize her at first – wiry dark hair heavily flecked with gray, her thin waist thickened some - but she'd grown more refined, better looking in fact than when they were in high school.

"Good yontif," he repeated mechanically.

"As I live and breathe, Terrence Jacov!" Lori said.

"Lori Wechsler," he said a moment later, recognition coming slow. He offered his right hand and looked around, not sure if he should hug her.

"Wechsler-*Steinmetz*!" she corrected.

"Steinmetz? Did you marry Freddy Steinmetz? Jeez, I haven't seen him since high school."

"You're not missing much. We split three years ago, but I kept his name for the boys."

"You had kids, huh?"

"Yep. Two beautiful boys. They're in junior congregation."

"Freddy Steinmetz," Jacov said again. "I always thought…"

His unfinished sentenced hung almost visibly between them. It really didn't need being said.

"That he was gay? Yeah, you and everyone else. Well, I didn't know. Maybe I suspected. Anyhow, it's a long story. Maybe I'll tell you some time."

Finally, like reels on a slot machine, Jacov's memory jogged. He had read her name outside on a glass-cased message board after the word president. The meek, pimply-faced girl he barely acknowledged in high school morphed into the accomplished woman standing before him.

"You graduated, what, seventy-six?" he said.

"Seventy-seven. You dated my girlfriend, Nickie Rohrbach. I guess you didn't know it, but I had the biggest crush on you."

"Nickie Rohrbach," he mused, half hearing her. "You still see her?"

"Every now and again. She lives in Howell. Five kids, divorced twice. You know the drill."

"Indeed, I do," he said. "But I've only taken that trip once and got away clean. Five kids, huh?"

"Yeah, three in college, two in high school. She's doing OK. Her first ex is a state trooper and he gives her like half his pay. They had four between 'em. Her second husband's a caterer and he pays his share but she has to stay on top of him."

"If I know Nickie that's what got her in trouble in the first place," he said.

Jacov hadn't seen his high school sweetheart in thirty years but felt a sudden twinge of jealousy.

"State trooper, huh?"

The look on her face told Jacov he wasn't scoring any points with Lori and that the conversation, as often happened with women, had taken a sudden turn for the worse.

He soon recalled that other juicy little tidbit about Lori Wechsler – that she was the one who started the Jewish singles group with the fruity name – the one JungleDotCom reportedly bought for millions.

"So, you're single," he said opportunistically.

"Happily. Which is ironic, considering I used to run a singles group."

"Kosher Kouples," Jacov said brightly.

"You've heard of it. Ever use 'em?"

"No, but I'm familiar. You still involved with that?"

"Nah, believe it or not I liked it better when it was small. I was a pioneer, one of the first to use classified newspaper ads for matchmaking. Then the Internet came along and it got out of hand. It was perfect for JungleDotCom though," she said.

"So I heard."

Their conversation flagged as other worshippers pressed through the doors, many of them hugging and greeting Lori personally, all of whom she handed a pamphlet.

"So how'd you get to be president?" Jacov asked.

"Well, I'm here all the time. My boys are in Hebrew school and I was active in the sisterhood. Then Herbie Cohen ups and dies."

"Herbie Cohen, jeezus christ! I *knew* Herbie. Baseball player. He was in my class."

"Herbie was in good shape, everything but his heart," Lori said. "Massive coronary three years ago on the tennis court. Just forty-five."

"Damn. Too bad," Jacov said.

"So, what are you up to?"

"Oh, this and that. Married, divorced. Lost, found. I'm doin' alright. I'm a general contractor down in South Jersey."

"Izzat right?"

"Yeah, I just renovated my entire synagogue – roof, drywall, alarm system, the whole sheh-bang, right down to the hardwood floors."

"You do all that yourself?"

"Nah, I sub out most of it, but I like doing the alarm stuff myself. It's like getting paid to play with other people's toys."

She gave him the ole once over a second time. Certainly had the build for construction. Dark suit smacked of management but something didn't fit, and it wasn't just the jacket - ten pounds of potatas in a five-pound sack.

"I always pegged you more for the military type," she said.

"Yeah, well, I did some of that, too. I'm still Ranger Reserves but they'll never call."

"Aren't you worried about Iraq?"

"At my age? Nah. I mean, they *could* call, but I doubt they will. The young bucks can handle it. This is their war."

Jacov said all this like the seasoned old vet he never was.

Now, from inside the sanctuary, the rabbi's mournful monotone hit the same hopeful notes it did every year – deeper faith in God and support of the State of Israel; piety, resisting temptation, and support of the State of Israel; blahbitty blah and blah blah blah and support of the State of Israel. His conclusion signaled the start of Yizkor – an exodus out for the youngsters whose parents were still alive, a steady stream in for the mourners who skipped the sermon. It also signaled to the synagogue president it was time to return to the bimah.

"Well, nice seeing you, Terry," she said.

"You too, but it's Terrence now."

"What's that?"

"Terrence. No one calls me Terry anymore."

"All-righty then," she said, turning away. What*ever*."

Jacov knew the conversation was over, shut down with the same *whatever* the little snot of a waitress used, but figured he'd go for it anyway.

"Hey, I'm up to check on my mom just 'bout every week. Maybe I'll give you a call some time."

"Uh… my plate's pretty full right now," she said. "But maybe we'll cross paths again."

Jacov wanted to remind her he wouldn't have given her the time of day in high school. Then again, back in high school she wasn't worth three mil. But then the moment was gone.

Stepping inside, he sighted Rueben and mother sitting toward the rear of the hall and excused his way over, bumping knees and backs in the narrow space between rows of chairs. He was warm about the face and neck and prayed most of all that the synagogue's air conditioning was working this year.

And, by the Grace of God and General Electric, it was. Cold air blew down upon him from a large ceiling vent almost directly above his seat. The chilled air was actually visible as he glanced up, colliding as it flowed from the vent with the mass of rising heat.

To his surprise, he luxuriated in the familiar readings and psalms, allowing them to wash over him along with the cool air.

But then it was gone. The air conditioner, suddenly but predictably, did just what Jacov hoped it wouldn't — it cut off. Within moments sweat beaded on his hairy upper lip, across his back and in his pits. He thought about stepping out for some water but he'd only been there a few minutes and did not relish climbing back over all the old men and women he'd just excused himself past. Meanwhile, the sermon he thought he missed must have just been a warm-up because the rabbi was building to a righteous conclusion, leading, as he always does, to a pledge drive for Eretz Yisrael, the Land of Israel.

"Mel Gibson... the Passion of the Christ... President Bush... terrorism... tourism...."

Jacov figured there was a thread connecting these disparate thoughts but damn if his sleepy mind could find it. Rabbi Finkle, a good-natured man with a great shaggy beard, rambled incessantly and Jacov forced himself to listen, struggling to find that thread.

"And so, give from the heart," the rabbi implored.

Jacov picked up a pledge card from beneath his seat and examined the preset amounts: $50, $100, $500, $1,000, $5,000, other. He folded the card and stuck it in his breast pocket, determined for the time being to mail in a check for "other."

<u>Chapter 20</u>

At this point Louis was still living at home, but barely. Twice in the two months since Janice began conversion lessons Rebecca thought she caught the scent of another woman on her husband and all but threw him out.

Again.

But he didn't sweat it.

Leaving the house for yet another rendezvous, he punched the accelerator and the massive engine came alive, breaking free the oversized tires in a cloud of acrid gray smoke. Rebecca hated the philandering bastard, his boyish giddiness behind the wheel of his new car, and peering from behind a lacey mauve curtain in their living room, resented him all the more for getting it.

The red Dodge Magnum for which he traded in his Crown Vic wasn't pretty in a traditional sense, but it was definitely bad. And Louis was all about bad. He went from driving a ride that emulated cop cars to one that was apt to attract them. Like they said in the commercials, you could open it up from both ends, and Louis surely did. The throaty roar of its engine emanating from chrome-tipped tail pipes was enough to give him a woody. And the spacious cargo area in his hopped up, modern day wagon gave him a place to use it.

The orchards around the Apple Hill of his youth, fields where Louis had once plied willing young high school girls, were long ago paved over and built up. So Louis, after collecting Janice at the train station, turned the car south, to the hills of Gloucester County. Even there, countryside once flush with farmland now sprouted one vast housing development after another. Termed "executive homes" by their builders, "McMansions" by those who could not afford them, the houses started around 400K and quickly climbed into the sixes. These neighborhoods were typically named for places they destroyed -- Lush Meadows and Running Creek -- and their homes sat upon an acre or more of rich, flat, former farmland. They did not, by and large, even come with city water.

Set upon barren, tasteless plots, the five and six-bedroom homes were to many an expression of all that is simultaneously right and wrong with America. On the one hand they stood for success, for making it in a downsized, outsourced economy. On the other they were a blatant example of excess, of debt-saddled Americans racking up ever more.

The ascetic landscaping surrounding these homes featured scrawny, helpless little trees secured to the ground with guy wires. If they survived to maturity the trees would provide shade and comfort - a point in time close to when the thirty-year note on the property came due.

Turning off the highway toward Mullica Hill now Louis blasted past half a dozen new neighborhoods and found a patch of woods with an old rutted dirt road. He followed the road to a field – one of the few not yet caught in developers' sights – where he parked the car and retrieved the bottle of cold California white he'd stashed between the seats. He and Janice passed the bottle between them like school kids and Louis went to work.

"Ohh, Rabbi," she cooed, spreading her legs slightly and revealing she was in a mood to be bad, too. Janice wore no panties beneath her supple leather skirt, so rich and smooth it practically melted into the car's buttery black seats. It occurred to Louis, as he slid a calloused hand between her thighs, that her ample slickness down there might spot his leather seats, but he only planned to take things so far up front. The Magnum's plush front buckets were for foreplay only.

"Step into my parlor said the spider to the fly," he said, getting out and motioning to the rear of the car.

They had grown ever more adventurous since Louis first took her that evening after studies on his big oak desk. Discussing the difficulties of mixed marriage, their hands brushed faux innocently and unleashed a desire that was building between them for months. Louis skillfully undressed her and entered Janice slowly while he stood, his good wool trousers bunched at his ankles on the floor.

The danger of getting caught – neither was sure the door was even locked – excited Janice and she came almost immediately, gushing all over his desk. But now, about a month into the affair, she was beginning to miss old fashioned romance -- candles, flowers, real dates with a man – and sneaking around, fucking on old farmland like high schoolers, fell kind of short.

"You know, we could go back to my place," she said. "I feel like a kid on prom night out here."

But Louis was already climbing from the driver's seat, the bulge in his pants making it hard, if not painful, to stand.

"I'd never make it," he said.

Janice saw the affair coming from the outset, possibly from their first meeting, and was ever more troubled by her role in the adultery. It was a sin, a violation of God's commandments, and she was a part of it. With a rabbi, no less.

As far back as high school she had gone out of her way to avoid so much as flirting with other girls' boyfriends, to demur politely if hit on by them and to walk away. She never imagined herself, wouldn't believe it if she had been told, that she would one day fall in love with a man who was cheating on his wife. But now, falling deeper by the day, she felt alone with her angst. For the first time in her life there was no one to talk to – not her sister (she wouldn't understand), not her mother (are you *kidding* me?), and certainly not her old priest ("YOU, Janice Marie Palumbo, are damned to hell!").

So she accepted Louis at his word that his marriage was a sham, kept up for appearances, and that Rebecca hurt him more than he ever hurt her. It wasn't just that Rebecca withheld sex – which she did, he assured her – but that she was an ever-loving bitch who put him out of his bedroom and even turned his own dog against him.

Nevertheless, a divorce at this stage of his career would ruin him, he said, resulting in a separation not just from his wife but from his job, his congregation, all he's ever known and worked for.

Janice believed his plausible half-truths but their relationship quietly gnawed at her and within weeks she began pressing Louis to make a choice.

"If it's that bad just leave her, Lou," she begged when he drove her home, the Magnum's big engine still rumbling outside her Center City row home. "I can't keep doing this."

"Please be patient," he said. "It isn't just about you."

"Well, it is on my end," she said. "You wouldn't be the first rabbi to get a divorce and I doubt, if things are so bad, the synagogue would can you."

"Janice, this is not open for discussion, at least not now," he said. "Let's give it some time and see if things take care of themselves."

"And what is that supposed to mean?"

"Let's just give it some time," he said.

<u>Chapter 21</u>

Shelly Tannenbaum noticed the change in his old racquetball partner almost from the start, in the way he carried himself, how he swung his racquet, how he played the friggin' game.

"Fresh tail doin' you some good, eh buddy?" he razzed.

Louis didn't take the bait but used it, drew strength from it, striking the small, hard rubber ball square and true, running away with the first game fifteen to nine. When he shot out ahead at the start of their second game Shelly only dug deeper.

"I'm starting to think Rebecca ain't the only one you're two-timin', Lou. You got another racquetball partner on the side, or what?"

Abrams eyed him crossly, took the shot and put his full weight into the smaller, trimmer man, driving him hard against the unforgiving side wall of the court. Shelly struck the wall with his upper back and head, a quick one-two blow that rattled his jaw and caused him to bite his tongue.

He hadn't been hit that hard since losing the Golden Gloves at Madison Square in nineteen-seventy-eight and picked himself up dazed. But just that quick he was in the rabbi's face, squaring off, ready to rock.

"What the fuck, Lou," he said, giving his friend a retaliatory shove. "You wanna take a shot?" Shelly knocked Louis off balance and was waving back toward himself in a gesture of bring it on.

Obviously, Louis meant to check his old friend but didn't mean to hurt him. And he definitely did not want to fight the one-time welterweight.

"Take it easy, Brooklyn," he said. "I didn't quite mean that. Just put a little too much English into it. You okay?"

Shelly blotted blood from his tongue on the right shoulder sleeve of his forty-dollar t-shirt, took a breath and calmed down. Then he harnessed his anger to kick his opponent's ass on the court.

"Go again?" Shelly said, his win cheering him despite the pain in his back and neck.

"Nah, I was gonna lift," Louis said.

"You think you need it, killer? You're already half jacked."

"You never know."

Louis was no punk but both knew Shelly would destroy him if it ever came down to it. But they were grown men, professionals, community standard bearers who did not fight like street scum to resolve their differences. Usually.

"You know I didn't mean so hard a check," Louis said again half an hour later amid the clanking iron of the weight room. He loaded a forty-five pound plate on one end of an Olympic bar and squeezed on a spring clamp while, at the other end, Shelly did the same.

"I know that Louie. Why else would I have stopped?"

As usual, they finished their workout trackside over coffee and bagels, watching young honeys scoot by in short shorts.

And, as usual, Yuri Marchenko was at the far corner of the track laying into the heavy bag.

"So should I ask how things are going again or will you feed me to that big fucking Russian?" Shelly said, seeking to ease the strain that still hung between them.

"Depends on what you ask. And how you ask it," Louis said.

Here Shelly proved that he was, at heart, a yenta, just like Louis had said, despite all his street smarts and toughness.

"Well, let's see. I wouldn't ask about your Eagles 'cause I don't really give a shit and they'll never be the Giants. I'm not gonna ask about your hemorrhoids because, again, I don't wanna know. So what do we have left? Oh yeah. Rebecca and Janice. How's tricks, lover boy?"

"I'd rather you ask about my hemorrhoids."

"Wish in one hand, shit in the other, you know ah'm sayin, dawg?"

Shelly couldn't resist talking smack, especially in "the voice." Downtown Camden by way of Bed Stuy.

"Could you *be* any fucking cruder?" Louis said.

"Yeah, coming from you. So talk to me, shmendrick. You alright?"

"Me, I'm good. Me and Bec? Another story. But that's how it's been for years."

"So what are you doing about it? I take it you're still seeing Janice or you wouldn't have put me into that fucking wall just for mentioning her."

Louis sipped his coffee and rolled his head side to side to crack his neck.

He breathed deeply, uninterested in rehashing either their argument or his history of infidelity but he couldn't very well turn away, change the subject or check Shelly into another wall.

Besides, Shelly wasn't just a friend and ally but a lawyer, *his* lawyer, and Louis knew that should he confide in him, attorney-client privilege could attach down the line.

"I think I love her," he said after a moment.

"Rebecca?"

"Yeah, Rebecca. *Jan*ice, you fuckin' half-brain!"

"Oh, for Chrissakes, Lou, you don't *fall* in love!" Shelly said, not exactly shouting but hardly sotto voce.

"Keep it down!" Louis said looking around, wary that worshippers or others from the community could be in hearing distance.

"Don't be so paranoid, Louie, there's nobody here. Just me, you and Ivan."

"I thought you said his name is Yuri."

"Whatever," Shelly said. "Don't change the subject. So you're in love? This is not the Louis Abrams *I* know. 'Schtup 'em and leave 'em', iddin that right? You're the one who told me that. You COINED the fucking phrase! And as long as I've known you, you've pretty much lived it. And here's another old Louis Abrams gem: 'love is for suckers.' Remember that? 'Love is for suckers, no pun intended.' Real nice, from a guy whose job it is to marry people."

The big Russian across the track continued brutalizing the heavy bag, glancing up every now and again at the Americans sipping coffee like a couple a Parisian school girls.

"So what is it you think he does," Louis said, avoiding the lawyer's line of questioning and glancing at the sweaty bruiser.

"How the hell should I know? He's got a good punch, I'll tell you that. I wouldn't want to be on the business end of it. I think he's a teacher. Or maybe a dockworker."

"Big fucking difference, no?" Louis said. "So it's Yuri what? And don't even tell me Zhivago."

"Yeah, he's Doctor Fucking Zhivago. Doctor Destructo is more like it. I think Marchenko. I dunno. Some shit. He's alright. Not a big talker. Big fucking schwanz."

"And why are you looking at his schwanz? Don't go turning fagelah on me."

"He-bro please. He walks around the locker room with no towel on. It's obscene. Like a friggin' club. I just didn't want to get hit by the thing."

"I should hope not," Louis said.

He drank his coffee, checked out some tail, asked again.

"So you really don't know what he does?"

"What's it matter?"

"It doesn't. He's just kind of intriguing is all. Must be the romantic in me. I thought maybe ex-KGB or Russian mafia. Maybe I'd have a job for him."

"A job? What d'ya want, bump someone off? Feed em your wife's meatloaf."

There was a shudder between them. Rebecca was a fine baker but she didn't give much time or thought to home cooking. Her famously bad meatloaf was a tasteless mound of ground chicken glazed with ketchup and topped with canned peas and carrots. Even the dog would barely eat it.

Louis looked around, stunned himself that he would even say it.

"That's who I'm talking about."

Like a punch to the gut, the words nearly took Shelly's breath away.

"Don't even, Lou," he said. "Even if you're fucking around, do not fuck around with me."

Louis paused, a rare speechless moment.

“C’mon, Shel,” he said. “Of course I’m fucking around. Don’t be such a putz.”

# PART III

<h1 style="text-align:center"><u>Chapter 22</u></h1>

Jacov wielded the utility knife deftly. He measured, drew a line across the paper backing and snapped the drywall clean, handing it to one of his underpaid Mexican assistants.

Louis was furious that the wall was broken and angrier still when he learned how. Jesse Kornhauser's ass struck it on one side and went clear through to the other. The little bastard, in his last year of Hebrew school and just one month from his bar mitzvah, provoked mild-mannered Michael Ginzberg for the last time. The final insult was a gobby spitball, launched from a straw at the back of the pimply boy's neck.

It wasn't the sting so much that inflamed Michael, even the yellow, phlegmy goo that he wiped from his neck in a wet string, but the expression of joy on Jesse's face. Seeing it, Michael launched from his desk, upended Jesse from his and hurled him into the wall. Jesse's coccyx struck between two studs and led his butt on a journey to the other side.

"Fucking dickwad," Jesse said, his ego as bruised as his ass bone.

"You're a bigger one."

As far as Jacov was concerned, the incident meant more work and for all he cared Jesse's ass could go through every wall in the school. As he'd noticed before, the more work he did for Louis, the more he seemed to get, and it wasn't because they were friends. In fact, he wasn't so sure they were.

If anything, Jacov was a bit too blue collar for Abrams' feigned urbanity, but the handyman was useful, on time and on budget and Louis didn't mind helping him out. He was also a moose. Louis, who built his skinny boyhood frame in the weight room, could barely move even half a sheet of the three-quarter inch wallboard Jacov brought over to fix the hole. While Jacov lacked the sinewy ropiness in his forearms that decades of free weights developed for Louis, his limbs were thick and powerful and ended in stubby ringless fingers. Louis watched in awe as he hefted a full sheet of drywall from the van, carried it inside and set it down gently in the hall with a grunt. He took his measurements, extracted the utility knife from a holster on his belt, slit the paper and broke off little more than half a sheet for the other side of the wall.

"Dusty work, eh?" Louis said, watching.

"This ain't the half of it," Jacov said. "Wait'll we start sanding the joints."

His assistant screwed the sheetrock into place and Jacov taped it up. He slathered a layer of smooth, batter-like joint compound into the narrow seams between the new rock and the old and embedded white strips of joint tape into it. Dipping a flexible four-inch putty knife back into the compound, a mixture so rich and sweet-smelling it reminded him of cream cheese icing, Jacov spread it across the tape he'd just laid. When it was cured a day later he would return to sand and re-spackle his work, feathering it out so that, when painted, it would blend invisibly with the rest of the wall.

Louis, never handy around the house, was impressed with Jacov's work.

"Stop by my office when you're done," he said. "I have another job you might give me a hand with."

Jacov finished the first layer of spackling, dispatched his assistant and headed to the rabbi's chambers.

As usual, the office was cool and musty. With its book-lined walls of old Hebrew and secular tomes the room smelled like the wing of a rarely used library. There was also that certain something he thought he sniffed on previous visits that hung in the air like a wraith. Despite

Louis's use of air spray, the sweet, skunky aroma of pot smoke lingered invisibly and Jacov breathed it in, hopeful but disbelieving in his own sense of smell.

Louis, his back to the desk, sat simmering over what to do about Jesse Kornhauser when Jacov came lumbering in. In the dim light of the office he didn't see Louis in his leather executive's chair and thought he entered an empty room when Louis spun around and startled him.

"You do fine work, Terrence," Louis said with a start, addressing him even before he'd turned around.

"How'd you know …"

"Terrence, you've got like forty keys on that chain. It was either you or the janitor and he always knocks. Besides, I did ask you to meet me, did I not?"

Outside the rabbi's office daffodils in bloom burst from a flower box below the window and yellow forsythia bushes screamed the arrival of spring. Just below the eve a small cadre of militant, single-minded wasps worked away at building their papery gray nest.

"You allergic to bees?" Louis asked.

"Hell no," Jacov said. "Excuse me, Rabbi."

"Quite alright. There's this wasp's nest I need knocked down and hoped you might give me a hand with it. I'd do it myself, but I'm allergic."

"No problem. But how do you know?"

"How do I know what?"

"That you're 'lergic."

"I got bit about ten years ago. Me and the missus were riding bikes when a yellow jacket flew inside my shirt. Before I could shake him out the little bugger stung me in the collar bone. By the time we got back to the house my head was swimming. My collar bone puffed all out and it burned like a lit match in my shirt."

"You gotta watch 'em, 'specially if you know you're 'lergic."

"That's what I'm talking about. My primary doc wanted me to go for treatments, but I was like forget it. Twice a week, an hour a pop, who has the time?"

"Well, if they'll help…"

"If the dog didn't stop to take a crap he would have caught the rabbit, you know I'm sayin', boychick?"

"Not really."

"Anyhow, c'mon outside and I'll show you that nest."

Jacov imagined the worst, a large, football-shaped cone of anger. He envisioned a home to hundreds, perhaps thousands of mean, pitiless wasps, their feathery, incandescent wings invisible in flight, sets of limp, paralytic legs hanging down.

He didn't actually know if he could remove such a nest and feared the fury such an attempt might unleash. Jacov recalled a children's book in which one of the characters, faced with such a challenge, donned an old diving suit to knock a beehive down. He considered the contents of the van and knew the closest he had to a diving suit was an old hooded sweatshirt and a pair of heavy work gloves. So he retrieved a short ladder, the hoodie and gloves and met Louis back by the eve.

"Is that *it*?" Jacov said, surprised and relieved by the sight of the nest.

"Should I call the bug man?"

"*Rabbi.*"

Jacov looked down, kicked the dirt, and tried to hide his smirk.

"You gotta broom? I'll knock that thing down right now."

"Whoa. Let me get inside," Louis said, sidestepping Jacov and heading for the door.

Foregoing the broom, Jacov simply donned the work gloves, climbed his stepladder, grabbed hold of the nest and crushed it in his hand. The pathetic little nest was as light and delicate as filo dough and so small he could fit two in a pack of smokes. A few wasps flitting about the thing were crushed when Jacov's hand came down around it and a third, witnessing the carnage, buzzed about and flew off for his life. The deed was done before Louis even got back to his office and he entered to the sound of the phone ringing. It was always ringing.

"Rabbi?" a small voice called from the receiver.

"Yes…"

"It's Jesse, Jesse Kornhauser. Rabbi, I can't make my bar mitzvah lesson today cause I need to go to the hospital."

"What's the matter, Jesse?"

"It hurts to sit. I guess you know about me and Michael Ginzberg and how he threw me through that wall."

"Funny you should call, Jesse. I wanted to talk to you about that very thing."

"Well I can't now, Rabbi. My mom is taking me to the hospital. She's outside waiting."

"You call me when you get back, Jesse. Better still, have your mother call."

Louis could have killed the little shit himself but hung up calmly, thrumming his fingers on the leatherette writing pad, his afternoon suddenly free. One hand strayed absently to the lump in his jacket pocket, a sandwich baggie folded over and rolled up, a finger-sized portion of good green weed.

"Good to go, boss," Jacov called from the doorway, rapping on the frame but just sticking his head in this time.

"I'm not your boss, Terrence. You do a job for me, I pay you. Even Steven. Let's not get into the whole 'yasser boss' thing."

"It's just an expression."

"I know. So what do I owe you?"

"For the nest? That was nothing. Glad to do it."

"Well let me buy you a beer."

"You want to buy me a beer?"

"Why not. My afternoon just freed up. The kid whose ass went through the wall called to cancel his bar mitzvah lesson. Said it hurts to sit and his mother's taking him to the hospital."

"What are they gonna do, put a cast on it?"

"Yeah right," Louis chuckled. "An ass cast. They'll give him some Tylenol, tell him to ice it and to sleep on his side for a few nights. That's if he's even going to the hospital. He can't sit for an hour with me, how's he gonna sit in the emergency room for three or four?"

"I dunno."

"I was being rhetorical."

"I know I should know what that is."

"You should. But never mind. So you want to grab a beer or what?"

"I'm game."

Jacov dusted himself off outside the door. Leaving the building he eyed the rabbi's new car, wondering, as Louis was, whether he should even get in.

"You're alright," Louis said, reading the look on Jacov's face.

"We could take my van."

"No way. Just brush that sheetrock dust from your shoes and get in."

As Jacov reluctantly entered the Magnum's leather cockpit he couldn't remember being in a car so fine.

"So where do you wanna go, Fridays?" he asked.

"Fridays? You think I'm gonna sit in a *mall*? I want some scenery with my beer."

"How 'bout Puffinstuff's?"

"Terrence, if I want to see the river I'll rent a friggin' boat. I want some *scenery*, you know I'm sayin'?"

Louis heard Shelly Tannenbaum in his voice, the streetwise, one-time welterweight and defender of hoods.

"Yo-yo," Jacov aped. "What cha got in mind?"

"The Den, baby," Louis said with a pause. "Delilah's Den."

Louis secretly frequented the Philadelphia go-go bar with the faux biblical name. Visiting it two, three, four times a month, he, like Hebrew strongman Samson, was seduced by Delilah but believed he could resist her charms. Like a junkie or a drunk, he could stop any time he chose.

At first Louis rationalized that trips to the bar were research, job-related, a study in men's needs and the lengths they went to satisfy them. There could be a sermon in this, he'd think, and in the beginning even recalled the story of Samson and Delilah en route to the club. In it, Phillistine beauty Delilah seduced the Hebrew warrior and plied him for the source of his great strength. Samson resisted, honoring his covenant with God never to reveal the secret, but ultimately relented, confiding in his lover that should his hair be cut so would go his strength.

According to the story, Delilah waited for Samson to sleep, sheared his hair and betrayed him to her people. The Phillistines captured Samson, enslaved him, and put him in chains. But in the end Samson prevailed. His hair re-grew, his strength returned, and he killed thousands of Phillistines when he brought their temple down upon them.

In the Philly market Delilah now stood for something else – hot babes and good times – and the bar that bore her name was nothing like going to temple.

* * * * *

It was just past four when Louis pulled into the lot, a wide, oddly shaped tarmac near the Delaware River in Philadelphia. The lot was pockmarked with tiny implosions in the asphalt and the loose, sticky filler material some second rate South Philly paving company shoveled in to fill them. Pieces of broken beer bottles shimmered on the blacktop like jewels, sticky, smelly and sharp in the afternoon sun. Already the lot was packed – Beamers and Benzes, a white Escalade with oversized tires and chrome wheel spinners, F150s and Infinitis. Louis wedged the Magnum into a spot near the rear of the building, narrowly missing the jagged green neck of a Heineken bottle some inebriate jackass broke the night before.

He sensed the heavy bump, bump, bump from Delilah's massive sound system through the walls and felt two urges – to head right in and to toke right up. He almost pulled the baggie out and did just that when two Philly beat cops in a roughed up squad car wheeled into the lot. The cops weren't vice per se but were on the lookout for it – blowjobs in the parking lot, fighting, yuppie stockbrokers doing a few lines, even a middle-aged rabbi smoking a joint.

"You ready?" Louis said, his mind made up for him as he pulled the kippa from his head. "Let's go."

He was no stranger to the joint and that was evident the moment they entered. It wasn't as if anyone knew him per se, not by name, anyway, but some – from two juiced up bouncers to the barmaid to at least one dancer – evidently recognized him.

"Jack and coke," Louis said, stripping three twenties off a roll and laying them on the bar.

Jacov thought he'd have a beer, but this was definitely a step up.

"Ditto," he said.

He reached for his wallet, but Louis stopped him.

"My treat."

"Thanks, Rabbi."

"Don't mention it. And tonight, just call me Lou."

"You got it, Lou."

The bar was a whirl of sound, lights and sweat tinged with the possibility of sex and danger. Delilah's was an upscale strip club, but with the crazy mix it drew there was always the chance, however slim, of being punched, stabbed, even shot for backing up too quickly and spilling the wrong guy's drink, even stepping on his toe. As for the possibility of sex… one could always hope, and tip heavy.

Out in the parking lot Louis had felt bass lines thumping through the walls. Inside they rattled his rib cage and blew up his hair. Above the stage a mirrored disco ball fractured strobe light a thousand different ways while, on either side of it, twelve-colored yoke lights swung wildly, out of sync with the flash of light cans hanging from a truss. Blue and red police beacons flashed intermittently at opposite ends of the bar and fog machines blew so thick a man could get lost in it. Taken together, the mood was kaleidoscopic, as if Walt Disney threw up, a mishmash of colors so bright and busy they almost became one.

Of course, the big attraction was neither the lights nor the sound but the girls - in cages, swinging from fire poles and wiggling, jiggling and giggling in customers' laps. Virtually all had fake tits, tiny waists and great legs. They were young - mid-twenties tops - and all, in a sense, for sale.

Off to the side, on a wide crushed velvet purple couch in the shadow of the bar, an enormously fat young man smiled wildly, his paw on the low back of a dancer as she rubbed up and down his crotch. Sweat beaded the man's face, neck and forearms, glistened on his big, fat head. The girl in his lap was repulsed by his sweat, his fat, his pink baby face, but she didn't let it show, not for five-hundred dollars a dance. As at most clubs he frequented, the going rate for a lap dance was fifty bucks for three minutes and Joey was good for a half an hour on a regular night. And this was no regular night. Tomorrow, as pretty much everyone one in the bar knew, the big man faced eight to ten, and where he was going there wouldn't be no lap dances.

"Hey that's Joey Stromboli," Jacov gushed like a fan at a movie opening.

"Joey Stromboli? Sounds more like a sandwich."

"You know who it is. Joseph Strombolini? Joey Stromboli? C'mon. Skinny Joey's boy."

"Skinny Joey" Louis knew. Joseph "Skinny Joey" Scarpati was a punk mobster whose South Philly crew made a name for itself after much of the city's established mob got popped in the nineties. They weren't *Goodfellas* so much as "Dumbfellas," a name thrust upon them by a local newspaperman for all the dumb shit they pulled. One of Skinny Joey's boys shot himself in the nut and thigh while shaking down a bar one night. He refused to go to the hospital and expired on his mother's couch. Another ran a four-way stop sign near South Street, ass-ending a patrol car. Hitting a cop would have been bad enough, but things got measurably worse when they found a body in the trunk. A third tried beating a pizza guy for a twelve dollar double cheese. Both went for their guns, but the pizza guy wasn't sitting around drinking beer and doing bong hits all night and capped the poor bastard before his nine even cleared the holster. In some neighborhoods, even the pizza boys packed heat.

"So there's a Skinny Joey and a Fat Joey?" Louis inquired honestly.

"No, he's a big fat fuck, but no one calls him Fat Joey. He's Joey Stromboli. Which, you know, is more or less the same thing."

The two were well out of earshot – in fact, they could barely hear themselves – but Louis considered the meaty mobster on the couch and glanced around cautiously.

"How do you know who this guy is?"

"Don't you read the papers? He's all over the Daily News. They've been running 'Stromboli Sightings' all week cause it's common knowledge Joey's goin' in da tank. He was supposed to be sentenced today or tomorra."

"Wasn't today," Louis observed.

"Guess not."

Jacov pulled a fresh pack of Marlboros from his shirt pocket, rapped the top against his palm several times to pack them and lit himself a smoke.

"So you ain't never hearda this guy?" he said, the cigarette dangling from thick, purple lips.

"We don't exactly move in the same circles."

"I know that but he's in the paper like every day. Don't chu read the *Daily News*?"

"Not if I can help it. I'll look at the Inquirer once in a while but that's about it. Usually I just read the *Times*."

Jacov scratched his head. This was not the rabbi he knew from Tuesday night rap sessions.

"Stromboli was in the *News*," he continued.

"Like I said, I read the *Times*. Still, it explains a lot," Louis said.

"What's that?"

"Why she's over there with him."

Saying the girl was over there with him was like saying a lap dance is like a dance. The girl rode Joey like a wave, bouncing her big wet tits in his face and rubbing him through his pants, but she did it for one thing and one thing only – the money.

Louis and Jacov sipped their drinks while a slim, coffee colored beauty just off the stage sidled up between them. Nineteen, twenty tops, her creamy dark skin was flawless, her body gym-tone perfect, her face worth fighting for. She was Halle Berry crossed with Heather Locklear, one serious piece of ass.

Louis picked a five-spot off the bar and slipped the money between the girl's delicate D-cups. Taking it, she squeezed her breasts together and gave Louis a feel, even her sweet, dark cherry nipples. Little Louie stirred.

"Thanks, baby," the girl cooed. "How 'bout a dance?"

"Not just now," Louis said, slipping an arm around her waist and pulling her close. "But maybe in a bit."

The girl pulled the five-spot from her bra and stuffed it into the strap of her G-string. She touched her snatch as she pushed the bill down there, brought her hand up and ran a finger along the rabbi's jaw line.

"We kin go in the back if you want," she said, still trying to make the sale.

"Maybe in a bit," he said again.

"Ah-eight, sugar, I'll be around."

Louis dropped a hand to the girl's ass as she stepped away and she glanced back, grinning.

Jacov couldn't help but be impressed.

"I wouldn't have made you for a Delilah's kinda guy," he said.

"What kind would you make me for, Chippendales?"

"No, c'mon. I mean, a *rabbi*? You're the first rabbi I've ever seen stick a fin down some chick's top."

"How do you know?"

Jacov thought on this a moment and adjusted himself.

"You've got a point there. Anyhow, might make a good topic for a Tuesday night, no?"

Louis gave him a severe look and swallowed his Jack and Coke.

"No."

"Just messin, Rabbi."

"Drink up, puss," Louis said, and ordered two more.

Louis tipped well and the second drink came stronger than the first, a toxic brew of sour mash and Coke, and he took a big gulp right off.

"Can I ask you something, just between you and me?"

"As far as I'm concerned, this whole night is just between you and me," Jacov said.

"Mah man."

Louis's simple response meant more to Jacov than Louis could have known. It was an affirmation that they, a poor working schmuck and a learned pillar of the community, were more alike in the rabbi's eyes than Jacov imagined. Maybe they were becoming friends after all. Louis stirred his drink, took another swallow and savored the bourbon buzz.

"You party, Terrence?"

"Whaddaya mean?"

"You know what I mean. You smoke grass?"

Jacov *knew* he caught a hint of pot in the air of the rabbi's office once or twice but always had his doubts. He doubted no more.

Pot smokers always tried to feel others out, to build a bridge over an everyday act that was still illegal in most places and publicly taboo. Because of his occupation Louis did so with extra caution, especially around South Jersey, but on ski trips and other out-of-town jaunts he was always game.

"Smoke em if you got em," he'd say on the gondola up at Killington or Stowe, pulling a spliff from his jacket and lighting up.

But he knew before asking that Jacov partied, too.

"You're dating yourself, Lou. Yeah, I smoke a little, but we call it weed now."

"Yeah, yeah, I know," Louis said, patting his coat pocket. "Let's go."

Jacov's eyes lit up big.

"Damn, Rabbi, uh… Lou, you *are* the man!"

Louis grabbed the bulk of his cash off the bar, knocked back his drink and winked at the girl who offered him a dance. But she had moved on, was rubbing up against other men now, and didn't even notice.

Leaving the cool, smoky bar they stepped into a typical summer's eve in the city. The air was velvety and thick, so humid it fogged Jacov's glasses. Philly smelled like most any major metropolis and Louis breathed it in, pleased and disgusted in the same breath.

Riding on the dense night air was a whiff of trash from a nearby Dumpster. Its stink mingled with the raw city smells of asphalt and exhaust but was tempered by the sweet, earthy scent of fresh cut grass and a nearby canopy of maples.

Horses clip-clopped along ancient cobblestones, dropping mealy turds and adding to the olfactory soup. A vendor hawked freshly baked pretzels on the sidewalk three for a dollar and the fragrant aroma from his cart spread out half a block around. The vendor himself was gross, unshaven, in a stained off-green Eagles tee and worn-out Reeboks. Louis couldn't imagine shaking hands with the man, much less buying food from him, but his hot pretzels sure smelled good.

Entering the Magnum's leather cockpit he considered leaving the parking lot to light up but opted instead to simply start the engine, turn on the air and fire up the joint.

"Looked for a moment like you'd take that little black babe up on a dance," Jacov said.

Louis took a hit, savored the weed like a fine Bordeaux, and blew it out slowly. He admired the even burn – evidence of his practiced rolling skills – and passed the joint to Jacov.

"Still might," he choked.

Jacov hit the joint and handed it back. It was little more than halfway smoked but Louis had had enough. He didn't want to get too stoned if he was going back in.

"You good?" he asked politely.

Jacov waved off the joint and Louis snubbed it out for later.

When they reentered the club their seats were occupied by a couple of suits from the Philadelphia Stock Exchange so Louis and Jacov ordered drinks at the bar and found a place to stand.

Stromboli's lap dance was over, but now he and his cronies yukked it up like the high school loudmouths they'd been. They hogged the dancers' attention as the women made their way around the bar for tips, the men, young and old alike, groping them cheaply and slipping them ones and fives.

"Watch my drink," Louis told Jacov. "I need to make a call."

A more sober Louis would never have phoned Janice from a strip club, but he was high, horny and close. She answered on the first ring.

"Are you at a bar?" she demanded right away.

"Not exactly," he said from the lot, his butt on the warm hood of his car, bass lines thumping audibly from inside.

"Don't B.S. me, Lou, I hear music."

"Actually, I'm outside a bar. Terrence Jacov did some work for me today but couldn't get his van started and asked me to drop him off."

"Drop him off where?"

"Some strip club. Delilah's something."

"Delilah's Den? Nice. *Very* respectable. I'm sure your congregation would be proud."

"I just did the guy a favor."

"Sure you did. And you're, what, just sitting in the parking lot?"

"Actually, I am."

"Don't play me for a fool, Louis. Why don't you go back in with Jacov, have another drink and call me when you haven't been feeling up strippers."

"Don't be like that," he said. "I'm just dropping him off and thought maybe I'd come by."

"It's 8:30 on a Thursday night and you're calling me from Delilah's Den. You're fucking kidding me, right? If you think you're coming over for a little booty call after sitting around drinking with Jacov all night, shoving bills down strippers' hoo-has, you are most definitely deluding yourself."

"No, that is not what I said. I said I'm dropping him off. I just wanted to see you."

"You know what? Save it, Lou. I do want to talk to you, but not tonight. Are you high? You sound a little spaced."

"No. All I did was drop him off. You're not listening to me."

But she did hear him and then some. Like the slur in his voice. His dumbed-down thoughts. And the bump, bump, bump.

"I don't want to see you now, Lou," she said. "But call me tomorrow. We do need to talk."

"About what?"

"Call me tomorrow, Louis."

Louis was the king of "we need to talk." He sensed break up but didn't dwell on it long because, on reentering the bar, his thoughts suddenly changed directions. There, at the foot of the stage, Jacov and another guy were about to square off.

The other guy, one of Stromboli's henchmen, was a thick-necked thug of about thirty. The thug stood to pick up some of Joey's action once he was packed off to prison and it was his idea to take Stromboli out for one last night – Delilah's Den followed by a coke-fueled cruise to Atlantic City. The thug had already done way too much blow for his dick to function, but his fists would work just fine and he was ready to give it a go.

Jacov, never the brains in the bunch, inquired about Stromboli's pending appointment with the judge and that was all it took to set things off.

"Big day tomorra, huh Joe?" Jacov called.

"What's that?" said the thug. "You'll mind your business, pally, if you know what's good for you."

But Jacov never did.

"C'mon, chief, Stromboli's a celebrity. I just wanna wish him well."

Half a smile crossed the fat man's face as the thug stood up and confronted Jacov. He was a head shorter, at least eighty pounds lighter, younger, quicker, tougher and way more seasoned. Jacov couldn't beat him on his best day.

Two other punks closed in behind Jacov, but he didn't notice them. If, by some chance, Jacov got the best of the thug, the others would beat him so bad out in the parking lot he wouldn't know his own name.

"Who you calling Stromboli, motherfucker?" the thug said, so close to Jacov's face he could smell the garlic and clams on the man's breath.

The others closed ranks and Jacov saw them now, one clutching a long neck Bud like a club, and Jacov winced for the coming blow.

Descending the stairs quickly Louis stepped up as casually and diplomatically as he could.

"Take it easy, fellas," he said, hands up in a gesture of calm.

"Who the fuck are you, his big brother?" the thug demanded.

"No, I'm his rabbi," Louis said.

The thug thought on this a moment, waiting for direction or inspiration on what to do next.

"Shoulda known. Coupla Goddamn Christ killers," he muttered.

Louis let it go.

"You're his rabbi?" Joey Stromboli called from the sidelines, amused with the sudden turn of events. "So what're you gonna do, say a little brucha?"

That this lard-ass, mobster wannabe knew the Hebrew word for blessing was curious, but Louis had no time for that now. He focused on the combatants.

"Look," he said, "We're not going to fight you."

"You got any sense you'd leave the 'we' out of it, *Rabbi*," the thug said. "If shit-bag here kept his mouth shut we wouldn't even be talking. You ain't got no say in the matter."

But Joey Stromboli did. He did not need a big public scene the night before sentencing, especially one involving a rabbi. In the morning he would face Judge Maxwell Kohn, a boyhood friend of the rabbi's. While Stromboli had no way of knowing this, he did know the judge was Jewish and that if he was involved in an assault on a rabbi – any rabbi – it would undoubtedly lead to the stiffest possible sentence Kohn could hand down.

"Peeps!" he roared to the thug, his baritone far more commanding than the shapeless image he projected, a voice that gave Louis reason to believe he might not be such a putz after all.

"Whaddup?"

"Let it go."

"Nah, man, I ain't gonna let this douchebag off that easy."

"Let it go!" Stromboli roared again. "I don't need this shit tonight!"

And Peeps did.

Jacov later mused that he could have taken him, that the only one Louis and the fat man saved was the thug.

"*Peeps*," he mumbled derisively, mostly to himself on the way back to Jersey. "I should have whupped his ass."

# Chapter 23

Three months passed since Rebecca banished Louis to their eldest son's former bedroom and they'd barely spoken since. As was their habit, she was up and out of the house before he was out of bed most mornings and he, between Tuesday night group sessions, couples counseling and community work, didn't often return till his wife was asleep.

But while Louis found himself banished – from their bed, from his wife's bakeries, from her company at synagogue Friday night – she suffered the split more. After all, it was he who was screwing yet another woman, he who violated the sanctity of their marriage yet again. And while Louis fell deeper in love with that other woman, Rebecca struggled to mask her heavy heart.

They were not legally separated but may as well have been. Rebecca's absence from synagogue, there in the front row in a smart new hat each week, was public pronouncement that something was amiss between the rabbi and his wife. Most worshippers knew better than to ask but didn't really have to. Apple Hill's Jewish community, easily the largest in South Jersey, was very tightly knit. That the rabbi was cheating on his wife was believable because so many knew his reputation. He was a philanderer and a flirt, the kind of man not to be trusted around one's wife, grown daughter, even grieving, widowed mom.

That said, Louis remained a strong, vibrant leader revered by many in his congregation. He was a dynamic speaker who connected with the younger generation, a man who roused worshippers to plant trees in Israel and led busloads to march on Washington in support of Jewish causes. His enthusiasm was catchy and, despite his own faults, sermonized on leading "le chaya tova" – a good life – the essence of Judaism.

"We are not, any one of us, perfect men or women, though some are more perfect than others," he said one Saturday. "I am not a perfect man. David Cohen, a mensch if I've ever known one, is not a perfect man. Sadie Libman is not a perfect woman, but she may be close."

Here he winked at the octogenarians in the front row, widow and widower, easily the cutest couple in the congregation, before going on.

"And that's okay, because God does not seek perfection from us. What he wants is for us to be good. To do good. To act good. Remember the old line, 'Greed is good'? Well, greed is not good. Good is good. You feel me?"

He believed his knack for mixing old movie lines with semi-urban catch phrases helped keep his sermons fresh and interesting, enabling him to connect with worshippers from different generations at once, to draw them in and hold them close.

"L'chaim – to life – is not just a toast," he continued. "To know l'chaim and to live l'chaim means to improve not just our own lives but the lives of those around us. When you help your brother and sister you help yourself. As they say, give till it hurts. But you know what? It doesn't hurt. It feels good. It is a mitzvah."

Outside synagogue Louis tried to practice what he preached but failed pretty much every day. The holiest of men might say failure is inevitable, that only God is perfection and man can never attain perfection and so, despite his best efforts, is doomed to always fail. But Louis's failures were repetitive. They were carnal, base, repugnant. Worst of all, he didn't learn from them, just kept repeating them, and that was his greatest failure of all.

And yet, to the world Louis was not just a popular clergyman but a Jaycee, an Elk, an adult literacy volunteer and a legendary Boy Scout leader. As scoutmaster of Troop 72, which met once a week for the past thirty years within the walls of B'Nai Tikvah, Louis was truly great. He'd shepherded more boys to Eagle, thirty-seven, than any other scoutmaster in South Jersey and so many boys wanted to join his troop year after year that at times they had to turn some away.

Tonight, his mind relieved of the tension at home by activity outside of it, he was excited by the premise of not one but three of his scouts poised to move from Life to Eagle, the ultimate goal in scouting. His son Seth, himself an Eagle at sixteen, now helped other boys reach that exalted goal, pushing them to earn merit badges, to formulate special Eagle projects and strive, like an eagle, ever higher.

Seth looked forward to the Wednesday night scout meetings because they were about the only time he and his dad spent time together anymore and Louis looked toward them, too.

Jonathan openly sided with Rebecca so he and Louis hardly spoke at all, but Seth knew enough to stay out of the mess that had always been their parents' marriage. He didn't want to know that his parents were on the outs again or that his father and mother did not share a bed –

again. He also did not want to know with whom Louis was screwing around.

"You OK, dad?" he asked, pouring coffee for them both from the big old electric urn on a table in the synagogue's all-purpose room. A thin paper runner covered the table's plain wood surface and, upon it, lay half-devoured trays of Mom's Bakeshop cookies, the better ones already scarfed up by the hungry young scouts. Louis knew Rebecca could never refuse her son so he sent Seth in his place before the meeting.

In his own way Seth found he could inquire about his father's well-being and slyly divine the situation between his dad and mom.

"I'm good," Louis said after a moment. "Fine."

"*Are* you good?"

"I'm good. Don't I seem good?"

"Yeah, you seem good. Too good, if you want to know the truth."

"What's that supposed to mean? 'Good. Too good.' What the FORK are you talking about, son?"

Seth let a moment hang between them, wondering what to say next. He wanted to keep things light.

"I dunno. You've got a spring in your step. Like you had prunes for breakfast."

"Maybe I did," Louis said with a wink.

Another explanation was that Louis was in love. Not puppy dog, tenth grade crush, holding-hands-in-the-hallway-and-hoping-to-get-some-after-school love, but the real thing. Thoughts of Janice consumed him, in waking hours and in his sleep. He cancelled bar mitzvah lessons if they coincided with her radio broadcast, abbreviated evening services so he could see her for late dinners.

He and Janice met for lunch near the Reading Terminal Market in Philadelphia that afternoon and went directly to her loft for dessert. There they made love twice in two hours.

"So…," she said, sweaty and flushed from the second round, her nipples puffy and full. She was eager to resume a conversation that started and stalled half a dozen times in the past few weeks and Louis knew full well what was coming next. It was still a conversation he just couldn't have.

"So, what?" he asked.

Her hand wandered as she spoke, gently roughing the sparse white hairs on her lover's chest.

"You know what," she said, pinching his upper arm for effect. "When you movin' in, lover boy?"

Janice had generously overlooked his call outside Delilah's Den and accepted his word, after some pleading, that he was just dropping Jacov off.

As for moving in, Louis wanted to ignore the question. He rubbed his thickening member against her thigh, almost ready to go again, and Janice looked down in disbelief, almost on the verge of anger, suspecting Cialis.

"Lou-iss," she sang. "I know you *hear* me."

Her tone was playful and calm, but Janice was serious. She would not be some casual piece he kept on the side. If they were to have any future at all, it would not be like this – an afternoon fuck on the sly and then back to wifey. No, ever since Louis called her that night from Delilah's she had been pressing him, with ever-increasing frequency, on when he was leaving his wife and moving in with her. Her intentions were clear and Louis could no more duck them forever than he could the awful encounter he'd ultimately have to have with Rebecca. Janice hadn't mentioned it, but he was certain that her long-term plans included marriage and children. She was, after all, in the twilight of her reproductive years and women want babies, whether they said so or not.

Leaving his wife was not an easy topic for Louis to discuss, but talking about it would, in fact, be the easy part. Making the move would be next to impossible. He thought of a passage on the institution of marriage he'd read somewhere and regurgitated it badly to Janice.

"You know," he said, "marriage is a funny thing. Those who are in want to get out and those who are out want to get in."

"Marriage? Who the *hell* said anything about marriage? Did I *mention* marriage? Have I *ever* mentioned marriage to you?!"

"No. You have not. But it's basically the same thing."

"It's not *even* the same thing! I'm talking about moving in, Louis, not getting married. I'm not looking for a ring, a cake, to wash your clothes, bear your children, none of it. I'm making it easy for you. What I'm asking of you does not even come close to marriage, but it's better than this."

"What's wrong with this?"

"Louis," she admonished. "Do not make me spell it out."

He tried to get closer, but she pushed him away and covered herself with the thin white cotton bedspread she used in the summer. The sex shop was closed.

Driving home from the scout meeting he thought about the conversation again and why leaving his wife would be so difficult. He believed – no, *knew* – that a formal separation and divorce would jeopardize his position with B'nai Tikvah. Though he had long been a womanizer, often within the confines of his own congregation, a divorce would doom him professionally. It was that simple. Divorces were public, messy and damning. Should he get divorced, especially on the grounds with which Rebecca would surely charge him, every rumor, hint, whiff of impropriety ever breathed in his direction would, he was certain, be confirmed.

But that wasn't the half of it. The biggest reason Louis couldn't fathom divorce was he couldn't afford it. What Janice didn't realize, what he couldn't possibly *tell* her, was that the bulk of the Abrams' assets belonged to his wife. Rebecca's parents left her, an only child, everything when they passed, within four months of each other, about ten years before. And that, coupled with her ever-growing business proceeds, gave her a net worth of millions.

Louis, on the other hand, lived pretty much paycheck to paycheck. If he and Rebecca were to divorce they would split joint assets like the house and cars, but the inheritance and business accounts were all hers.

Sure, he made a decent salary as chief rabbi, but it was no king's ransom, enough to cover his share of the bills, lunches, dinners, and a bit left to play. Problem was, he'd played too much of late. There was the new car, which he didn't need and could ill afford, but also the trips to Delilah's. They'd become twice weekly and went very well, like a glass of red wine and a thick, juicy steak, with his love affair in Philadelphia. He'd spend a few hours at Delilah's, then give it to Janice but good. Squiring her about town also did not come cheaply, but she had no idea how tightly it squeezed him.

To help make up the slack Louis started tapping the synagogue's expense fund. The fund, created some twenty years before, was intended as a ready source of cash for day-to-day repairs without the need for board approval. After all, the board of directors had reasoned in the seventies, if you can't trust your own rabbi, whom could you trust? It was a question they would soon have to answer.

For, with this fund, Louis had hired Jacov for all manner of jobs and it wasn't long before they worked out a scheme. Jacov quoted a price, wrote it up twenty to thirty percent higher, cashed the check and turned the excess back over to Louis. Louis's only concern was the annual audit and that, done within weeks of the scheme's commencement, checked out fine. The bean counters found numerous odd jobs, written estimates, and checks cut to match them.

Louis stifled his guilt over cheating the synagogue by reasoning that as chief rabbi he was as much a CEO as a man of God. And, as such, he deserved certain perks, gosh darn it. So he rewired the alarm system, fixed broken walls, re-glazed windows, mended leaky pipes, painted classrooms, tuned up the HVAC system and became a regular at Delilah's Den.

* * * * *

The light in the kitchen gave Louis pause as he eased the Magnum up the steep slope of their drive, careful so as not to scrape the stainless steel exhaust. He clicked the remote fob for his garage door and idled the car in. Rebecca should have been fast asleep, but there at the kitchen table, drinking a cup of strong black coffee and watching the tube, his wife sat waiting for him. He assumed she had been counting the day's register receipts because there on the table sat a fat canvas lock bag ready for deposit.

"Another late night, eh?" she said.

As with most of her queries to him of late this one was rhetorical, but Louis answered anyhow.

"Not so late. We got three kids makin' Eagle."

Rebecca stirred her coffee and glanced up at Action News. Fight outside a bar in West Philadelphia. Man rushed to Penn, dead on arrival, gunshot wound to chest.

"So I hear. Seth called a few minutes ago."

"Did he? I just left him. What'd he want?"

"He didn't want anything. Can't a son call his mother?"

This Louis didn't answer.

"He says you look good," she said. "Says maybe I should eat more prunes, too."

"Sounds like his grandmother," Louis said.

He drew a glass of chilled water from the dispenser in the fridge door and wondered why his wife was up drinking coffee.

"I told him it wasn't the prunes," she said.

Louis felt queasy because he knew a fight was brewing, but when he turned back he was all business, unashamed and unrepentant.

Rebecca was staring at the screen but didn't really see it, hardened as she was to the news and by the numbness of her own life. She felt black, resigned, certain that if things didn't change for the better, and soon, she wouldn't just feel dead, she would in fact *be* dead, rotted from the inside out.

After so many years she knew everything there was to know about the man standing before her except what he'd do next. Would he deny the allegation outright, ignore her, storm out of the house or just stand there, mute and pathetic? It didn't really matter.

"Look, I'm not doing this again," she started, surprising even herself with her calm.

"You're not doing what?"

"Naomi Kahan, Paula what's-her-name, Janice whoever-she-is, I don't really care."

"I don't know what …"

"I DON'T CARE!"

Rebecca's strong little fists balled up on the table and squiggly blue veins plumped along her neck and forehead. Her eyes, now that Louis could see them, were muddled and red, but she would not cry.

"Janice…" he stumbled. "Re-BEH-ka."

Rage gripped her so powerfully she could have stabbed the bastard, plunged a fucking kitchen knife into his chest and ended the bloody thing then and there, but she steeled herself and soldiered on.

"Just. Please. Go."

And long perfidious Louis, struck by his wife's dispassion and conviction, said not another word, just packed a quick bag and went.

<u>Chapter 24</u>

Louis packed so quickly that he forgot his phone on the kitchen counter. He could have stopped to call, but finding a pay phone was almost impossible anymore – half his congregation didn't even know what they were – and instead surprised Janice on her doorstep half an hour later with a duffle in his hand.

"Sign outside says room available," he said.

Standing there in the doorway, she glanced back at the phone off its cradle near the couch.

"My sister," she said, and hustled back to the couch to cut the call short as Louis stepped in.

"So, I didn't expect *this* so soon, not after today," she said on her return.

"It's what you wanted, right?"

"I didn't think it's what *you* wanted."

"It's not that it's not what I wanted. It's just, you know it's … "

"Don't even say it's complicated or I may have to bust you upside the head."

She was only half joking.

"Well it *is* complicated. I'm still married, I'm a member of the community, a …"

"I get it, Lou," Janice interrupted. "So you're still a married man, you're still a member of the community. What exactly do you want from me?"

For the second time in an hour Louis was certain a woman in his life wanted to hit him, or worse. He thought what he wanted was obvious but for a moment he just stood there, mute, duffle in hand, door closed behind him, neither fully in nor out.

"Well? What's changed?" Janice asked again.

Louis knew honesty was not always the best policy, at least not for him, yet sometimes, when you're tired enough, beat enough, *desperate* enough, it was just easier.

"Rebecca threw me out," he confessed.

Janice stood silent a moment. She leaned against the couch back, her pale yellow socks slipping on the polished pine floor.

"This wasn't what I meant when I asked you to move in," she said. "Be here because you want to be here, not because you need a place to crash, because your wife threw you out."

Louis set the duffle down and embraced her, somewhat against her will, but she let him pull her close.

"That's not what I meant. I want to be here. Do you want me to leave?"

"Where you gonna go? It's eleven thirty at night."

"That wasn't the question."

Both looked as the phone rang again but Janice just let it ring.

"Probably Rosie again," Janice offered without being asked. "She and Tony are having problems. He wants another baby and she wants no part of it."

"Ahh, to be forty again," Louis said.

"Not even. Rose-Ann's only thirty-five. But she's done with the whole babies thing. If Tony wants another kid, he's gonna have to have it on his own."

Louis held Janice and she softened. She wrapped her arms around his waist and laid her face against his chest.

"How 'bout you?" he asked.

"What about me?"

"You done with the babies, too?"

"Am I done? I never got started."

"Doesn't mean you're done," he said.

Janice long ago stifled a maternal drive that, she imagined, would impede professional success. Since graduating St. Joes she had simply been driven to succeed and she finally was. *Driveways,* her daily talk show, was steaming toward syndication. As for babies, they'd still have to wait.

"You want some coffee?" she said, extricating herself from his grip. "I'm gonna make decaf."

Louis followed her into the kitchen, a hip little room no bigger than his walk-in closet that was so pink it made his head swim. With its pink ceramic sink, lighter pink and black tiled backsplash and pasty white ceiling the room reminded him of Good-n-Plenty. Though small, the kitchen had all the accouterments of young urban chic: Kitchen Aid mixer, Krups cappuccino maker, wooden Ikea dish strainer, quality German knife set.

"So what're ya gonna do?" Janice asked as the coffee cooked.

"About what?"

"Don't *fuck* with me, Abrams," she said with a little shove.

"Maybe I *like* to fuck with you," he said.

Louis pulled her close again and kissed her. He tried to hold her but she wriggled free, turned and fished a tin of good English shortbread from a cabinet above the sink.

She wore the same tight corduroy jeans she had on the first time he met her - at the art exhibit at the Y - and his eyes tracked as she reached further up into the cabinet for blue packets of sweetener. She felt his eyes upon her.

"Don't get any ideas, Rabbi. You already got yours today."

"It makes me horny when you call me rabbi. And I could use a little more."

"You're always horny. And I'll be the judge of who gets more," she said.

They sat together at a small round table inlaid with broken pieces of glass. Ignoring the cookies before him, Louis reached across the table and took Janice's hand. She was glad he had come, and he could tell.

"So you gonna answer me or what?" she said.

"About what?"

"About what? About your wife, that's what."

"I dunno. Get a lawyer, I guess. Not like I have much choice in the matter."

"Oh, you've got choices, Louis. Get a divorce, don't get a divorce. Stay here with me or go back home to Rebecca. It's a little thing called pee or get off the pot. Speaking of which, I'll be right down."

"More than I need to know," he said.

Louis watched as she ascended the stairs, but his eyes fell to the phone near the couch. Something in

Janice's manner told him it wasn't her sister on the line when he arrived. He went to the phone, lifted it from its cradle, and checked the Caller ID.

<u>Chapter 25</u>

Louis heard little in the community about his pending divorce, but that was sure to change once the paperwork was filed. Today, New Year's, he took the train back to Apple Hill for Shabbat services but hurried back to Philly to meet up with Janice for the Mummers Parade up Broad Street.

He glanced at headlines in a newspaper someone left on the Speedline but set it down quickly as scenes of South Jersey raced by. Sitting in a backward facing seat, his ride was disorienting, dizzying, and reading the paper only made it worse. He looked forward to the parade, a Philadelphia tradition that predated the Revolution, a gaudy spectacle of sequins, strutting and drinking in about equal measures.

Speeding through Haddonfield, Westmont, Collingswood and Camden, he marveled at the deterioration in quality of life, the rapid digression from prosperity to poverty, of million-dollar homes in Haddonfield giving way, less than five minutes down the track, to the broken squalor of Camden, block after block of burned out rubble, and the happy suburbanites safe on the train who chose not to see it.

The parade, when he got to it, was an unlikely sea of humanity. Beer swilling South Philly Eagles diehards bumped elbows and bellies with suburban parents and their children. People of all stripes – black, white, yellow and brown – lined up behind wooden police barricades as stringbands, fancy and comic brigades strutted by. More colorful and buoyant than a thousand drunken peacocks, the Mummers filled Philadelphia's cold gray air with spirit but clashed with the stoic stone walls of Broad Street. The parade was the city's wackiest, gaudiest, liveliest tradition, and Louis, recently separated and on the verge of a new life, lost himself in it gladly.

"Drink up, buddy," a young man said, proffering Louis a half-drank beer.

Louis turned it down but no sooner had he done so than the young man offered it again, this time to a passing Mummer. The man grabbed it mid-strut, upended the long-necked bottle and drained it in one swig, dropping it with a clang in the street. All around, revelers still buzzed from the night before drank openly, plastic tumblers sloshing back and forth as they bumped along.

Louis himself was hung over and nearly hurled from the stale smells of beer and cigarette smoke along the parade route. He cringed each time some kid with a plastic flugelhorn blew it in his ear and farted when Janice walked up from behind and surprised him with two fingers to the ribs.

"Yowza! You step on a duck or just glad to see me?"

"Just glad to see you," he said with a kiss, hugging her deeply.

"I do bring out the best in people."

They stood for a few moments while the Kensington String Band strutted by, a nightmarish collection of men in yellow, orange, pink and green costumes. Some of the troupe carried saxophones, their faces painted white, pink and blue, heads topped with three-pointed hats like medieval jesters on acid. Others sported banjos, long, yellow Goldilocks braids, and flowing, knee-length lavender dresses. Like the other troupes, virtually all of Kensington's brethren reeked of booze and machismo, bad-ass attitude and that famous Mummers strut, the combination of which contrasted badly with all their women's makeup, girly-girl dresses, sequins and fluff.

Though Louis and Janice had a pretty good vantage point curbside at Broad and Pine they left it for the grandstands near City Hall where, they figured, they could sit and watch the parade. But there the crowd thickened so much they couldn't see the sights at all. Louis thought about forcing their way back to the spot they'd left but knew, by now, it would be filled, like water finding its level, so they circled City Hall instead, caught a bit more of the parade, and headed to China Town for noodle soup and dumplings.

Darting into a small restaurant off Arch Street, Louis cast his eyes quickly about the place. Though many in his congregation weren't kosher, he still hoped no one he knew would be inside. He *was*, after all, a rabbi and would rather not be seen eating traif.

He ordered for them both and, in a few moments, a waiter brought a platter of good steamed dumplings and hot bowls of soup with shrimp, pork, chicken, noodles and greens.

"So how were services?" Janice asked between slurps of her soup.

Working her chopsticks badly, she dropped a dumpling into a shallow bowl of dipping sauce that splashed up onto Louis's glasses. He removed the glasses, wiped his lenses with a crisp linen napkin and answered her question before looking up.

"Not bad," he said. "But it's like I got cancer. People know something's wrong, they just don't want to ask."

"Don't say that. It's not like you have cancer, it's like you're getting a divorce. And half of them have been through it themselves."

"I know. I helped half of them through it. The other half I married. Some I married *and* helped through a divorce. But I'm the one up on the bimah. I'm the example. I'm the one they're talking about."

"How do you know they're talking about it? Are they talking to you?"

"No. But I know."

He glanced about the restaurant making double sure no one he knew was within earshot.

"Rebecca's not in shul and they know it. They're muttering during services. They're talking about it."

"So what. You be the leader. Just let them talk."

* * * * *

When Rebecca filed the papers three weeks later it didn't come as a surprise, but sitting in Shelly's office Louis was thunderstruck nonetheless. She sought pretty much everything – the house, her car, virtually all of their combined savings, even their beloved dog Buster. About the only thing she didn't seek was his hot rod Sedan Delivery, a vehicle she referred to in the paperwork as "loathsome and creepy," a description that pained him.

"I'm not gonna lie to you, Lou, this is gonna get ugly."

"*Gonna* get ugly? Whaddaya call this! You're not going to let her get all this, are you?"

"No, we're not going to *let* her have it all but it may not come down to what we want. She's claiming you abandoned her, that you're in the midst of the latest in a string of not-so-secret affairs, that you've publicly humiliated her and that most of your stuff is hers."

"I know what the fucking thing says, Shel. What I want to know is, can she get away with it?"

"Well, she's betting a judge will side with her and she may be right. The short answer is I don't know."

"You don't know? What am I paying you three-hundred bucks an hour for?"

Louis rose from his chair, stomped about the room, raked his hair back and muttered beneath his breath.

"Calm down, Lou. I just can't know for sure at this stage of the game."

"Believe me, Shelly, this is no fucking game. She wants to ruin me and what I want to know is, can she get away with it?"

"I'm sorry, pal. I know it's no game. My point is, it's early. A judge will decide but we'll have an opportunity to try to make it equitable. The thing of it is, and this will be tough to get around, you did abandon the marriage."

"I didn't abandon anything. She threw me out."

"Yes, and you went. I'm not going to sugarcoat it, Lou, because that won't help. She's been tailing you. Probably for some time. I had lunch with Goldberg yesterday and he said she knew for certain about Janice weeks before she threw you out."

"You had lunch with him? Whaddaya, dining with the enemy?"

"Louis, c'mon. We're lawyers. It's a small club. He gave me copy of the decree as a courtesy but he's filing it soon."

"How soon?"

"I don't know. The thing is, you have to decide what it is you want to do."

"What I want to do is keep my house, Shel. She's the one with all the fucking money."

"I don't see that being the issue and a judge won't either. You walked out and she's still there. Possession is nine…"

"Yeah, yeah. Do me a favor, Shel, for what I'm paying you, don't sit around dropping fucking clichés."

Louis sat, put his head in his hands and tried to get his mind around the situation.

"Our goal is to negotiate," Shelly said. "It's possible we work something out where you sell the house and split the proceeds but I don't see Rebecca going for that. The house is still her home."

"Well, there ain't much to negotiate then, is there?"

Louis sat in silence, the gravity of his situation washing over him. He really could go broke.

"You know they've got pictures of you and Janice coming in, going out, carrying bags of groceries like a couple of Goddamn *newlyweds*? They've got pictures of you and her at the *Mummer's Parade*, for Christ sakes!"

"I swear, Shel, by all that is fucking holy, I will fucking kill her!"

"LOUIS! Now listen. I am your lawyer. You are a rabbi. Do not start talking shit. I know you're upset. You have a right to be. But keep your cool and we're gonna get through this."

"*We*. Uh-huh. Good one. Feels a lot more like *me*."

Shelly pulled a bottle of scotch from a cabinet and poured shots for himself and Louis. He took a slow pull, but Louis gulped his down.

"What we say is between you and me, Lou, you know that. But I don't want you to say shit even in jest because it's a slippery fucking slope. You start talking shit in private and before you know it you say something to someone and word gets around. I know you're just venting, but don't. The last thing you need is some not-so-veiled threat against your soon-to-be ex-wife getting back to the judge.

"What we need to do is be grounded and focused," the lawyer continued. "Just remember the standard: 'equitable division of assets.' That is our goal. What I want you to do is keep your cool and let me do my job."

"Equitable" sounded well and good, but Louis didn't see things turning out that way, not by a long shot. He faced an ugly divorce. Losing the house, the dog, the vast majority of their assets. He imagined losing his job.

He imagined killing his wife.

Sure, as Shelly said, he was just talking shit in the office, but now, the more he thought of it, the more it made sense. If he could pull it off he wouldn't lose a thing. He would gain, gain, gain. The house would be his. Joint assets, all his. Baking business, his again. And, if anything, the tragic loss of his beloved wife would make his job more secure. People would feel for him, want to do well by him, Poor Rabbi Abrams who lost his dear wife. Sure they had their struggles, but who didn't? Surely he didn't want this.

When Jacov arrived early that Tuesday night Louis was the one with questions - about Jacov's security business, how his worker, the one who got burned rewiring the alarm system, was making out, about his aging mother, what he actually did in the military.

His mother, it turned out, was OK, better in fact than when his old man was around. Jacov heard Simon Gonzalez was doing well but hadn't seen him in months, not since he got out of the hospital. As for the alarm business, it was just one more thing he'd gotten into after the gold rush.

"But you *were* in the military, weren't you? They had to teach you *some* usable skills."

"They taught me some skills all right. I don't know how usable but they taught me."

"What, like carpentry and stuff?"

"Something like that."

Louis doubted Jacov ever did anything in the service worth all his winks and nods but he let him have his fun. Besides, the job he had in mind would take more will than skill.

"Like what? C'mon, I want to know."

"You don't want to know."

"Terrence, I ain't some civilian here. I'm former Navy chaplain corps. Back around sixty-six, sixty-seven, we saw action. Some heavy praying. Davening like you wouldn't believe."

"You're kidding me, right?"

"Little bit. So really, what'd you do? Recon? Wet work?"

Jacov's head was down but he looked up over the tops of his glasses, the corners of his mouth twisted in a silly put-on grin.

"I really can't talk about it."

Coming down the hall Naomi Kahan warbled like a small furry mammal. She entered the room with a friend in tow, the long-promised Rini, but long-suffering Alex was nowhere in sight.

"Check with me tomorrow, will you?" Louis said. "I have a proposition you might find of interest."

* * * * *

They didn't set a time per se so Louis went about his daily business – service in the morning, a look at the papers, bong hit around ten. He'd just smoked up when there was a rap at his door.

"One moment!" he shouted, opening a window and spraying some pine scented air freshener as he stashed the bong beneath his desk.

Going to the door reluctantly, he saw through the mini blinds that it was Jacov and let him in.

"Just on the phone," he said, offering his hand.

Louis closed the door quickly, relieved it was Jacov and not some really unwanted surprise, and turned the lock behind them.

Jacov sat heavily in a big leather wing chair and sniffed. As it turned out, he wasn't mistaken before and certainly wasn't now. Besides, after the night at Delilah's, Louis's little secret was secret no more. This morning Louis had a much bigger bomb to drop and could use another hit to get through so he pulled the glass pipe from beneath his desk and offered it to Jacov.

"Hmmm, the ole wake and bake. Gee, thanks, Rabbi Feelgood, don't mind if I do."

Jacov took a big hit, exhaled as completely as he could but hacked loud and painfully.

"Keep it down!" Louis said.

Jacov returned the pipe to Louis who smoked it expertly and passed it back. Jacov took a moment to catch his breath and took another hit.

"Good shit," he said, exhaling completely this time so he wouldn't cough again. "'Bout time you came clean."

"What do you mean? We smoked that night in Philly."

"I know. Well, even before that I thought I knew. Half the time it smells like Panama in here. Of course I knew."

It had been a warm February and outside the synagogue snow crocuses were starting to bloom. Planted in the fall, bunches of gold, white and purple flowers seemed to have burst from the ground overnight and smattered the frosty earth with color. Louis rose from behind his desk to look at them and suddenly needed to get out.

"Let's take a walk," he suggested.

A craggy old hilltop cemetery abutted B'nai Tikvah's property and Louis led Jacov toward it. For generations, students skipping school went up there to smoke cigarettes, drink beer and fool around, but Louis just liked the view, especially when he was high. Reaching the top he felt invigorated, but the big man behind him wheezed like an old asthmatic.

"You gonna make it?" he asked.

"I'm alright," Jacov said, brushing off a rotted old tree stump for a seat and fishing out a pack of Marlboros.

"That oughta help," Louis said.

Jacov didn't reply, just lit up a Cowboy Killer and breathed in deep.

Louis looked around. Though he hadn't thought about it in years, this was where he and Rebecca first made love, two horny kids fumbling with clothes and body parts, not quite sure what to do. It had been warm, late spring, and their smells and tastes mingled with the fresh sweet scents of grass and clover, intoxicating the young lovers.

"This is where Rebecca and I used to do the deed when we were first dating," he offered.

"Oh yeah? What deed is that?"

Louis looked oddly at the oaf, realized he was ribbing him, and smiled despite himself. The sun was high now, burning off the morning's early frostiness, and it felt balmy, spring-like and good. Jacov continued to smoke but Louis just gazed about.

"She's divorcing me, you know."

Jacov flicked the stub away, sat for a minute and fished out another smoke.

"No, I didn't know."

"I thought you might have heard."

"How would I have heard?"

"People talk. It's not official yet, but we're separated."

"That something you want, a divorce?"

"No. Most definitely not."

"Can't imagine it's gonna look so good, what with you bein' a rabbi and all."

"Yeah, well, that in itself isn't the problem. Truth is, it ain't the half of it."

"What's the other half?"

Louis picked up a stick and dug at the ground like a sandlot quarterback sketching the next play.

"Rebecca's trying to ruin me. She wants the house, the majority of our assets, the bakery business, pretty much everything. And my lawyer thinks she'll get it."

Jacov sat a moment reflecting. He was enjoying the high, his smoke and the warmth of the sun, but the conversation was a sudden downer.

"Well, you still have your job, right? It may not look so good you gettin' a divorce and all but you'll still be a rabbi, no?"

"I dunno. Yeah, for now, I guess. But I've got a sneaking suspicion that once the fit hits the shan that'll be on the line too."

Now Jacov was the one looking askance, but he knew what he meant.

"Why's at? You wouldn't be the first rabbi to get a divorce."

"Well, the thing of it is, I haven't exactly been faithful to Rebecca. You know I'm seeing Janice, right, but there have been others."

"Janice Palumbo? NPR Janice?"

Louis rolled his eyes. He thought that much was obvious.

"Yes. Listen to me, Terrence. There have been others and Rebecca is leveraging it to get what she wants. She hasn't filed the paperwork yet, but her lawyer gave my lawyer a copy of the decree out of professional courtesy. Once it's filed the word will get around fast and people will talk."

"And?"

"And I've *shtupped* half the fucking congregation!" he snapped. "Rebecca doesn't know about everything, but what she knows, it's in there."

The rabbi's meaning finally dawned on Jacov.

"And once that comes out you think they'll can you."

"I dunno. Maybe. They will. I'm sure of it."

Louis jabbed at the ground still searching for the words. He thought of abandoning the whole thing, of going back inside and losing himself in another hit, of becoming really, deeply, stupidly stoned. And then he thought of Janice. If he lost his money, his home, his assets, if he lost his job, surely he would lose her, too. Louis steeled himself and went on.

"I want you to do something for me, Terrence."

Jacov liked that the rabbi called him Terrence. It was respectful. Not Terry, not Jacov, and certainly not Jack-Off.

"Name it."

"I was hoping you'd say that. What I'm about to ask of you is more than a favor. Way more. It's a job. But it's bigger than that, too. You do this for me and it will change both our lives forever, for the better."

The tip of Jacov's cigarette got very bright as if, to listen closely, he needed an extra deep drag.

The stick stopped moving across the crumbly, fertile ground and Louis looked up calmly.

"I want you to kill my wife," he said.

He waited a moment for the gravity of what he said to sink in, to penetrate Jacov's famously dense noggin. They sat there a moment, stoned, the biggest sentence either had ever heard hanging in the air like smoke.

"She's been ill anyway," Louis lied. "But you do this right, just the way I tell you, and we'll both come out fine, better than fine, set for life. You hear what I'm saying?"

And still Jacov just sat there. He didn't inhale for a moment or two but the cigarette continued to burn, singeing the hairs on two fingers and making him wince, mute, stoned and stunned.

"Terrence!"

"I heard you," Jacov said, looking down at his feet. He suddenly regretted all the Army guy allusions and "wet work" references he'd wrapped himself in. A job – a real job – was finally at hand, and he was not up to it.

"You want me to do what?"

"You heard me."

"Rabbi, listen. I know I brag about being in the Army and all but this, this…"

"Terrence, I know I'm asking a lot of you but you can do this. I know you can. It will be clean. No mess. And when you're done, when all's said and done, you're going to be a hundred thousand dollars richer and no one will ever know."

"A hundred thousand?"

"A *hundred* thousand."

"Wow."

"I know, wow. And you can do this. You can and will be able to do this."

<u>Chapter 26</u>

One hundred K.

Jacov could barely get his mind around the figure but not for lack of trying. In fact, since Louis proposed the plan, it was pretty much all he thought of. A hundred K. One hundred large. One hundred *thousand* dollars!

With that much scratch, he could lose the hunk-a-junk broken-down piece-of-shit van he putzed about in and get something nice. Something new. Maybe a full-size Chevy Express. V-8, power windows, CD, the works. Fuck that. With *that* much dough, he could stop salivating over the Sunday circulars and buy a badass pickup - maybe a lime green Dodge with big block Hemi.

The plan itself was simple, almost perfect, really. Enter house through unlocked side door sometime after nine. By then Mrs. A will be home, at kitchen table, doing paperwork and counting receipts. She works late Tuesdays and Thursdays so Jonathan will have the dog. Use element of surprise. Approach from rear, grab around neck. Snap. Take money bag, leave.

It wasn't wet work per se and that was a relief.

And he would get paid immediately, two-thousand to three-thousand –whatever cash was at hand -- so the motive, naturally, would appear to be robbery.

He'd wear gloves, ditch his clothes afterward, go home, shower, shave, grab a steak somewhere and have himself a drink.

Louis told Jacov he would be paid in full once the claim on Rebecca's life insurance came through – anywhere from three to four weeks from the time of her death.

What he didn't say was how much he, Louis, stood to gain. He and Rebecca both carried million-dollar policies, nine tenths of which he would collect after Jacov was paid. But his big windfall would inevitably come from the house, her business and the hefty savings she'd socked away – two to three million dollars if a dime.

He didn't know the exact amount because it was a subject Rebecca refused to discuss. Her goal, until recently, was to save enough for the two of them to retire comfortably. She'd tried to make peace with his earlier betrayals because she didn't know what else to do. As for their golden years, she'd considered him her soul mate and believed retirement together could be very good, not predicated on sex alone.

But with his latest humiliation everything changed. Worse, it proved once and for all that nothing had changed. So, in addition to the divorce decree that Goldberg drew up, she also had him change her will.

* * * * *

Descending the hilltop cemetery the irony was not lost on Louis that he had just planned a death in a place of death.

Like many Jews he was not hung up on the notion of heaven and hell. Unlike Catholics and Muslims, Jews didn't obsess with the afterlife but emphasized leading a good life for its own sake. Still, when one plans a death, when one does the most unholy thing one can do, one cannot help but consider the consequences – for this life as well as the next.

Louis and Jacov parted ways at the synagogue's door and Louis entered his study shaken. He Googled some literature on the afterlife and was not heartened by what he read. Rabbi Moshe Chayim Luzzatto, a renowned 18th century scholar, addressed the issue clearly:

*"Gehenom, Purgatory, is the place for souls that are suited for punishment, and there they receive pain and suffering in relation to what is applicable to them ... And*

*there are different levels of pain as there are different levels of pleasure, and with this pain the sinners shall bear their iniquities. If they are worthy of reward, after this, they will be purified and go to rest. If not, they will be punished until they are obliterated. And this thing will not occur to a descendant of Israel, a Jew, except in the most infrequent of cases."*

Killing one's wife, Louis was certain, had to be among the most infrequent of cases. But what did this Rabbi Luzzatto know? Louis shut the computer, left his study and went for a drive, determined not to dwell on it.

<u>Chapter 27</u>

Tuesday night.

Rebecca dropped the green canvas lock bag on the table with a bang and let Buster out of his room.

"You been good boy? You miss Mommy? Yeah?"

The big dog jumped nearly three feet vertically to kiss her across the lips, then bounded to the back door, his whole body wagging with his tail.

She opened the door and Buster bolted out – "Mommy's big pit bullet" – and raced around the yard till he found a place to pee and poop.

While he was out Rebecca prepared his meal – some leftover brisket and a little water – microwaved for twenty seconds and mixed with a bowl of kibbles. Buster was nothing if not consistent: he'd eat, prance about the room with a chew toy in his mouth, stretch, rub up against the couch, and have a good burp. Then he'd curl up on his bed in the kitchen while Rebecca did her work.

Sometimes, when she wanted a long, hot bath, she returned him to his room after dinner while she soaked. Buster was long past the point of chewing furniture, but in his own room he was safe, secure, unable to get into trouble, and she was glad to have him tonight.

Immersing herself in the tub Rebecca nearly got up for the phone in the next room but let it go. She leafed through a recent issue of Vanity Fair and started to unwind when, ten minutes later, the phone rang again. This time she rose from the cooling suds, wrapped a thick terry towel around her and went out to take the call. She reached the phone on the fourth ring but heard only a click as the other party hung up.

In an old beater van across town Terrence Jacov chewed his nails and smoked compulsively. A flaky bit of skin hung on his right cheek and he scratched at it inanely, digging at the thing till it bled.

Clearly, he had his doubts. The whole plan could go awry. Was it even worth the risk? He could fucking *fry* for killing the rabbi's wife. But here he was, en route, on his way to do what he agreed to do.

He needed to clear his head but the window jammed as he tried to roll it down. Long broken, he'd discarded the original crank and replaced it with an old set of vise grips. Now, in order to open the window, he had to twirl the handle of the grips, but sometimes – like now – the cable inside the door slipped or got stuck. He cursed the fucking thing, slammed his hand on the steering wheel and headed to see Mrs. Abrams.

White-knuckled, sweating and nearly paralyzed with fear, Jacov forgot part of the plan – a little part that said park down the street – pulled up almost directly in front of the house and killed the engine. He looked about, paranoid, tried willing himself calm. He had to pee really bad and his stomach was so roiled he thought he might puke. Jacov swallowed back the bile, turned the key to restart the engine and almost ditched the plan entirely when two things happened that convinced him to stay.

First, the engine failed. It cranked, turned over once and backfired. The engine might have started on the second try, but now that would have to wait. A light came on in the living room and the lace curtains moved.

"Fuck," Jacov hissed. "She *sees* me."

He ducked down in his seat -- as if that would hide him -- and steadied himself while he waited for the shadow at the window to pass. Then he climbed from the truck.

* * * * *

Though he tried to conceal it, Louis could not hide the fact that something was amiss tonight. He was jittery, ill at ease, not himself. A casual observer might not have noticed, but Naomi Kahan was no casual observer. She knew this man almost as well as he knew himself.

"Where's boychik?" she asked, gesturing to the empty seat that usually contained the bulk of Terrence Jacov.

"Terrence? I think he's out of town this week."

She looked at him, puzzled.

"He and Rini went out, you know."

"Izzat right? How'd it go?"

"It went great, or so she thought. Then the louse didn't call her. You men are all the same."

Louis forced a grin.

"Take it easy, Betty Friedan," he said. "Maybe something came up. His mother's been sick; maybe he went up to see her."

Naomi, who caught the tail end of the conversation between Louis and Jacov the previous Tuesday, thought this odd. Only last week his mother was fine. In fact, the old bird was better than fine. She was thriving.

"So where *is* Rini tonight?" Louis went on, changing the subject. "Didn't she enjoy herself last week?"

"She liked it well enough," she said. "I just don't think she wanted to run into Oaf."

"C'mon, Naomi," Louis said. "Can't we all just get along?"

She huffed, disregarded him, stood and got herself a decaf.

Soon Sol and Toby Kimmelman shuffled in, followed by Steve and Ester Frank. The two older couples took their regular seats near one another and looked up eagerly, ready to start.

"So, Rabbi, vaht's the vord?" Sol said.

"Oh, Solly," Toby said, slapping her husband's wrist and shushing his phony accent. "You'll hear when you hear."

Louis stood and dragged a lectern over to lean against.

"Open forum," he said. "Tonight I thought I'd let the inmates run the asylum."

Louis looked uneasily at the clock on the wall, raked a hand through thinning hair and down across his beard.

"Let's talk… sex!" Sol said gleefully, his bald head shining, dark eyes a-twinkle. "Sex in your seventies! Orgasms at eighty!"

"Oy vey!" Mrs. Kimmelman said, slapping her husband's wrist again.

Louis, who other nights might have initiated such a topic himself, stood silently at the front, his long face drawn. With Americans living longer and the vitality of Viagra (now *there's* an ad slogan, he thought despite himself), this topic was ripe for the picking. But tonight, it swept past him. He simply stood there blank-faced, alone with his thoughts.

"So, what of it, Rabbi?" Naomi chimed in. "Orgasms at eighty? Nookie at ninety? How 'bout... humping at a hundred?"

The two older couples looked at the attractive younger woman and blushed, but Louis barely moved, a forced half smile frozen on his lips. At that moment the phone on his belt buzzed. He checked the number, excused himself and stepped into the hall.

* * * * *

Jacov was almost comical creeping across the lawn in the dark. He was a parody, a cartoon character, Spy vs. Spy. With each step he drew his knees up high as if, in so doing, he would not leave a mark in the grass as he moved toward the house. He glanced at the living room window, uncertain now if anyone had been there at all, and treaded up the hilly drive and around the back as instructed.

Little details threw him, and pissed him off greatly. He stumbled on one of the cobblestones that lined the driveway but caught himself before he fell. The rabbi might have told him about the God-damned cobblestones, he thought. Then there was the stubborn lock on the high wooden fence gate that didn't want to open. He jiggled the thing once or twice, finally realizing he had to lift the latch and push at the same time.

"Small fucking detail, *no, Rabbi?*" he growled.

As for himself, a little practice in this sort of thing would have helped. Perhaps, instead of just talking shit, he might have actually done something, but, truth be told, Jacov had never actually *killed* anything, besides maybe a spider or a fly. Even then, no matter how big, hairy and ugly, he didn't like to do it and more often than not just let the thing be.

On the other hand, and it was an awfully big fucking hand, there was something to the prospect of a major payday. He had the right. It was his time. And the bitch already lived long and well, better than he ever did. Besides, like the rabbi said, she was ill and he could do this. He could do the old lady, snatch her money and get away clean.

He eased the wooden gate shut and secured its tricky latch. There were no lights on in the back of the house as he made his way to it, quietly, like the rabbi told him to do. He reached for the doorknob, half expecting it to be locked, but it turned. His heart pounded so heavily he thought someone would hear, but Jacov cracked the door slowly and stepped in.

"Louis?" Rebecca called, startled.

Her bath time disrupted, Rebecca sat at the kitchen table just where she was supposed to be, wrapped in a clingy pink robe, her breasts fairly visible through the sheer material, hair bundled in a towel.

Jacov stood for a moment in the outer doorway, paralyzed with fear, neither in nor out.

"Louis, that you?" Rebecca called again.

Jacov barely took a breath. Then, in one decidedly non-oafish move, he closed the door and stepped forward, crossed the small hallway from the door to the kitchen in two long, smooth steps and entered the brightly lit space. Rebecca, one hand on the adding machine, the other turning receipts, swung round to confront her soon-to-be-ex-husband for having the gall to show his face but found instead a hulking, unkempt Terrence Jacov. And he was moving toward her.

Rebecca screamed, dropped the receipts and stood up awkwardly, her leg catching the end of the table and nearly tripping her. She'd seen this man before but wasn't sure where. At any rate, she didn't have long to think about it. Jacov lunged at her, but Rebecca sprung from his path. The plan, thin though it was, called for a surprise attack with a small window of opportunity, but Jacov realized now that the window had closed and that his target was up and moving.

He nearly fell over the chair that Rebecca, fleeing, shoved in his way, but he pursued her. She shrieked again but moved surprisingly quick, skirting the kitchen island and reaching for the phone. Buster, closed in his room, heard the commotion and barked angrily, clawing at the door and throwing his big body against it, but Jacov had no time to wonder why that part of the plan – the part that said no dog would be home – was bungled, too.

Rebecca snatched the phone from the wall, but Jacov fell on her and pried it from her hand before she had a chance to dial. She let out an ear-splitting wail as he grabbed her from behind, but she fought him with feet, elbows and fists, the full strength of her being. With surprising fury and strength she stomped the top of his foot, fracturing small bones, tendons and ligaments, kicked back at his shins and elbowed him in the throat and gut. Jacov, forced now to cover up, tried to restrain her, but Rebecca reached back, knocked the glasses from his head and clawed at his face. She was winning.

Injured now and barely able to see, Jacov almost lost his grip, but with one strong hand held tight. He pried one of Rebecca's wrists behind as if to put her in cuffs, but with her free arm she reached across the island and grabbed a knife from the block. Jacov heard a metallic hiss as the knife pulled from the block and whipped it through the air toward his face.

But Jacov, younger, stronger and much heavier than she, held his edge. Clamping down tight on her left wrist he put his full weight into her right shoulder and drove Rebecca down hard. He slammed his fist into her forearm and the knife fell to the counter with a clang.

Now Jacov pulled Rebecca's other wrist behind her back and, holding both there with his left hand, covered her mouth with the right. He would have wrenched her neck in another moment, but that moment never came. She bit down hard on the fleshy part of his lower right palm and, for the second time in seconds, almost broke free.

But Jacov would not fail. Not again. Restraining the struggling woman bodily he reached for the black leather sheath at his belt and drew out his utility knife. Then, with the flick of a thumb, he exposed the sharp, strong blade and, just as surely and cleanly as if cutting a length of drywall, drew it across her throat.

Rebecca gasped, blood gushing from the wound, and fell to the floor with a groan. She thought of the family and friends she loved, her children and grandchild, how she'd never see them again. She was dying.

*****

Jacov fled the scene covered in blood, glasses askew, wheezing and stunned. He limped to the van and started it on the first turn. He was a mile away when he realized he didn't even grab the cash.

<u>Chapter 28</u>

Things had gone wrong, terribly wrong. But now, flying through the wet streets of Apple Hill, he didn't know what to do. Wasn't there a plan? *What* was the fucking *plan?*

He mopped his face, neck and arms with a rag from the floor of his van. Like chocolate melted and taken from the heat, the blood on his skin set fast and cakey and he had to rub hard to remove it. Bits of sawdust from the folds of the cloth clung to his skin, in the sticky, sparse weave of his hair and in the corners of his eyes. Panicked, he did what they agreed he couldn't do, wouldn't do, no matter what. He called Rabbi Abrams.

And Louis, reading the incoming number on the screen of his cell phone, nearly crapped his pants. As calmly as he could, he excused himself from the Tuesday night rap session, stepped from the room and took the call.

"Don't say a word," he instructed Jacov.

It was a stupid thing to say and he knew it. It was, after all, a phone call.

"It's all fucked up," Jacov cried, slamming his hand on his forehead in punishment for what he'd done. "It's all fucked up!"

"Terrence. I don't know what you mean, but I want you to calm down. Have yourself a drink, get something to eat and I'll stop by later to talk."

"No," Jacov said, and Louis could tell he was sobbing. "It's all fucked up and I shouldn't have done it. I shouldn't have done it!"

Louis had assumed Jacov was home but realized now he wasn't. As they spoke a dirty white box truck braked without warning ahead of Jacov and he braked hard to avoid it. But the Chevy's worn old bias-ply tires didn't grip and his brakes locked up. His tires squealed on the wet asphalt as the van skidded sideways and slammed into the back of the truck.

"Terrence!" Louis called, stepping from the hall out into the night.

He called his name again, but Jacov, the senseless, hapless oaf, was gone.

Louis looked about and breathed deep, unsure what to do. He couldn't simply leave. The group was still meeting and, besides, his keys were inside. So he went back in and, just as casually and quietly as he could, told the group a version of the truth.

"I have to cut it short tonight," he said apologetically, knowing a breath later he should have muddled through. "Family emergency."

Now there were two things on his mind and Louis didn't know how to deal with either. Rebecca was dead, that much he was fairly certain, but so may be Jacov. If both were gone that might OK, but if one or the other lived there could be a problem.

A shrewder, more patient man would have sat tight till the end of the meeting, but Louis wasn't thinking shrewdly and he was rarely patient.

So now he was out, rumbling across town in the old sedan delivery, cherry red with chrome wheels and muffler tips, "Mom's Bakery" emblazoned on the side, anything but subtle.

Pulling up to the house, the first thing he noticed was how dark it was. Buster, who rarely ever barked, alternately howled and whimpered somewhere inside.

Louis reached the door and called tentatively for his wife. He assumed Rebecca was in the kitchen when Jacov arrived, but why, he wondered, was it completely dark? Panicked, Jacov evidently hit the lights on his way out.

Entering the kitchen now Louis didn't see much at first and aside from Buster there was nothing to hear. But he could smell. And the smell was so strong he could taste it.

In the few long, heart-thumping moments while his hand scrambled for the switch, a tangy metallic scent caught in his nose and he gagged. His stomach clenched and bile oozed in the pit of his gut.

Pulling a tissue from the wad in his suit jacket he put it to his face, found the light switch, and wished he hadn't.

The room, antique white with ice-white waist high wainscoting and chair rail, was as if finished in blood. Blood sprayed across one wall and up onto the ceiling in a horror movie arc. There was a thick, mucky puddle on the island countertop, bloody handprints that slid down the side, and a big dark pool coagulating on the floor.

Then Louis saw Rebecca and his stomach clenched again, this time with a force that expelled his coffee and cake. His poor innocent wife, so long the victim of infidelity, was now, ultimately and finally, a victim of violence.

"Rebecca?" he said, kneeling beside her and taking her hand.

Her eyes were open and clear and her breath gone, but a last vestige of air bubbled from the slash at her neck when he touched her.

"Rebecca… Rebecca!"

He held her hand, wrapped his arm around her and wailed softly.

"Oh, Gott im Himmel," he said, rocking his wife gently. "What have I done? What have I *done!*"

Louis cursed himself. He cursed Jacov. He sat and cried and cursed some more. Then he called the police.

"9-1-1 operator. What's your emergency?" a toneless voice responded.

"Please send someone," Louis beseeched.

"Sir… What's your emergency?"

"Send someone now!"

"Please calm down, sir. What is the nature of your emergency?"

"My wife's dead. She's been murdered. Please! Gott im Himmel! Send someone now!"

Louis went back to Rebecca and rocked her some more, alternately crying and wailing.

Had he expected death to look any different, really? Just how much "cleaner" would things have been if they'd gone according to plan? Was strangulation prettier? And just what the fuck went on here? While he couldn't answer these questions, one thing was certain: Jacov could, and did, do this.

In the few short moments before police arrived, banged on his door once and entered the house, guns drawn, Louis thought he might kill the bastard. Then he realized he ought to just kill himself.

"Apple Hill police!" the big sergeant shouted. "Don't move!"

Louis, who was nearly as bloody as his wife, looked up to see two cops staring at him behind huge black semiautomatics.

"Someone killed my wife," he said sotto voce, his voice so faint the officers could barely hear him.

Patrolman Tracy Brody and Sgt. Mick Nalepka could see that, but their immediate concern was him. Did Rebecca's killer sit before them? Did he pose a threat to them? And did they need to cuff him?

Gun still drawn, Brody reached down and felt Rebecca's wrist for a pulse. His eyes said she was gone as he called for the bus: lights, no siren. There was no rush.

Nalepka helped Louis to his feet and rested Rebecca on the floor.

"We see your wife is dead, Mr. Abrams," he said a moment later. "What we'd like to know is why. Can you help us with that?"

"Rabbi," Louis said, looking up.

"What's that?"

"I'm a rabbi. Rabbi Louis Abrams."

The cops exchanged a glance.

"OK then. *Rabbi* Abrams. Can you tell us why your wife is dead?"

"Someone killed her."

Nalepka removed his hat, scratched behind his ear and glanced about the room. He noticed the scattered register receipts on the table and floor, the green canvas lock bag stuffed with cash. In another room a big dog alternately whimpered and howled, scratching at a door.

Nalepka holstered his gun and, with a nod, instructed Brody to do the same.

"Yes sir," the sergeant continued. "We're trying to establish why someone would."

Louis had seen enough cop shows to know these guys would work quickly to secure the area, preserve evidence and attempt to solve the crime at the scene, possibly with a confession. But there was a big difference between having a penchant for police programs and being a suspect yourself, sitting there on the floor cradling your dead wife, her throat splayed open like a maw. Clearer thoughts would come later.

"What's that?" Louis said.

"Can you tell us why anyone would want to kill your wife?"

Louis seemed confused, disoriented, as the cops helped him to a seat at the table where they could better keep control.

"Major Crimes will be handling this, Rabbi," Nalepka continued. "What I'd like to be able to tell them, when they arrive, is why someone would want to kill your wife. Do you know of anyone who might have a reason to do this?"

"Of course not," Louis said.

"Did you have a reason to want her gone?"

Despite his guilt, the question hit Louis like a musket blast, or so he made it seem.

"What did you say?"

"It's just a question, sir," Brody said.

"Did you have a reason to want your wife gone?" Nalepka repeated.

"No! Of course, not!" Louis said, rising, but the cops motioned for him to sit.

"I am a *rabbi* for Christ sakes," he continued. "What is *wrong* with you?"

The cops exchanged another suspicious glance.

"Rabbi Abrams," Nalepka said patiently. "This is a murder investigation and there will be many more questions before it is through. Outbursts and confrontation will not make it go any smoother."

Louis looked at Rebecca and, once again, started to sob. But there were fewer tears now and he regained his composure more quickly.

"Listen, you," he said, wiping his eyes on his sleeve and blowing his nose on a napkin. "My wife is dead. Sure, we have our problems, everyone does, but I did not kill my wife."

Nalepka took a seat beside him at the table and set his hat on one knee.

"I didn't ask if you killed your wife, sir," he said. "All I asked was did you have a reason to want her gone."

"And I told you no."

Outside, the quiet tree-lined street was aglow in flashing red light. Four additional squad cars arrived within moments of Brody and Nalepka, two of which blocked traffic to that part of the street, and the arriving officers were mechanically efficient. They quickly established their perimeter and roped off the nascent crime scene with wide yellow police  tape.

Almost immediately, neighbors began pooling outside the tape, whispering among each other how they knew something was wrong but never expected this. That they didn't yet know what "this" was didn't seem to matter. The level of police activity coupled with a waiting ambulance from Kennedy didn't portend well.

"He's a cheater and a louse," Toni Sachs whispered to her husband, Alfred. "Always has been."

"Oh, you don't know that," Alfred responded. "You're just feeding the rumor mill."

"I know what I know. The latest is some shiksa radio broad. The whole synagogue's talking about it. This is him covering up."

"Talk is cheap," Alfred said. "For all we know she suffered a heart attack."

"All these cops? I don't think so. Besides, if it was a heart attack the guys in the ambulance would be doing something, not just standing around pulling their putz."

That she was right became evident when, moments later, police began probing the neighbors for info.

"I know this much – he's a cheater and a louse," Toni repeated to a handsome young patrolman fresh from the academy.

Just then an unmarked midnight blue Ford sedan rolled up, a flashing red strobe in the windshield the only visible sign it was a cop car. The Crown Vic stopped directly in front of the Abrams' house and Camden County Prosecutor Solomon P. Jeffries climbed out, escorted by three armed investigators from the Major Crimes Unit.

Jeffries, a casual acquaintance of the rabbi's and a worshipper at B'nai Tikvah, visited few actual crime scenes anymore. He'd usually dispatch an assistant prosecutor – one of the hot shot young attorneys in his office looking to build their case even before a suspect's arrest.

In what promised to be an explosive case – like the one in which a sixteen-year-old gangbanger fired two rounds through a Camden living room window, killing one little boy and paralyzing his brother – Jeffries sent his first assistant.

But, upon getting the call that Rebecca Abrams was dead, her throat slit in her own kitchen, instinct told the prosecutor that this case would be way beyond explosive. The fallout would be nuclear.

Jeffries, a former defense attorney, had been a natural predator inside the courtroom but he'd rarely gotten his hands dirty on the outside. His appointment to county prosecutor eight years before changed all that, exposing him to things he'd never expected, or wanted, to see.

In one case his first year a construction worker murdered his supervisor over a three-hundred dollar paycheck the victim had just cashed. Lying in wait, the worker bludgeoned his boss with a fourteen pound sledgehammer he used earlier that day to bust concrete. Then, in an attempt to hide the crime by dismembering the body, the suspect took a power drill with a paddle bit and gouged holes from the man's neck. Failing to behead him with the drill, he took a construction grade circular saw and cut the head clean off. Co-workers discovered the suspect covered in blood, saw still spinning, standing above the corpse.

Described in newspaper accounts as "the demo-site demon," Cooper Williams scribbled quietly at the defense table throughout his three-day trial, unperturbed by crime scene photos, admonitions by the judge to pay attention or the assistant prosecutor's portrayal of him as the devil himself. To everyone's relief, including, it seemed, Williams' own attorney, he was convicted and sentenced to life without parole.

Entering the Abrams' house now, Jeffries was bolstered by such experiences but still not prepared for what awaited. There was an inordinate amount of blood and the sight of it made him queasy. Deputy coroners had covered Rebecca's body and were loading it onto a collapsible stainless gurney when Jeffries reached the kitchen.

He glanced at Louis but huddled briefly with Sgt. Nalepka and the chief of county detectives before walking over. The C of Ds suspected Louis from the start.

"I'm so sorry, Lou," he said, extending his hand to greet him. "How you holding up?"

"Rebecca's dead," Louis said, as if that needed to be said.

"I know, Lou. What I'm concerned about, for now, is you. We need to get you out of here. Have you spoken to your boys yet?"

Louis shook his head.

"We really need to call them before they hear this on the news," Jeffries said.

"I haven't spoken to Jon in months," Louis admitted.

"I'm sorry," the prosecutor repeated, but it wasn't clear if he meant because Louis wasn't on speaking terms with his eldest son or because his wife was dead.

"Nothing will make it better for them, but this will be easier coming from you."

"You think this is going to be easy?"

"No, Louis," Jeffries said. "Just better than seeing it on TV."

Louis nodded, sniffed, and said he'd make the call.

"My investigators need to speak with you, but they can't do it here. Can you ride back with me to the office?"

"Do I have a choice?"

Jeffries took a seat at the table. Looking up, he told two investigators shooting the crime scene to give him and Louis a moment.

"Of course you have a choice. We're gonna get the son of a bitch who did this, but we need your help. We want to speak with you about why someone might have done this and who it might be."

As he contended with Brody and Nalepka, Louis said he hadn't a clue. But a moment later he offered one anyway.

"Rebecca brings a lot of money home some nights when she doesn't make a drop. I guess some of her bakery people knew that."

"That's the kind of stuff we need, Lou, but not here. It's not a healthy place for you to be right now."

In the next room Buster whimpered and clawed at the door. Jeffries, a dog lover who recently rescued a pit bull himself from the Camden City Animal Shelter, glanced in that direction.

"Your other boy's not going to take this well."

"No, he won't," Louis said, blowing his nose and wiping his eyes. "He's very attached to her. I need to let him out."

"Why don't you do that," Jeffries said. "Walk him around the yard, around the block, whatever. Can one of the neighbors watch him for a couple hours?"

"I don't know. Maybe Toni and Al next door. Can't I just leave him here?"

"No. The lab guys will be here half the night."

Louis got up to take the dog out and Buster, who hadn't seen him in more than a week, wet the floor in excitement. Louis put him in his harness and led him out back, but the dog froze at the sight and smell of so much blood. Though he hadn't seen the crime, Buster heard what went on, sensed it, and his agitation was palpable.

His fur rose in a ridge along his spine and he growled at the crime scene investigators tip-toeing gingerly around Rebecca's spilt blood.

Louis, who often just slipped a steel choke collar around the dog's neck to walk him, was glad now he opted for the harness and dragged him bodily to the door. Once outside the dog's agitation eased enough for Louis to lead him around the block. There, from his cell phone, he placed his call -- not to his boys but to Shelly Tannenbaum.

For most people, gaining entry to the office of the Camden County Prosecutor was a little like entering jail itself. A brick fortress in the middle of the "most dangerous city in America" -- a moniker Camden hadn't been able to shake three years running -- the building's exterior was monitored from every angle and there was but one entrance through which visitors came and went. Once inside, a small anteroom opposite a walk-through metal detector contained all visitors until they were buzzed through a second door and formally escorted in, usually by a man wearing a gun.

The experience was arresting enough for visiting media, but for suspects there on official business – an interrogation likely to end with an overnight stay – the arrival itself could be downright portentous.

As far as Louis was concerned, he was not a suspect. He was a presumed innocent and carried himself with dignity, bore the countenance of an aggrieved loved one and sat proudly in the anteroom waiting for his lawyer, even accepting a cup of coffee.

He would have insisted on waiting at home for Shelly and driven to Camden with him but the lawyer told Louis this was not the time to fight. Be amicable, accept the prosecutor's offer of a ride to his office and KEEP YOUR MOUTH SHUT. He'd be there as soon as he could.

It was after midnight when Shelly arrived, spoke briefly with his client, and sat down with Louis and the county prosecutor. Louis thought it a good thing that Shelly and Solomon Jeffries knew each other and got along well, but it wasn't long before the shine came off the apple.

Almost as soon as the pleasantries ended, a dour Lt. Gerald Nickerson entered the room, a huge cup of Dunkin' Donuts coffee in one hand and a file folder in the other.

Unlike the functional-but-soft, county-issue seating in the anteroom, the interview room had four heavy wooden chairs and a plain, no-nonsense gray desk. Nickerson pulled the last empty chair out and it skidded across the floor with a shriek. He got in front of the chair, dragged it back under him, and sat down heavily.

On the cusp of retiring, Nickerson was exhausted, not just from the long day he'd had but from thirty-four years of them. He knew in his heart that his career in law enforcement had done some good, but days like today always made him wonder how much. Sure, he'd helped catch and convict his share of bad guys. He'd brought piece of mind to families after loved ones were ripped away and discarded. It was that part of the job -- helping those families who died a good bit with their lost loved ones -- that kept Nickerson's sense of right and wrong, guilt and innocence, sharp as a pencil. But knowing that his moral compass was better than the system itself wasn't enough. No matter how many murderers, rapists, robbers and thieves he helped put away, there were always more, a fetid, festering stew about to boil over.

Nickerson looked across the table at Louis and considered the case before him, the brutal slaying of a fifty-seven-year-old mother and grandmother in her own kitchen. What sickened him most wasn't the death, the gore, the bloody mess at 3232 Applewood Terrace. No, what sickened him most was his private conviction that the tweedy jack-hole in front of him, this so-called holy man with the fancy Haddonfield lawyer, was behind it. And, just as sure as he sat there in that hard, unforgiving wooden chair, he *would* nail the fuck. For the time being, however, Nickerson let his boss do the heavy lifting, sat back and observed.

"Rabbi Abrams," Jeffries started, "I think you met Lt. Nickerson at your home tonight. Lieutenant, this is Shelly Tannenbaum, Rabbi Abrams' attorney."

Observing the file Nickerson laid upon the table Louis assumed at first that it was for another case. But the file, replete with digital crime scene photos, preliminary statements from neighbors, police observations and initial reports, had one purpose and one purpose only -- to catch Rebecca's killer.

Her name and date of death were scrawled with a red Sharpie on a white label that Nickerson crimped on the tab of the folder, a simple file that would come to contain the crux of the case.

"I needed to speak with you right away, Rabbi, because spouses of murder victims almost always provide the most crucial information in helping us close the case, but we need it at the outset," Jeffries continued.

Louis couldn't help notice that the prosecutor's informal use of "Lou" earlier in the evening had died on the ride over from Apple Hill.

"Whatever I can do," Louis offered, overeager to help.

His response drew a frown and a showing of hands from Shelly who non-verbally told him to slow the fuck down.

"Of course he will," Shelly continued. "But what I need to know, Sol, is why tonight, right now. Rabbi Abrams lost his wife tonight. Doesn't he deserve a little time to grieve?"

It was nearly one in the morning, but the prosecutor's pin-striped trousers bore a crisp, fresh-from-the-cleaners pleat, his white button-down shirt was immaculate and his striped ocher tie pulled all the way up. Jeffries' non-verbals were clear too: he was here to work no matter what time it was.

"They're separated, Shel. But of course. And I appreciate both of you taking the time to come down."

More non-verbals. We're talking. Tonight. Like it, don't like it, I don't really give a shit.

"Rabbi," the prosecutor continued, "I don't recall if I said so at your house, but I'm terribly sorry for your loss. Rebecca was a fine person. That said, and Shelly's handled enough murder defendants to know this, we must start our investigation *immediately*, lest the trail grow cold. I'm sure you can appreciate that."

"What, I'm a *defendant* now?" Louis said defensively.

"Take it easy, Lou," Shelly interjected. "We're just talking."

"Shelly's right, Rabbi," Jeffries said. "Poor choice of words. My apologies. My point is only that your attorney has been around this block once or twice and knows how we work here. We're friggin vampires when we need to be."

He motioned toward Nickerson and his vat of steaming coffee.

"Exhibit A, if you will. He'd take that stuff intravenously if the union would let him."

The joke had a calming effect on the room and it enabled Jeffries to redirect, as it were.

"Rabbi, I'm going to be frank with you, but I need you to just listen for a moment. You have not been read your rights and no one's trying to jam you up here. Everything we do is out in the open and our only motive -- one I'm sure we share with you -- is catching Rebecca's killer. We good so far?"

"Yeah, fine," Louis said.

"Good. Now, as I started to say, we have no choice but to start right away. We could have interviewed you at the house, but considering what went on there this evening that would have been inappropriate, not to mention in the way."

Jeffries paused a moment, looked across at Louis, then continued.

"Our initial investigation has raised some questions that you should be able to help us clear up. I'm going to keep it as brief as possible so you can turn to more pressing matters with your family."

Louis and Shelly remained silent but watchful.

"Now, Rabbi, we understand that you are in fact separated from your wife. Is that not the case?"

"I don't understand what…"

"Yes," Shelly answered for his client.

"Thank you. Now, it was past nine when you showed up at your wife's home tonight. Considering the separation, why were you there?"

Louis looked at Shelly, who nodded his OK to answer. This they anticipated.

"I was stopping by to get a few things… It's still my house."

"I see," Jeffries said, jotting in his yellow legal pad before pressing on.

"Our men spoke to some of your neighbors outside the house, one of whom, Antoinette Sachs, said she hasn't seen you there in weeks."

"Yeah, Toni Sachs. She lives next door."

"Got it. But regarding Mrs. Sachs, she wondered why tonight, especially at such an odd hour?"

"Who says it's odd?" Louis answered. "As I stated, I needed a few things, and again, it's still my house. I had my Tuesday night rap session tonight and after it ended I decided to stop by."

"Rap session?"

"Yeah. It's a couples group basically. We talk issues. And it's 'Ms.'"

"What's that?" the prosecutor said.

"Toni. She goes by 'Ms.' The whole seventies thing."

Stomach acid churning in his gut, the prosecutor was in no mood to be corrected. His crisp suit and calm demeanor belied an exhaustion borne of sixteen-hour days that of late had become routine but he popped two Tums and soldiered on.

"Ah, the seventies," he said with a forced grin. "I'd like to say I remember them well, but hell, you boys were all there, you know what went on."

For a moment, the room was nearly soundless, the quiet broken only by the scratch of notetaking by the opposing attorneys and Jeffries' chief investigator.

"Now, you *are* separated, you and Rebecca. Did she expect you tonight?"

"Sol. They're separated," Shelly said. "I think we've established that. And Rabbi Abrams, as he has stated, was just stopping by."

"Right. You seeing anyone, Rabbi?"

"I date."

"But no one steady?"

It was another question he and Shelly anticipated, one that was sure to come up given the public personas of the people involved. Shelly nodded his OK to answer.

"I don't think I've 'gone steady' since high school, counselor, but yes, I'm seeing someone. That a problem?"

"Not for me, but I'm not married to you."

From the moment they sat down there was veiled hostility in the room but the mask was coming off. Jeffries paused another moment, then went on.

"I understand she's on the radio," he continued.

"That's right," Louis nearly boasted. "Janice Palumbo, from NPR."

That her show was not quite "NPR," a non-syndicated but popular local public radio program, went unchallenged.

Nickerson looked up in recognition. He still didn't say a word but took copious notes while a boxy old tape recorder turned on the table before him.

"And you and Janice are intimate?" Jeffries said.

"Again, I'm not in high school anymore. What's your point?"

Shelly's face went blank, but before he could admonish his client the Camden County Prosecutor did it for him.

"Rabbi Abrams," Jeffries said, placing his pencil down sharply and looking Louis in the eye. "I think you should understand a few things before we go any further. Number one, I'm not some twelve-year-old kid in for his bar mitzvah lesson, you *feel* me? Number two, your wife was murdered tonight, her throat sliced open like a fucking watermelon. There was no sign of forced entry, no evidence of a *robbery*, nothing pointing at anyone but you. You are a fifty-six-year-old man with a long and colorful history of philandering *and* you're fucking a glamourous younger woman almost half your dead wife's age."

The prosecutor retrieved the pencil and thumped its eraser on the desk to emphasize his points.

"Are we going to find a major life insurance policy on Rebecca? Are we going to find a connection between you and whoever did this? *These* are the things you ought to be thinking about and not some innocuous inquiry into whether you're banging some Philadelphia disc jockey."

"She's not a disc jockey," Louis corrected indignantly. "She's a radio personality. And I'm fifty-seven."

For Shelly, the time for chitchat was over.

"You charging him?" he asked the prosecutor.

"Not right now."

"Let's go, Lou," Shelly said, standing. "Meeting adjourned."

It was the biggest story of the year -- perhaps any year -- and Bob Jackson just got beat on it in his own backyard. But it wasn't just Bob who got beat. The entire staff of the *Carrier News* stood around in shock, mumbling about the lead story in the morning Inky.

In a darkened office just off the newsroom, executive editor Eric Frost sighed audibly. He rubbed a palm over neatly trimmed chin whiskers but said nothing, just stared at the one-word headline on page 1A of the competition:

SLAUGHTERED!

Eric's office was often darkened, but this morning, a cadre of subordinates silent around him, the mood inside was as bleak as the story. No one said a word out of fear his wrath be wakened and directed at them. Even chatty-Cathy features editor Oliver Detweiler, who followed Eric to three papers and whom many on staff suspected as his longtime lover, was stoic as a statue.

Eric, tall and ghoulish, his humped back more pronounced than usual, stooped above his antique walnut desk as he studied the story in silence. With every word it just got worse and he knew, in the minds of his corporate masters, that his nascent stewardship of their paper would be coming into question.

Given the state of newspapers, a medium he'd loved since before he had his first paper route, Frost figured the dark days would someday come, but he'd pleased the suits in the beginning. One of his first acts as executive editor was to slash three positions from the news staff: the librarian (a fifty-six-year-old widow who had been with the paper twenty-four years), an assistant metro editor, and the late-night cops reporter.

But now, beaten badly in his own backyard, the turkeys came home to roost.

This morning, as he scanned the headlines over sissy-sweet coffee, Frost felt ill. The lead story in the *Inquirer* was one he should have had.

SLAUGHTERED!

*Wife of Prominent Apple Hill Rabbi Slain at Home; Throat Slashed*

*Rabbi Louis Abrams Questioned by Police*

The *Carrier*'s lead story? Team coverage of the *American Idol* finale on TV.

"It's the essence of 'real news, real people,' " Frost heard himself telling the small group of sycophantic junior editors huddled around a table during Tuesday afternoon's news meeting.

The concept of "real news, real people" was the latest dream scheme of parent company Danette to attract and keep readers – a losing proposition for nearly every paper in the country. Boiled down, it made sense on paper: fewer stories about local politicians and bureaucrats and more about Joe Six-Pack. But Frost, a rudderless company man if ever there was one, misinterpreted it to mean filling his pages with more crappy fluff.

So, while half his staff was out covering the outcome of a television program, something anyone interested in would have simply tuned in to, the competition was out covering real news (with real people!) in the *Carrier*'s hometown.

The *Inquirer* reporter who broke the story, Erika Brenneman, had been a *Carrier News* staffer under Frost's predecessor, Grover "Flip" Houseman, a blond-haired golden boy who came up through the Associated Press and ran the paper like an AP news bureau. He encouraged his reporters to take chances, to "make news and break news," and under his tutelage the paper shined.

Covering Apple Hill schools and government, Erika broke stories about hate crimes and neo-Nazism in the largely Jewish community. Producing piece after hard-hitting piece about local corruption, she cast fear into the hearts of township council, the school board, even the longtime mayor, a slick political operator whose penchant for deep and meaningful ass-kissing led to a position with the governor's office.

Brenneman left the *Carrier* for a job with the *Inquirer* within months of Flip's return to the AP. Though she had claimed to be happy enough at the Carrier, her first real job out of college, Erika seethed over her forced pairing with Vanessa LeConti, an editor virtually no one on staff could work with. Nessa, as she called herself, was a toxic, pear-shaped Texan whose journalistic skills were about on par with her interpersonal ones. She was prone to weeping and once openly berated Erika for the way in which she pursued a story. The crime? Erika went behind an elementary school to observe, for herself, swastikas and obscenities scrawled on a cafeteria wall. Her hands-on reporting led to an award-winning piece.

"I was just trying to get the story," Erika told Nessa at the time.

"That is not the way we do things at Danette," Nessa cautioned. "We do not sneak around, prying where we're not supposed to be. We have a little something called an ethics code. Have you *read* the code?"

Erika had, in fact, read the code, but believed chasing stories, even if that meant going places where the authorities did not want you to be, was the essence of journalism. And if hands-on reporting wasn't in the "Danette ethics code" that didn't mean shit. But she'd already had one brush with the bitch that week and wasn't in the mood for another.

"Whatever," she mumbled.

"Don't 'whatever' me, missy!" Nessa hissed. "I am *talking* about our code!"

Walking through the newsroom, Flip overheard the conversation and shut it down quick.

"Give it a break, Nessa," he said. "And nice job, Erika. Keep it up."

Despite Frost's decision to cut the late-night police reporter position, the *Carrier* still should have had the Abrams story.

Like many papers around the country, Apple Hill's *Carrier News* and the *Philadelphia Inquirer* both paid for a police scanning service that notified subscribers via pager when police or fire activity broke. The *Carrier's* pagers carried the exact same info the *Inquirer's* did, but when they started buzzing around ten-thirty the night of Rebecca's murder, there were no *Carrier* reporters on duty to hear them.

The first message, which came across as a domestic call to 3232 Applewood Terrace, was quickly upgraded to possible homicide. By the time the pager announced "coroner en route" Inquirer police reporter Erika Brenneman, working the six p.m. to two a.m. shift, was already on scene. Across town her *Carrier* counterpart, Bob Jackson, didn't even have his pager with him while his ass polished a high-backed wooden bar stool. As virtually every available cop in town raced to Applewood Terrace, Jackson sucked down his fourth pint of Guinness and a big plate of extra spicy hot wings. Even a breaking story on the eleven o'clock news playing in the bar two towns over didn't pique his attention.

"… And the big story tonight -- police activity on the 300 block of Applewood Terrace in Apple Hill, N.J.," iconic *Action News* anchor Jim Carver reported. "Our Dave Cuevar has more."

Normally attuned to Apple Hill news when it was covered on TV, Jackson hardly even heard it. After all, his shift was over and his commitment to daily journalism was met -- he filed a piece on local reaction to the *American Idol* winner -– so he paid his bar tab and headed home.

* * * * *

"What time is Jackson in?" Frost growled to his subordinates once he'd found the breath to speak.

"Usually by eleven," city editor Barry Rosenfield said.

Frost checked his watch. It was ten-forty.

"When he stumbles in, grab him!"

Rosenfield, another AP transplant and a leftover from the Flip Houseman era, was as hard news as they come. But it didn't take Edward R. Murrow to know the murdered rabbi's wife story was The Big One, a journalist's dream.

"We need everyone we can spare," Rosenfield told his boss. "Jackson's a good reporter but this is too big for him alone. Let him cover the police angle but get Touhy to drop whatever he's doing for neighborhood reax and have Laughlin handle reaction in the Jewish community."

He glanced at the *Inquirer* on his editor's desk and wondered if the man even heard him. Rosenfield considered mentioning that he'd argued against cutting the late-night cops reporter *and* against throwing so much manpower at the *American Idol* finale. But considering the lightning quick interactions on which careers rise or fall, this was hardly an I-told-you-so moment.

So Barry just stood there, waiting for his editor's response.

"That it?" Frost snarled.

By now the rest of the editors had slithered out the door leaving the two of them alone. Rosenfield reviled the corporate suck-up, but considering the morning news, a little placation couldn't hurt.

"They may have gotten the jump on us, chief, but come tomorrow we *will* own this story."

Frost looked up from beneath Dollar General reading glasses. A decent reporter himself once, he remembered the thrill of chasing a big story, the sense of heading out the door, pen and pad in hand, a rush so strong it made him giddy as he headed to the scene. But the feeling was vestigial, practically at odds with the never-ending stream of Danette corporate directives he'd come to embrace as journalism these past twenty years.

"Yeah," he grumbled, quietly determined to place blame anywhere but on himself. "And send me Jackson the moment he shows his face. I want his head on a plate."

<u>Chapter 29</u>

On Thursday the front page of the *Carrier News* carried everything Rosenfield promised. Its main bar was a nuts-and-bolts police story telling readers about the murder, and sidebars offered reaction to it in the neighborhood and Jewish communities. There was even a business story that explored how Rebecca Abrams created a multi-million-dollar baking business from scratch and contemplated its future without her.

In short, the *Carrier*'s coverage was must-see -- for anyone who didn't watch TV, listen to the radio, read the *Inquirer* or talk to friends, family, neighbors or strangers.

The thing of it was, by Thursday morning most South Jerseyans with even a weak pulse had done one or more of the above so the *Carrier*'s coverage did nothing to move the story forward. The nuts-and-bolts it provided were, by this time, rusty, and the full package taken together just one more reason people don't read newspapers anymore.

By contrast, the *Inquirer*'s coverage brought some newness to the morning news. Sure, it recapped what ran

Wednesday, but it pummeled the *Carrier*'s pedestrian reporting, a series of stories supervised by Frost himself.

Working overtime, Brenneman returned to the Abrams' block after filing her Day 1 story and learned that more than one neighbor saw a broken-down beater van in front of the house at the time of Rebecca's murder. Curious, she thought.

Then she learned through simple conversation with police sources – "So, what else went on last night?" – that a similar broken-down, piece-of-shit rust bucket van was involved in a nasty crash shortly after the murder.

Curiouser still.

"What, you think there's a connection?" she asked Sgt. Nalepka over Krispy Kremes at the stationhouse.

In addition to being a smart, streetwise reporter, Erika was a bit of a hottie -- blonde, twenty-six, cute little bod. She was a Columbia J-School grad who answered the phone like a rising star -- "*This* is Erika" -- a tone that gave callers the impression she was giving of her valuable time, so don't waste it. On the other hand, her attitude conveyed the sense that since they were speaking with her, the conversation must be important and that made them important, too.

She had a flirty, intuitive interview style and spoke with a slight lisp that sounded kinda sexy -- Cindy Brady all grown up. She also possessed an indefinable libidinous quality that was lost on neither the cops she cozied up with for information nor the insecure, less attractive female bosses she answered to. Case in point: Nessa, that shapeless, poisonous mass of moody.

Nalepka eyed the young reporter cautiously before offering his thoughts on the crash-killing connection.

"We're off the record, right?" he said.

"Off the *charts*," Erika conspired, polishing off one of the Krispy Kremes she brought like she meant it.

Nalepka liked the girl. She had sauce. So he rose from behind his desk, adjusted the bulky police belt half-buried by his gut, and gave her the lead of a lifetime.

"May-be."

"Meaning what?"

"Meaning, if I were an enterprising young reporter, I'd find the owner of that junker work van that crashed last night on Route 70 and see if maybe he knows the good rabbi."

Nalepka stepped away from his desk, returned with a file and set it down, open, atop the assorted paper, pens and miscellanea covering his workspace. He then walked away ostensibly for more coffee and left, for Erika to view, the unfinished police report on the previous night's crash.

Sensing another big scoop, Erika scribbled as fast and nonchalantly as she could, her heart fluttering like the wings of a hummingbird, as she collected information on drivers involved, vehicle types, summonses issued, etc. She closed the file, whispered thanks across the room to Nalepka and threw him a wink as she headed out the door.

As every reporter in South Jersey knows, victims of serious motor vehicle crashes generally go to Cooper, a university hospital in Camden with a Level 1 trauma center. But Erika, on a hunch, drove straight to Apple Hill's Kennedy Hospital, assuming because of its proximity to Jacov's crash that that is where they took him. And there she hit pay dirt. Alone in room 304, bed B, a broken and bruised Terrence Jacov was flipping through the afternoon dreck on TV.

"Mr. Jacov?" Erika said meekly, offering a tentative hand as she inched up to his bed.

Jacov rolled his head toward the young woman and muted the TV. Then, with his left hand because it was not hooked to an IV, he reached up and took hers.

"Excuse me if I don't get up," he mumbled through clenched teeth, but that's not what she heard.

"Excooth ee ih eye oh eh uh," is what came out. "Do you know me? (Ooh u oh ee?)"

"Not really," Erika answered honestly. "I'm kind of a friend of a friend. I thought maybe you'd like some company."

At this point Jacov would have welcomed the cleaning lady. A morphine drip still had him kinda groggy, but he was coherent enough -- as much as he needed to be for Maury or Springer. He'd had no visitors since his admittance late Tuesday night, but a nurse called his mother to tell her about the crash.

Now, despite his injuries, he leered at his visitor carnivorously. He pushed his heavy framed eyeglasses up the greasy slope of his nose and cupped a hand in front of his mouth to check his breath. He hadn't brushed since Tuesday.

"Have a seat," Jacov tried to say, motioning toward a low green leatherette chair.

Erika pulled the chair close, still not sure what she'd say. She really had no idea who she was dealing with, what connection, if any, he had to Mrs. Abrams' murder, no inclination she was within choking distance of a recent killer.

"Terrence Jacov (terrenth day-co)," he said, offering his hand again.

"Erika Brenneman," she said, accepting it again.

She didn't identify herself as a reporter and Jacov didn't ask; she would be ethical another time.

Erika's biggest fear starting out in the news business was that she wouldn't have the proper questions when the time came. Early on she thought of movie-of-the-week courthouse scenes, pushy reporters jamming microphones in defendants' faces, and how the journalists always had questions. Questions, questions, questions. And she never thought she would.

But now, five years into it, Erika realized that coming up with questions was as simple as having a conversation -- so long as one was prepared. And her preparation for this interview included calling B'nai Tikvah and speaking with the junior rabbi, Jeremy Miller, who confirmed that a member of his congregation was hurt in a car crash Tuesday night and who thought it nice that Erika Brenneman, a busy *Philadelphia Inquirer* reporter, would even take the time to ask. He told her right off he could not say anything about the Abrams case and that, Erika assured him, was fine.

"Tho, whooth or fend?" Jacov queried.

"Rabbi Miller," Erika answered but Jacov just shook his head.

"Jeremy Miller," she prompted. "The junior rabbi at B'nai Tikvah?"

"Doan know im."

"You sure? He said you help make the minion some nights when they're short a man."

Jacov thought on this a moment.

"Oh yeah," he mumbled dumbly. "Wabbi Miwwer. Goo guy."

Jacov still had not released her hand, but she let it linger a few moments longer. There was a bathroom down the hall where she could wash when she was done.

"He likes you, too. Anyhow, he heard about the accident and thought you could probably use some company. I think he said he'd stop by later."

"Coo," Jacov said, grinning at her as best he could, a letch despite his condition.

Erika glanced up at the muted TV where a large bald guy on the Springer show eased an enormous, toothless, half-clad woman back into a chair, her loose breasts nearly falling from her dress.

"So, you help make the minion," Erika continued. "That's nice. How often does he call you?"

"Wabbi Miwwer? He don't. Wabbi *Abams. He oothuay callth.*"

"Rabbi Abrams? I don't think I know him."

Jacov's mind felt sluggish and numb, his head a big, lolling block. But he was glad for the company. He'd chitchat a bit and then fall back asleep.

"Chief wabbi. I do thtuff 'round the thul for im."

"Oh yeah? Like what?"

Jacov tried to force his eyelids up, but they were heavy. Between the morphine drip and the accident, he'd forgotten about what immediately preceded it and was just glad an attractive young woman was interested in his well-being.

"Oh, ooo know. All kindtha thtuff."

Erika had enough of a confirmation that Jacov knew Abrams but sat a moment longer. She wondered how she might couch a direct question about his involvement in the murder, at least about why his van was at the Abrams' house the night before. She glanced at the TV again and smiled. Pure, unadulterated, white-trash bullshit. God Bless America. She felt like fucking singing.

Then Jacov's grip loosened and she heard him snore. She stood, pushed his hand back inside the chromed metal guardrail and headed for the ladies' room.

Racing to her car, Erika rewound her Olympus Pearlcorder to make sure she clearly caught Jacov on tape, then dictated her lead into the machine. By the time she arrived at the newsroom her story was half written and, just as she'd hoped, there was space set aside for it on 1A.

*Police Probe Crash Link to Rabbi's Wife's Murder*
by
Erika Brenneman

APPLE HILL, N.J. -- Police are investigating a possible link between the murder of Rebecca Abrams, a successful businesswoman and spouse to a leading South Jersey rabbi, and a motor vehicle accident moments after the slaying, sources told the *Inquirer* Wednesday.

Abrams, whose throat was slit during a violent struggle in her home Tuesday night, was the founder and proprietor of Mom's Bakeshop, a popular confectionery with stores in Voorhees, Apple Hill and Philadelphia. She was the estranged wife of Rabbi Louis Abrams, chief rabbi of Congregation B'nai Tikvah in Apple Hill.

Still-stunned residents in the Abrams' Tony Orchard View neighborhood said Wednesday they noticed a beat-up work van in front of the Abrams home moments before the slaying and, looking back, found it suspicious.

"There are workers in this neighborhood all the time but for it to be there on a dreary Tuesday night, that was a little odd," resident Dina Versacchio said.

Versacchio said county detectives questioned residents about the van on Wednesday but did not acknowledge a suspected link to the murder.

Speaking on condition of anonymity, police sources confirmed that the van seen in front of the Abrams house before the murder was, in fact, the same van that crashed on Route 70 a short time later.

The van's owner, Terrence Jacov of Apple Hill, was driving the van when it struck a delivery truck just after 9 p.m., police sources confirmed.

Not only is the van the same, but Jacov is a personal acquaintance of the rabbi, worships with him, and does odd jobs for him, Jacov said Wednesday.

Jacov, 48, of Apple Hill, said from his hospital bed that Abrams often calls him to help make a minion, a quorum of 10 needed for daily services, as well as for odd jobs around the synagogue.

"I do all kinds of stuff," Jacov said.

He did not comment on the type of work he does for Abrams, but a Yellow Pages ad for his business, Jacov Home Repair in Apple Hill, lists a variety of handyman services, from drywall to plumbing.

Abrams, through his attorney, declined comment.

Camden County Prosecutor Solomon P. Jeffries, questioned about whether Jacov's van was, in fact, the one seen parked in front of the Abrams' home moments before the slaying, also declined comment. He further declined to say whether authorities have interviewed Jacov, if he's considered a suspect, or about his relationship with the rabbi.

"This remains an on-going criminal investigation," Jeffries said. "As in all criminal investigations, my office is following every lead but will not discuss the progress of the investigation until its conclusion."

# Chapter 30

Slowly it came back to him. On impact Jacov went flying, tossed about like a pull-tab in a crumpled can of Coke. The front right corner of his van caved in and before the vehicle came to rest on its side at the curb the air inside was a dangerous swirl of broken glass and construction tools.

A heavy red steel box full of hammers, screw drivers and other gear went aloft and struck him in the face and collarbone. Paramedics pulled Jacov from the wreckage bloody, broken and barely breathing.

Now, two days later, he felt like the loser in a bull fight. His right wrist had an IV drip, his left a shiny metal bracelet by which he was fastened to the bed, and Dr. Arnav Mitra was checking his vitals when Jacov came around.

"Ah, Meester Jacov, nice to see you back among the living," the doctor said.

Jacov wanted to speak but couldn't. He jaw was evidently wired shut. Breathing was labored and painful from three cracked ribs and a fresh white dressing covered the stitches in his face. His right ankle and shin were sheathed in plaster and held together by a network of titanium pins and screws.

Casting his eyes about the room Jacov saw that medical personnel weren't the only ones attending him. There in the corner, on the same green leatherette chair that Erika Brenneman so nicely graced a day before, sat the chief of detectives for the Camden County Major Crimes Unit.

Lt. Gerald Nickerson munched the last of an egg white omelette on a sesame bagel and washed it down with cold chai tea. He held a wide yellow legal pad on which he was scribbling thoughts and observations.

"Hello, Mr. Jacov," Nickerson said after Mitra left the room. "I'm Gerry Nickerson with the Camden County Prosecutor's Office."

He gave Jacov a moment for the introduction to sink in.

"I know you can't speak just yet, but I want to fill you in on what we've got. Do you recall much of what happened Tuesday night?"

Jacov didn't so much as nod. He throbbed all over, from his rattled head to his fractured foot, and two days of morphine muddled his thoughts. He knew there had been an accident but still couldn't remember it or the preceding couple of hours.

As the detective sat grinning beneath a big, droopy mustache, Jacov slowly recalled the events leading up to the crash -- the rabbi's proposition on the hill, plans to snuff Mrs. Abrams, his apprehension that, despite the promise of a major windfall, he shouldn't get involved.

"I don't mean to upset you, but based on that cuff on your wrist and this old cop sitting here, you've no doubt drawn some conclusions of your own. You're in a lot of trouble, Mr. Jacov."

Jacov felt claustrophobic as he pulled at the manacle fastening him to the bed. He yanked at it and the clang of metal on metal echoed off the hard, institutional flooring and out into the hall. Try as he might he couldn't open his mouth fully and that heightened his sense of claustrophobia. Moving his leg or shifting his position in bed caused tremendous pain in his rib cage so he just lay there, a salty, viscous tear pooling in one eye and dribbling down his cheek. With both hands immobilized he couldn't even wipe it.

"Strange as it may seem, the crash almost saved you," Nickerson continued, casually scribbling on his pad. "You were so covered in your own blood that we might not have looked for Mrs. Abrams'. If it hadn't been for that beat up, broken down shit wagon of yours being parked as it was in front of her house when you slit her throat, nobody would have known. Then again, you also seem to be quite the blabbermouth with women of the Fourth Estate. Which brings up a fine point. What the *hell* were you thinking?"

Jacov remembered the plan more fully now and looked away, the whole murderous memory flooding his thoughts. He thought he'd spoken with an attractive visitor but now wasn't even sure about that. He did remember chairs flying on TV.

A nurse popped in and Nickerson turned amiable, still scribbling but nodding cordially, the good-natured uncle come to visit. She left and he went on.

"So, you crashed the shit wagon, the same broken down van that was parked outside the home of an upstanding citizen at the time of her vicious, bloody murder."

Nickerson leaned close and turned his voice low.

"Now, I'm no fucking *genius*, Mr. Jacov, but it wouldn't *take* no fucking genius to figure this one out. We tested your knife and you know what? That utility knife from your belt, the one you use to cut sheetrock and wire and God knows what else? It was caked with the blood of Mrs. Rebecca Abrams. Yessir. The blood on the blade, in the corrugated grips of the handle, in the little springy thing that lets you pop it out all slick and smooth? That was, in fact, her blood."

A bent old woman with an aluminum walker pushed by and Nickerson looked up, smiled, and gave her a "How do ya do?" Then he turned back, eyes focused, darkly serious.

"Are you *crying*, Mr. Jacov? Now, I know it ain't cause you're starting to feel all cathartic and what not from this little heart-to-heart. You're concerned. Well, you ought to be."

Some clarity returning, Jacov sensed the southern roots of his soft-spoken interrogator, a long-transplanted Virginian with a great love of Robert E. Lee, through mild inflections of his voice.

"You're crying from regret. From lives wasted, hers and your own, ain't that right? It's okay. Ah've seen it. But you know what, Mr. Jacov? Regret is a funny thing. Most often, like now, it's too little, too late."

Jacov pulled again at his restraint. Exasperated, he tugged at his right arm, the one attached to the IV drip, and the tall chrome stand it was suspended from nearly toppled over.

Surprisingly agile, Nickerson jumped to his feet, caught the stand on the fly, and righted it. He turned back toward his chair but then pivoted to the bed, rested his palms on the metal rail and spoke quietly within smelling distance of Jacov's foul breath.

"What I'd like to know is why. The rabbi – I know you know the rabbi, you do work for him, or so we're told, so I've *read* in the mornin' paper – he seemed to think whoever did this thing did it for money. A robbery. Problem with that theory, between you and me, is whoever did it didn't rob good Mrs. Abrams. Whoever did it left a big ole fat bag-a-money there on the kitchen table. A course, they could a done it for money, a robbery, let's say, and got all freaked out when things went awry. I don't know about you, Mr. Jacov, but the sight of all that blood freaks me out. I been doin' this job thirty-four years and it *still* freaks me the fuck out. Amazin' just how much blood comes out a human body when it's cut right. But I ain't tellin' you nothin.' You seen it. Hell, you was practically swimmin' in it."

Jacov, who had the presence of mind not to incriminate himself further by cooperating, even non-verbally, tried to turn away but couldn't. Between his busted ribs and shackled wrist, the best he could do was shut his eyes, lie there and listen.

"We'll want to talk some more but right now it feels a little one-sided," Nickerson concluded. "But you just get used to the feel of that drip, Mr. Jacov, 'cause it won't be your last. Your last will be your last, if ya know what ah mean, son."

Four days later Jacov was released, not to the comfort of his Apple Hill Towers apartment but to the rank, semi-sanitary medical ward of the Camden County Jail.

# Chapter 31

"No, I'm not gonna see you today."

"Why not?"

"You're kidding me, right? Your wife is dead five friggin' days and that Goddamned Jacov killed her."

"You don't know that."

"What's it, just a coincidence he was at your house moments before Rebecca was killed? That fucking deviant is your buddy, Louis, and he killed her."

"He's not my buddy. He just does work for me."

"Yeah, so I read."

"I read it, too," Louis said. "So, what. The fact that he was there, if he was there, is circumstantial, at best. It doesn't mean he did it and it's got nothing to do with me."

"Nothing to do with you? For Christ sakes, Louis, he's your goddamned handyman."

"Would you *mind* refraining from that expression?"

"Whatever. The *circumstances* are that this fucking Jacov was at your house Tuesday night and your wife was butchered. He slit her fucking throat! It's more than a little 'circumstantial'. And let me tell you something, Louis. There's nothing wrong with 'circumstantial.' Lots of people get convicted on circumstantial evidence. It's a little thing called The Law. They were there, they did it, *those* are the circumstances! And if he was there, they're going to prove it."

Louis felt like smashing down the receiver, breaking the fucking thing altogether. Instead he pulled the phone from his ear, rested it on his shoulder, glanced out the window and took a deep breath. Somehow, despite the shit storm his world had become, it was still a beautiful morning. Male cicadas wooing their mates chirped wildly, outdone only by the songbirds. An overnight storm washed the world anew and the smells of summer -- sweet cut grass, moist black earth, chlorinated pool water -- filled up his senses. But now, pulling into the lot, came an unmarked detective car from the Camden County Prosecutor's Office.

"Fuck," Louis said.

"Whatsa matter?"

"There's a guy from the prosecutor's office just pulled up. I gotta go."

"Louis?"

Janice wanted to ask him, flat out, if he had anything to do with Rebecca's murder, but she didn't want to know. She already did.

"Can I stop by later?"

"Maybe better just call."

As Louis hung up the phone he saw that it wasn't just one investigator who pulled into the lot but three -- Nickerson followed by two armed deputies in a patrol car from the Camden County Sheriff's Department.

He'd no sooner begun to dial Shelly when there was a brusque knock on the frosted glass of his office door. Warrant in hand, Nickerson did not wait to be invited in.

"Rabbi Abrams," he intruded, "we have a legal search order signed by Superior Court Judge Clement Browne in an on-going criminal investigation. This warrant covers your offices, your cars, your home and all your cellular communications."

Rejected by Janice, Louis moments earlier hoped to lose himself in the glorious early summer sun, a bong hit and a walk with the dog -- maybe even a ride down the Shore. He thought of Wildwood, all the young babes in thong bikinis, tattoos and piercings -- the best of which you couldn't even see -- and their jiggly little bottoms and tops. He yearned for not just the sights but the smells of the boardwalk – fresh, hot pizza from Macks, the air redolent of salt and sea, and the strong, male scent of tar wafting up from between the boards. Then he thought of the annoying yellow people mover, a caterpillar on wheels working its way north and south along the boards, picking up and discharging passengers -- swallowed up here and spat out there. The big ugly thing had been startling pedestrians for decades with its monotone mantra -- "watch the tramcar, please, watch the tramcar, please" -- and tourists, the only ones who seemed to ride it, both hated and loved the thing, a summer rite of passage no better or worse, really, than a mild case of sunburn. But the babes, the boards, even the big ugly yellow thing, would have to wait.

As the call rang through to his attorney, the two humorless deputies set stiff cardboard boxes on Louis's desk and, without asking, started piling stuff in. Beginning with the sparse desktop, they took Louis's leatherette writing pad with calendar, spiral-bound organizer, even family photographs of Rebecca, Jonathan, Seth and Buster.

"What do you need those for?" Louis protested, but he was ignored.

Shelly had just taken the phone with a "Yeah, Lou," when one of the eager young deputies found the bong.

"Oh, for Christ sakes," Louis said.

"What's going on?"

Louis turned away from the cops, cupping one hand over the receiver.

"Nickerson and his goons are here with a search warrant. They just found the bong."

"Jesus CHRIST, Lou!" Shelly said. "OK. Stay put. I'm coming down."

"That yours?" Nickerson asked, coming over.

"Well it ain't the Avon lady's."

Unlike his boss, Nickerson would not erupt over insolent remarks. An oldschool lawman, he generally just smiled at the offender and took whatever action he could.

"Rabbi Abrams," he said calmly, producing a shopworn set of Smith & Wesson handcuffs, "You are under arrest for possession of CDS. Place your hands behind your back sir."

"I'm on the phone with my attorney," Louis protested.

"Good, because you're going to need him. Now put your hands behind your back. I won't ask you again."

"Now you wait a damn second," Louis started, but Nickerson, with the same surprising agility with which he caught and righted the IV stand in Jacov's hospital room, grabbed the flat of Louis's right palm on the fly, turned it back and over, and threw him face down on his naked desktop. In the next moment, Louis was cuffed and on his way out to the patrol car.

"This is Lt. Gerald Nickerson," the investigator said into the dropped phone.

"Lieutenant, Shelly Tannenbaum. What the hell just happened there?"

"I've arrested your client, Mr. Tannenbaum."

"On what charges?"

"Possession of CDS and resisting arrest, for starters."

"Resisting arrest? I heard the whole thing. He did no such thing."

"Mr. Tannenbaum, I am not going to debate you on what took place here, what you did or did not hear. Rabbi Abrams is on his way to Camden where he will be processed and, mostly likely, arraigned. I suggest you join him there."

"Very professional," Shelly hissed. "This won't be the last of it."

"No, sir, I don't suppose it will," Nickerson said, unruffled, the courtly Southern gentleman he'd always been. And, just as calmly and courteously as he could, he hung up the phone and followed his men out.

* * * * *

Louis's arrest was a lesson in humility and that, he presumed, was the point. It started with that smug fuck Nickerson slapping the bracelets on him, "Hands behind your back, sir," and having his subordinates lead him out, cuffed, for the whole world to see.

But it went beyond humiliation. From the hands-behind-your-back thing to the silent escort by the deputies out to the waiting patrol car -- did it really take two? – the lot of it, Louis was sure, was about control.

As he passed, Louis's secretary dabbed at her nose with a shredded tissue and sobbed -- something she'd done a lot of the past few days. Tears rolled down Anita's cheeks, streaking old, papery skin so fine and delicate one could practically see through it.

"It's okay," Louis said. "Shelly's going to meet me in Camden. This is just a frustrated old cop trying to make a name for himself before retirement."

"Rabbi," Nickerson said a step behind, ignoring the slight. "It is not my good name you ought to be worried about. But now that we're chatting there is something I'd like to tell you."

"Yeah, what's that?"

"You have the right to remain silent."

"Whatever. Call Seth and let him know what's going on," he continued to Anita as if they were alone. "Tell him this is a joke. It's less than a joke. And tell him to call Shelly on his cell."

"... Anything you say can and will be used against you in a court of law. You have the right to be speak to an attorney, and to have an attorney present during any questioning. If you cannot afford a lawyer... "

"You'd better hope *you* can afford a lawyer, friend, because you're the one who's gonna need one."

"... one will be provided for you."

Nickerson, still a pace behind Louis and the deputies, jumped ahead to open the rear door of the squad car.

"Why would *I* need a lawyer?" he asked, pushing Louis's head down so it didn't bump the frame and give him something to sue over.

"You never know," Louis said. "You just might find yourself in a jam some day."

"That's funny coming from *you, friend*," Nickerson said. "Because your day has come."

Like many kids Louis grew up with, he'd done a number of things that might have landed him on the wrong side of the law before now. There was the pot, of course, numerous instances of drinking and driving (but he never hurt anyone and never got popped), and then there was the time, at seventeen, when he heaved a cinder block through the window of his high school's guardhouse on an especially drunken Friday night. Again, got away clean. But his closest call came on a borrowed motorcycle, speeding around Cooper River Park as an undergrad one morning when Louis suddenly approached a cop going the opposite way. Startled and knowing he was moving way too fast, Louis hit the brakes and fishtailed the bike in a plume of gray smoke, its tail swaying like a flag in a gale. The cop threw on his flashing reds and swung around after him but Louis regained control, took a few quick turns and dodged into a nearby neighborhood. Several blocks ahead he peeled up the hilly drive of some absent homeowner, killed the engine behind the house and jumped into the woods where he hid for the next forty minutes until three or four of Apple Hill's finest gave up the search.

But now, as Nickerson noted, his day had come. Louis squirmed uncomfortably in the backseat of the cruiser, hands still cuffed behind him, on the ten-minute ride to Camden. The so-called "Hooker Highway," a mile-long stretch of Admiral Wilson Boulevard that Gov. Whitman sanitized and papered over for the 2000 Republican Convention in Philly, passed without notice. The squad car flew past crack and whore houses, their doped-out denizens spilling off broken brick stoops into the once-cobbled streets of Camden. Though some improvements actually took hold these past ten years -- a first-rate aquarium, a minor-league ball field and an outdoor concert hall -- the ride to the Prosecutor's office carried Louis past none of them and he wouldn't have noticed if it had.

Once there he was led not through the secure vestibule that contained him the night of Rebecca's murder -- with its soft seats and complimentary coffee -- but through a solid steel door and into a hyper white holding area. Inside, uniformed and plain clothes cops buzzed about like bees. Off to the far end an inebriated, unshaven, middle-aged Latino snored upright on a bench, one hand cuffed to a rail. The man's boozy breath permeated the air around him, competing with his own body odor for the local stink title. Two gobs of spittle hung in strings from his mouth and Louis hoped vomit wouldn't soon follow because it was next to this man, on the same short bench, that he was sat.

"I want my lawyer," Louis said to no one in particular, one wrist cuffed to the rail with his neighbor.

"Hey! I want my lawyer!" he repeated, louder and more hostile.

Nickerson, who drove to Camden separately, entered the holding area just as Louis opened his mouth.

"Welcome," he said, ambling over. "Now, you're going to need to behave yourself son or you're gonna lose this luxury box seat. And, believe me when I say this, we put you back in that pen back there you'll think this was the fucking Hilton."

Fucking Hilton. Another time, another place, Louis might have found a joke in the remark but not here, not now. He accepted Nickerson's word that he could make things very bad, very fast, and acquiesced, piss and vinegar dissipating like air from a leathery old balloon.

"I just want my lawyer," Louis petitioned again, quieter and more sensibly.

"I understand," Nickerson said calmly, "and your lawyer is on his way. Now just you behave."

Five miles east, Shelly punched through the gears of his heavy silver Benz as he left Haddonfield for Camden.

Just minutes apart, there was no greater contrast between the haves and have-nots, the ever-rising rich and the permanent poor, that close in proximity, in all New Jersey, perhaps all of America.

In Haddonfield one didn't find big money, diamond-crusted-dog-bowl rich -- the Gates', the Rockefellers, even the Trumps -- but for South Jersey it was close. Here, contemporary brick fortresses and lavish, ten-bedroom Victorians insulated the well-heeled from even their neighbors with massive blue-green lawns and dense thickets of shrubs. Chest-high security fencing contained some of the properties and virtually all boasted state-of-the-art alarm systems.

But as in all places with a confluence of rich and poor, fencing and high technology couldn't keep all the low earners out. One saw few of Camden's blacks or Puerto Ricans shopping the town's jeweled boutiques, but scads of Mexican laborers tended the pools, the lawns, the landscaping and the roofs.

With Haddonfield but a glimmer in Shelly's rearview now he considered Louis's jailing and how he might get him out. That Nickerson was a sly one, no question about it. Surely, he hadn't gone to the synagogue looking for pot paraphernalia but finding it was a Godsend, no pun intended. And, Shelly figured, charging Louis with possession was but a provocation that found its mark. Had Louis said nothing, just kept his fucking mouth shut and resigned himself to cooperating, there'd be no bail to speak of, just a misdemeanor embarrassment and quick release. But now, held on the more serious charge of resisting, he faced an overnight stay in county if Shelly couldn't secure a quick hearing, something over which he had no control.

"What the *fuck* was he thinking?" he muttered, fingering his cell phone for messages and gulping lukewarm Wawa coffee. He flipped on KYW for word of his client's arrest but the AM news station didn't have it yet. For the briefest of moments, he considered calling the media to put his own spin on things but that was pointless too. The *Inquirer* all but put the knife in Louis's hand and the Carrier was still trying to play catch-up. Give that Jackson bastard a scoop and Shelly was sure he'd use it against him.

* * * * *

"Abrams!"

Louis nearly jumped off the bench, startled by a squat black deputy calling his name from an old brown clipboard.

Silvery bars midway between the woman's right elbow and wrist indicated rank of some sort, but Louis didn't know what they meant and, at this stage of the game, couldn't care less. His attention was fixed on the woman's small, square mouth, her even white teeth, and the enormous sound emanating from between them. He didn't have much time to think about her, or even respond, when the hole opened and roared again.

"Abrams!" she bellowed, a ridge of dark hairs above her lip twitching at having to call his name twice. Her small black eyes were capable of kindness but, Louis could see, not regarding him.

Despite his situation, he reeled at the woman's address without his proper title in the way most doctors do, even doctors of chiropractic (like his own son) or education (somehow the worst offenders of all).

And yet, he felt entitled. After all, to his way of thinking, he was in for possession of a pot pipe, no more. The charge notwithstanding, he didn't *really* resist arrest. It wasn't like he puffed up his chest and menaced a cop and he certainly didn't kick, punch or scream at one. He didn't threaten a cop, dig in his heels and refuse to go with a cop and he most definitely didn't spit on, curse out or otherwise abuse a cop. No, in his mind, the charge of resisting was more formality than reality and a judge would certainly see it that way, too. In fact, he believed, any sane, reasonable, *educated* person would see it that way even if some short-timer, good-ole-boy with a badge like Nickerson did not. This surety gave Louis some wiggle room and the will to remain cocky, an attribute that didn't exactly serve him well lately and surely would not now.

"It's *Rabbi* Abrams," he said, digging his shit hole a little bit deeper.

Deputy Sheriff Carmela Jones sniffed. She intuitively disliked the man – connected as he was to his wife's brutal slaying despite the penny ante charges they hauled him in on -- and his correcting her did not exactly hit her sweet spot.

"I don't care if you Grandma Moses," she retorted, leering at him, incredulous.

Louis didn't answer, but the silence between them was palpable. Cops, criminals, even the half-drunk bum on the bench beside him looked up as one, mouths closed, the storyline still unfolding.

"You really think you somepin' special, don't you?" Jones said, visibly revolted. "Well let me tell you somepin', big stuff. In here you ain't no priest, you ain't no mullah, and you *ain't* no rabbi, you feel me? In here, you just *Abrams*."

His neighbor on the bench pulled himself in tight as if to shield himself from what would come next, a blow of some sort or a rain of obscenities. He knew diminutive Deputy Sheriff Jones did not come looking for a fight but that she wouldn't turn from one, either.

"Now, I need to get your ass fingerprinted," she said. "What *you* need to do *Abrams*, is git your long, sorry ass up slowly, left hand behind you, and don't make me mace you 'cause I *will* fuck you up but good."

The deputy didn't wear her service weapon but attached to a wide leather belt was a medium length T-stick, a non-lethal tazer and a canister of professional grade pepper spray. Her hand now rested on that very can of spray.

Never one for actual, physical confrontation even if he wasn't so woefully outgunned, Louis stood as directed, left hand behind him, and Deputy Jones un-cuffed him from the rail. Without another word, she pulled back his right wrist, locked it tightly to his left and led him back for fingerprinting.

# Chapter 32

It was a hell of a day to come before Judge Clement Browne.

Scheduled for a three p.m. colonoscopy, Browne hadn't eaten since the night before. He was worried about what the test might find but he was also hungry, irritable and, by this time, fully purged. The Fleet Phospho-Soda cleansed his bowels like a water spout but tasted like a double dose of battery acid, roiling his insides and leaving a horrid, rusty feel in his mouth.

Most patients prepping for the snaky invasion would have stayed home and suffered in private, and Browne might have done the same had the doctor's office accommodated his request for an early morning procedure.

But it had not, and Browne wasn't most patients. Just forty-three, he was the youngest judge on the Superior Court bench of New Jersey and accustomed to doing, not thinking about doing. Months earlier he'd viewed with great interest a certain intrepid morning show host getting scoped live on TV, the whole world watching, after her husband died young of colon cancer.

Upon viewing the show, Browne decided to have the procedure as a precaution but accelerated his decision at the first sign of bright blood in the bowl. The doctor who would perform it, a petite, attractive, bohemian woman who shuffled about her office in flip-flops and peasant skirt, shifted some patients around to accommodate his request for the soonest possible appointment but could only squeeze him in for a late afternoon procedure.

So, Browne came in to work for a few hours.

He postponed testimony in a robbery trial scheduled that morning but ruled on a variety of preliminary hearings and arraignments, one of which brought Rabbi Louis Abrams before him.

"Good morning, Judge," Shelly began, Louis at his side behind a plain wooden defense table. "Sheldon Tannenbaum for Rabbi Abrams."

"Morning, Counselor," Browne replied.

Already familiar with the case -- it was he who'd signed the search order for Louis's home, office, cars and phones -- the judge was glancing through a sheaf of papers when defendant Abrams addressed him directly.

"If I may, your Honor," Louis started to say, and Shelly could have killed him himself. "It seems there's been a mistake. I didn't actually resist..."

"You may not!" Browne shot back, his hand gripping and slamming a stout wooden gavel.

"It's just that…"

"Silence!"

The judge's belly gurgled and he slammed the gavel again. The taste of Fleet Phospho-Soda rose in his throat and he spit onto a Kleenex.

"Mr. Tannenbaum. You will advise your client that in this courtroom I speak first, last and always, unless I say otherwise, is that clear?"

"It is, your Honor."

"Please also advise Rabbi Abrams that this is not a trial and that he has no right to address the court at this time. Is THAT clear?"

"Yes, your honor."

Shelly turned to Louis and whispered in his ear but his message, as if it needed to be said, was less legal translation and more shut the fuck up.

"Now," the judge continued. "For the sake of expediency I'm entering a plea of not guilty on both charges, unless you have a problem with that, so we can move on to the bail hearing."

"No, your honor. Thank you, your Honor," Shelly said quickly.

"On the lone count of possession of CDS, this is a misdemeanor offense in the state of New Jersey and no bail is required," the judge ruled matter-of-factly.

"Thank you, your honor," Shelly repeated.

"On the count of resisting arrest... bail is set at two-hundred thousand dollars cash, no ten percent."

Shelly was stunned.

"Your honor, my client is an upstanding member of the community," he interjected. "The defendant has no criminal record. He acknowledges possession of the pot pipe but offered no physical resistance during his arrest. His access to that kind of cash would be impossible at this juncture and I respectfully request you reconsider the ten percent option."

The judge removed gold-toned eyeglasses that looped in soft semi circles around his ears. He was prematurely gray and balding on top, features that somehow didn't age his lean, boyish face. Placing one of the loops from his glasses in his mouth he looked down upon Shelly and Louis, rested his chin upon his hand, and smiled benignly. Or maybe it was just gas.

"Yes, I understand he is quite the pillar of society," the judge continued. "That said, your request for ten percent is denied. Bail stands at two-hundred thousand dollars cash."

And, at the third slam of the gavel, a bailiff led Louis to jail.

<u>Chapter 33</u>

Louis steeled himself as best he could for that first night in custody, but there was really no way to prepare for it.

He expected the indignity and unpleasantness of a body strip/cavity search, but before things even came to that was nearly worn down by basic redundancies. There were metal detectors and pat-downs, security checks and interviews, locked doors and ever more clicking, bolting, slamming steel doors. The huge, teaming facility was a nonstop series of compartments, locked down, video monitored and rebar-reinforced.

To his relief, once inside the Camden County Jail the first impression made upon Louis wasn't that of the dreaded cavity search. Nor was it the labyrinth of compartments or feral stares from prisoners (though they chilled him to his core.)

No, what struck Louis the moment he entered the jail was the smell. For lack of a better word it smelled... almost... *clean*. If he tried it wouldn't be hard to train his nose to the stink of humanity, to forty plus years of pent-up rage and frustration, loose bowel movements and urination, nervous, sulfurous sweating and close quarters breathing. It wouldn't be hard to detect the smell of men in cages, of hierarchy, of order, of, God help him, rape.

Surely, those aspects of prison life existed here, as they did in prisons everywhere, but Louis at first sensed none of them. No, assaulting his palate, front and center, was the strong industrial scent of bleach. The chemical clean smell of good old Clorox permeated the corridors and offices, the restrooms and kitchen, the mess hall and medical ward. The smell was aloft in the lobby, behind the thick green bulletproof glass of the guard booths, down on the floors and up on the walls. It wasn't a clean-kitchen, doctor's office scent per se but the sour odor of an adult movie house; that or the men's rooms at Veteran's Stadium on Monday following a big Sunday game.

Louis didn't have long to ponder the odor, just take it in and move on, because there was business to attend to. Led into the admissions center he was paired with a senior corrections officer for intake paperwork and processing.

This was serious business, no question about it, but he marveled at how casual, even jovial, things could be here.

Across the pale green intake room an enormous uniformed corrections officer frisked a frail, drunken man who stood, spread eagle, against a wall. Amazingly, once the search was over the guard and inmate, evidently a returnee, yukked it up over one thing or another -- the Eagles or Phillies, food in the joint, maybe even the fact that he, the inmate, was back again.

Unlike the drunk, Louis was in no laughing matter.

"Should I be worried?" he queried the guard handling his paperwork. It seemed, even to him, a stupid question. One might say rhetorical.

A wiry, middle-aged man just months from retiring, Lt. Oxford Wilson assured Louis everything would be fine.

"You be ah-eight," the officer told him, mannerisms and inflections all South Jersey. "It ain't all like on TV."

"It's not?"

The man looked up and Louis saw kindness in his weathered face, in the wet, gray-blue eyes contrasting crackly dark brown skin.

"Not as much as you might think."

Wilson checked Louis for scars, tattoos and other identifying markers for a searchable nationwide database. He asked a series of questions, some of which, like Louis's religion and address, seemed hopelessly redundant but were intended to help determine every new inmate's state of mind and disposition. Was he in denial? Did he know where he was? Did he know who he was? Did he pose a threat to himself? These were things the jail authorities needed to know.

Louis surrendered his personal items and was issued a two-piece yellow uniform, its color signifying low security risk.

Finally, Wilson told Louis where he'd be housed -- in a seven-day holding ward containing thirty-seven cells and a central open space. The Center, as the men called the central square, was a general hang out area where Darwin ruled. It was also a place where, until recently, the men could smoke and it was a dark day across the state prison system when that small privilege was stripped away.

Wilson told Louis he would not go into protective custody -- solitary confinement -- even if Louis wanted it (he did), because he didn't fit a profile. Unlike police officers who found themselves on the inside, Louis's occupation did not make him a natural target for violence and he was not, evidently, someone likely to stir things up.

During his time there -- which was likely to be short, depending on how soon he could make bail -- he would share a cell with one or two other men, neither of whom would be violent offenders, and that last bit of information comforted Louis. Still, he understood his cellmates and everyone else on the block would likely be younger, stronger, tougher and more streetwise than he. And he was aware that pretty much any of them could hurt him bad.

"I'm scared," Louis admitted, his voice tremulous, his face ashen with fear. He worried that at any moment he might cry.

"You be ah-eight," the man said again. "Don't worry none 'bout what you heard 'bout this place. People do love to talk. Just chitter chatter."

The CO's voice had a nice musical cadence and Louis found his words calming and true, his nature almost clerical.

"But you ain't gone be mixing it up none wif the real bad boys, no how," Wilson said. "They in a whole 'nother ward."

Louis nodded appreciatively.

"You be respectful and straight with them other cats on the block, just like you want 'em to be wif you, and you be ah-eight."

The man flashed a jack-o-lantern grin, bright and toothy but full of gaps as Louis, no longer cuffed, sat quietly in a standard-issue office chair next to the man's desk. He looked about and concluded that, aside from all the husky guards coming and going, the entire office was pretty much standard issue -- smooth institutional flooring and old-fashioned upright cabinets – and the ordinariness was comforting to him. The office was filled with big, clunky desks and chairs. Some of the desks even had computers, if you could call them that. With blinky green diodes on inky green-black screens, the old tanks were little more than paperweights, good for nothing but basic word processing and data entry and their throwback simplicity was oddly calming and comforting, too.

Wilson took a pull off a cold bottle of spring water and turned back to the job at hand.

"Little respect go a long way in heah, know I'm sayin', Rabbi?" he continued. "Shoot. Half these knuckleheads woulda learnt that when they was young they wouldn't be here no how."

Louis sensed that this was a kind and compassionate man. He believed that, despite the harshness of his job and a life lived largely inside, Wilson remained, at heart, decent. The thin gold band on his left ring finger seemed to counterbalance the maelstrom Louis presumed his work life to be and he appeared older than his fifty-two or fifty-three years. But the fact that Wilson was still here, doing the same job he'd done for a quarter century or more, suggested one thing – that he was a survivor. And Louis wanted to learn from him. He wanted to know, in five minutes or less, how he might get through a day or two in this awful place. He sought more of the man's kind, paternal wisdom before he, Louis, was cold and alone, left to his own defenses in a place without friends.

But then their time was up.

Locks clicked and a heavy steel door slid open and slammed into a wall. A younger, much thicker C.O. sporting a goatee and lots of fancy ink stepped inside to collect the new inmate.

Louis stood as instructed, the tremulous feeling in his belly back and stronger than before, and tears welled up in his eyes. He stuck out his hand to the admitting officer as he was led away.

"You be ah-eight," the man said yet again, accepting Louis's long, soft hand as he would a child's. Wilson possessed power but it went beyond the physical. He lived within the beast, was wary of it, but did not fear it.

"Just treat 'em like you wanna be treated," the man repeated lyrically. "Treat 'em like you wanna be treated. An' if they got a problem after that, just tell 'em to come see me. Tell 'em ole Ox sent ya."

"Thank you, sir," Louis said. "I will sir."

* * * * *

During that first long walk to the block Louis somehow held his head high but avoided eye contact with everyone, guards and inmates alike. Still, over the next two hours, he felt whiter and weaker than ever before. He'd spent so much time in the gym, towered so completely over so many people, that Louis somehow mistook himself as bad. But he sure didn't feel bad now.

The inmates, most of them black, leered at him from behind steel bars and heavy screen mesh. Many had rippling physiques, bluish green jail tats that stood out weakly on blue-black skin and experience way beyond their years.

The big C.O. led him to his cell and wished him luck, then left him alone with the other cons on the

415

block. To Louis's surprise, the block was only about half full, its tenancy mostly a mishmash of street-level drug dealers, petty thieves and drunken drivers.

But when Louis arrived, all eyes turned to him. Here was a true outsider, an educated man of means, and the yellow two-piece jail suit didn't hide that. He was the type who wouldn't see any of them if they passed him on the street, in the mall, even at the stadium -- he off to box seats, they to stand and watch from the aisles or sit in the nose bleeders they paid for. He was precisely the kind who didn't do well behind bars and they smelled the fear on him.

For his part, Louis assumed virtually all the inmates were gang members – Latin Kings, Crips, Bloods, it didn't matter -- and that none of the men on his block, black, white or brown, made it past the tenth grade. At ease only with his own white-collar lifestyle, he believed everyone else at the jail (including most of the guards) were hustlers or dealers, two-bit career criminals so far beneath him he could barely see them. (In that sense, the other inmates were more right about him than he was about them.)

Beliefs about his fellow inmates aside, what he knew for sure was that he had to pee so bad he could taste it.

In fact, what he really needed was to move his bowels but didn't dare bare himself for that most private of acts. He waited as long as he could, pacing the cold eight-by-ten cell, and finally found the nerve to take a leak. With great relief, he loosed a torrent at the small circle of water in the crusty old bowl and splashed not a drop outside of it. When he was done, Louis wiped the rim with a wadding of rough toilet tissue, closed the lid, and stalked the cell some more. He simply did not know what to do with himself, glancing beyond the cell but not daring to venture out into the square.

Louis eyed what evidently was his bunk but made no move to sit down or lie upon it. The top in a set of bunks, his was just a cold steel frame with pitted springs fanning out from one side to the other. A moldy, inch-thick cushion lay rolled up on top, wedged between the frame and the damp cinder block wall.

Beneath the bunk a morose thirty-something white man picked at callouses in his strong, leathery palms as well as at snots deep in his nose. He glanced up when Louis entered the cell but didn't so much as acknowledge him. The man also didn't offer one of two thin woolen blankets that comforted him, one of them evidently belonging to the tenant of the top bunk.

Louis, whose first formal act in his new abode was to pee in it, thought it now time to meet the locals.

"Guess we're roomies," he said amiably, his eyes casting between the man and the cell's opening onto the block.

Still working his nose, the man angled a finger nearly to his knuckle and extracted a rich, slimy booger, dry and crisp where it stuck to his fingernail and trailing a wet strand of goo. He rolled the treasure between two fingers and flung the soft greenish ball against a wall.

"We ain't shit," the man said flatly.

Louis glanced down at his own two feet and up again at the man. He was stymied with what to do with himself and wondered in a nanosecond if he could take him.

"Look," Louis said, his voice as flat and cracked as a dry pond, "I'm just trying to make conversation."

"You want conversation, go make it with them niggers."

Louis didn't like that word but a lesson in political correctness was not at hand.

He glanced up at the bed roll and noticed the missing blanket. He'd want that blanket later and the dead of night would not be the time to come asking for it.

"I'm Louis Abrams," he tried again, proffering his hand.

But nothing.

Out in the Center a couple of punks milled about, pants yanked low and drawers pulled high. Others worked out continually – sit ups, crunches, pushups and dips – further armoring lean young frames with layers of muscle.

Two or three sat bullshitting on bolted down table tops, bored and evidently angry, conspiring in ghetto street slang. Louis's few paces toward the door were met with stares from these young men – many just boys, really, nineteen or twenty, tops -- but the stares were more like dares.

Louis looked out again and one of the punks caught his eye and stood up.

"You want somethin', motherfucker?"

"What?" Louis said. "Uh, no, I'm good."

"Keep lookin' at me, *motherfucker*," the kid said, "and we'll see 'bout good."

Louis turned back toward his bunk and figured he'd climb up into it. There was nowhere else to sit in the cell beside the cold, hard floor and he wasn't going out for a seat on a bench.

"Look," he said to his cellmate, "I think you've got my blanket. I can see your taking it when no one was here but now that I'm here I'm gonna need it."

The man didn't answer, just sat there, feet flat on the floor, eyes ahead on the wall.

"I know who you are," the man said a long moment later, drawing air through gapped teeth as he spoke.

"I don't think you do," Louis said.

"*I* think so. You that Jew rabbi had his wife kilt."

Louis looked at him a moment, incredulous.

"Excuse me, sir, but you've got that all wrong," he said. "Now, if you don't mind, I just want my blanket."

"You're the one's got it wrong, mister."

Now the man stood and Louis saw that he was much smaller than himself, shorter and thinner than he appeared sitting down but wide in the shoulders and back, almost triangular. As he ascended from the shadows Louis noticed that the man had a harelip and that half of his top front right tooth was gone. His complexion was bad and he had greasy hair and a powerful stink from not showering since his arrival five nights before.

"What're you saying, motherfucker? You calling me a thief? You think I'm a retard? I don't know how to read?"

He looked up at Louis, breathed in his face, and didn't flinch.

"I'm not sayin' nothin'," Louis said.

"That what you're sayin'?"

"Look, all I'm sayin' is I want my blanket. I ain't lookin' for trouble."

Fact was, now that he saw his cellmate, now that he *smelled* him up close and personal, Louis wasn't so sure he wanted the blanket after all. Who knew what might crawl out of it.

"You want it, take it," the cellmate said, stepping aside.

So Louis, towering above him, bent between the bunks to retrieve the cleaner-looking of the blankets, the one that had been wedged between his cellmate and the wall.

And in the moment that followed, a split second in which Louis took his eyes off him, the man drew back his fist and laid into the side of Louis's head.

The punch felled Louis before he even reached the blanket and his face caught the side of the steel bed frame on the way down. The blow hurt, no question about it, but the unforgiving bed frame did the real damage, carving up the meat under his left eye and fracturing the bone beneath it. Louis crumpled to the floor like a fallen leaf, spitting up blood, a few teeth and a big hunk of flesh from inside his cheek. He tried covering up, protecting his head and face with his hands, but the man kept coming, kicking and punching and kicking and punching and kicking.

The black boys from the Center joined in the ruckus now, cheering the white boy on. They didn't know the man under attack and really had nothing against him but a show was a show.

"Hit 'im, yo!"

"Fuck dat nigga *up!*"

A third joined in, punching and upper-cutting the air like Batman. "Dag, nigger, hit 'im. Bam! Whoop his ass!"

The soft flesh of Louis's torso was like hamburger beneath the rain of the man's kicks and punches, but what satisfied his attacker most were the cracks and shifts beneath his blows and Louis's muffled, bloody grunts.

A million miles away locks clicked but Louis didn't hear them as a small battalion of guards rushed the square and secured it. They herded the prisoners back to their pens and tended to the injured man.

As for Louis, the hesitancy that he felt to move his bowels when he first entered the cell was gone now. There was moist, foul warmth about him, familiar but nearly forgotten, a feeling he hadn't known for fifty years or more. And the stink was all his own.

<u>Chapter 34</u>

Ribbons of sun filtered through thickets of barbed wire and heavy steel mesh and bars, finally reaching the semi-sterile medical ward of the Camden County Jail. As they did everywhere, the ancient rays seemed to carry glittering specks of dust and gave this abysmal room the tiniest sense of normalcy and well-being. The sun's rays didn't just warm the pale green ward but energized it and subtly cheered the sick and injured.

A full day after his beating Louis felt these rays upon him and sensed them through the bright private crimson of his inner eyes. They reminded him of childhood, of sitting on a hooked, circular rug in his parents' living room, his belly full from breakfast, playing quietly with his Lincoln Logs. He would have stayed in that moment forever – suspended, blissful, at ease – but forever would have to wait.

"Rabbi," someone said, and they were touching him.

Dried gluey tears fastened his eyelashes together and he had to consciously think about opening his lids. When he did, the bulk of Terrence Jacov filled up his view and blocked out the gentle warm sun.

"Terrence," Louis rasped, his throat too parched to speak.

Jacov was still badly beaten from his brush with the truck but rose painfully to offer Louis a plastic tumbler of water. Louis sipped a teaspoon or two and closed his eyes again but his moment of bliss on the carpet was gone.

"What are you doing here?" Jacov wanted to know.

Louis held up one hand and glanced about the room. There were no cameras in view and, for the moment, no guards.

"I got beat up."

Jacov glanced around, too.

"I can see that," he said. "But that's not what I mean."

A moment or two passed.

"How you feelin'?"

Louis coughed once and it almost killed him. His eyes watered as he rested one hand on Jacov's thick, hairy forearm, a signal that, despite his condition, he'd be OK.

"What I meant was what are you doing *inside*?" Jacov said.

"You didn't hear? I'm sure it was in the papers."

Terrence paused a moment to bolster the weight of his response.

"I must've missed it," he said. "This ain't exactly a library."

Breathing was painful for Louis and talking excruciating, but he muscled through.

"Jeffries sent his goons over to my office and they found the bong."

Jacov thought on this a moment. It was curious that, considering everything, the rabbi would leave out a smelly bong, paraphernalia that by scent alone could easily be found, but he let it go.

"You couldn't make bail for a bong?"

Louis sipped some more of the water. He cleared his throat and attempted to sit up but cried out in pain from his busted ribs. As much as it hurt to breathe, he prayed to God he wouldn't have to sneeze or, God forbid, move his bowels, but that would be coming, too. He wiped his eyes with the side of his hand and settled back down.

"They said I resisted arrest and the judge bought it," Louis said. "Two-hundredd K. No ten percent."

"I still don't understand."

"I didn't have two-hundred grand."

"No, I mean the bong. Why'd you leave it out? Wasn't that asking for trouble?"

Jacov looked around now, visibly agitated, and trained his voice to a loud whisper.

"They know I know you!" he hissed. "They say they know what I did! Rabbi -- I don't remember. I didn't talk to that newspaper girl. Rabbi -- "

He looked around some more, his voice on the brink of hysteria.

"They said they're gonna give me the needle!"

Louis, his hand still upon Jacov's forearm, dug his nails in.

"You need to calm down," he growled.

He pinched deeper and Jacov winced, pulling his arm back without a word.

"You calm?" Louis said.

"I'm calm."

"I needed to speak with you."

"I don't get…"

"I didn't just leave the bong out! I needed to speak with you and this was the only way."

"What are sayin', you set yourself up?"

"Listen to me, damn it. When they see I'm awake they *will* split us up, do you understand? What I'm saying is, I knew they were coming. It was only a matter of time. And I had to speak with you. I didn't expect that fucking halfwit to come after me in the cell like he did but talking to you inside was the only way. As it turned out, he delivered me to you."

"Don't worry about him," Jacov said. "I'm gonna wrench his neck."

Louis was exhausted. He wanted to rest, or die, but what he had to say wouldn't wait.

"Forget about him. Do you hear me? Forget about him, I mean it. What I want you to do is sit tight. I want you to believe me when I tell you this -- you are *not* getting the needle. The only way you get it is if I get it, too, and the only way that happens is we turn on each other."

"It ain't gonna happen."

"I know it's not. We're gonna get through this but you have to believe me and you have to just sit tight. It's our word against theirs. That's all they got. Our word against theirs. For all they know, it was a robbery gone bad. No witnesses, no motive, no nothing."

Still, Terrence was worried that they had more. A lot more.

"Nickerson said they got DNA," he said.

"Nickerson's full of shit," Louis said. "DNA takes six weeks, not six fucking hours. He's bluffing."

"He said they got it from the truck. Said my knife was full of her blood."

Louis cringed. He knew, of course, that he was responsible for what happened to Rebecca, but wanted no details, now or ever. He simply didn't want, or need, to know.

There was movement at the far end of the ward where another low-risk inmate pushed open the door and slid through with a bucket of bleachy water. Louis noticed that Jacov's garb, unlike the man's with the bucket and his own, was not yellow. His red jail suit signified that he, Jacov, was a greater security risk, one who required closer observation, and he knew that someone, somewhere was watching.

"Believe me when I tell you this, Nickerson is full of fucking shit," Louis repeated. "Your van was a wreck, Terrence, and the only blood they found in it was your own."

The man with the bucket swabbed closer but stopped and turned to look when the door he'd come through opened again.

"You with me?" Louis asked. "I gotta hear you say it. You need to be with me 'cause divided we fry."

"I'm with you, Rabbi," Jacov repeated. "Divided we fry."

* * * * *

For Louis, the short-term worst of things was over. He'd take his meals through a straw for a few days, maybe a week, but at least he wasn't raped.

Bone heals, cheeks heal, any third-rate dentist can pop in a few new teeth. But dignity? Loss of self? Fear of AIDS or actual infection? Those things don't simply knit so Louis, as far as he was concerned, escaped intact.

Shelly filed an immediate appeal to the judge's refusal of ten percent and Judge Browne evidently reconsidered. It wasn't as if he had an epiphany there in the O.R., the colonoscope wriggling so far up his bowels he practically felt it in his throat. No, Browne's change of heart was grounded in the reality of the bench. He did not wish to be overruled by a higher court on a matter he knew would not stand.

Besides, by the time he returned to the bench a day and a half after his ruling, soon enough to reconsider the matter but not long enough for the Appellate Division to hear it, justice had been served. It wasn't ultimate, incendiary, damn-it's-hot-down-here justice, the type he knew Louis deserved -- but temporary, as much as could be meted out on charges of bong possession and "resisting" arrest. So Browne acceded to the ten percent and Shelly sprung Louis free.

By the time Louis got home, the physical investigation of the crime scene at 3232 Applewood Terrace was complete and the now-clean house bore a semblance of normalcy. Jonathan and Seth, unable to cope with the dried, lingering horror of their mother's death, had the home professionally scoured. Soiled carpets were ripped up and replaced and the kitchen ceiling and wall were cleaned, primed and repainted.

As Louis and Shelly entered through the rear kitchen door, the sweet scent of fresh paint filled up their senses. They had barely crossed the threshold when Buster leapt into Louis's arms, nearly knocking him down. Louis cried out and fell to his knees in agony, his ribs recoiling as if a knife was stuck between them. He pushed the dog away, but Buster, blissfully unaware he'd hurt him, bounded back, relentless, his big, muscular body contorted into a happy kidney.

Louis could barely breathe. Speech, for the moment, was impossible. So he just sat there and wept. The eighty-pound pit bull sensed something was wrong and backed off, a hurt, quizzical look crossing his clownish face.

"You alright?" Shelly asked.

"Yeah," Louis said. "Just give me a minute."

When at last Louis could stand, Shelly helped him to a stool at the island where Louis pondered his future. Resting his head in his palms he felt a cold, clammy sweat, the kind borne of sickness, fever, or fear.

Shelly found a few bottles of water in the fridge, opened them, and handed one to Louis.

"I saw Jacov," Louis said a moment later.

The lawyer stopped drinking mid-swig.

"Please, God, tell me you didn't talk to him."

"Of course I talked to him," Louis said. "He's the reason I was there."

"Indirectly, yes. But you were there because you left the God damned pot pipe out and the cops found it."

"And why would I do that?"

"Leave the bong out? I dunno. You tell me, Lou. You're the one's got it all figured out."

"That's what worries me, Shel, that you don't."

"Hey, Lou, if you're feelin' froggy, jump. There's lots of lawyers around. It's not like you're married to me."

"Fuck you!"

Shelly thought about Rebecca, how she'd been a friend to him, cooked meals for his family and shared holidays with them. He was sick with memories of her autopsy photos and sicker still to be standing literally in the spot where she was killed.

Louis just sat there brooding and black.

"I'm sorry, Lou. I shouldn't have said that."

"No, you're right, Shel," Louis said. "We ain't married. You want out, there's the door."

"Fine, asshole."

Shelly threw his plastic water bottle into the sink, but it swirled around the inside, up and out onto the floor, and without even stopping to pick it up he bee-lined for the door.

"Just explain to me why you left the bong out," he said, turning back.

"I already did."

"No, you didn't."

Louis sat there brooding a moment more, testing Shelly's patience, but finally continued.

"I had to talk to Jacov and they weren't going to let me just walk up and see him through the glass."

"So you found a way in. You damn near got your brains bashed in but you got to see Jacov. Brav-O. And what exactly did it get you? These charges aren't going away and if I know Jeffries they're just the start. He's coming for you. The last thing you want them to see is you talking to Jacov."

"Let him come," Louis said. "All he's got on me is possession and resisting, and that's a big fucking farce. He needs Terrence and, guess what, he ain't getting him 'cause I've got him."

"Is that right?"

"That's right."

"Well, you really do have it all figured out, don't you?" Shelly said. "Sounds like you don't need me."

"I just thought *you* would have figured all this out, too. You're the one went to law school."

"Get some rest, Louis," Shelly said. "You're gonna need it."

He turned again and headed for the door.

"So, you're still my lawyer?"

"I don't know, Lou," he said, pausing before going out. "You may need a bigger gun than me. Get some rest and we'll talk tomorrow."

Rest didn't come easy the next few days, but scotch and Percocet worked wonders. Janice, who refused to see Louis before he was locked up, now refused even to speak with him. On Louis's third morning home Shelly called and told him to sit tight – he'd be stopping by.

Water was on for tea and Buster had just come in when there was a brusque knock at the door.

Louis went to let Shelly in but found instead Det. Gerald Nickerson. Behind him stood two armed deputies and, behind them, two patrol cars hummed on the sloping drive, lights flashing but silent.

Nickerson had in his right hand a writ of some kind or other and, in his left, his pitted old set of cuffs. He didn't say a word, but he was grinning.


The End

# About the Author

For nearly 30 years, Steve Levine has been a full-time writer – an award-winning journalist with news outlets in New Jersey, New York and Pennsylvania, an advertising copywriter, and a higher education public relations professional. *Bad Rabbi* is his first published work of fiction.

# Acknowledgements

I'd like to thank my friends and family who supported and encouraged me during the writing of *Bad Rabbi* and my search for a publisher, especially my wife Yvonne, my sister, the writer Eleanor Levine, my step-daughter Jessi, whose help improve the already strong cover design by suggesting the smoke flourish, my brothers Allan and Michael, my editors at Unsolicited Press, who did a great job and were terrific to work with, and my late parents, Jack and Hilda Levine, who loved my writing even in the third grade and encouraged me to do more of it.

# About the Press

Unsolicited Press is an independent publishing press based out of Northern California, Portland, and Chicago. We focus on literary fiction, creative nonfiction, and poetry. If you loved Steve's novel, then you may enjoy reading:

*Dick Cheney Shot Me in the Face* by Timothy O'Leary

*The Amendment* by Anne Leigh Parrish

*A Few Small Stones* by Marilyn Ogus Katz